SORROWS
YIELD

SORROWS YIELD

THE PAST IS EVER PRESENT

DIANA O'NEIL

First published in 2024 by Diana O'Neil, in partnership with Whitefox Publishing

www.wearewhitefox.com

Copyright © Diana O'Neil, 2024

ISBN 978-1-916-79756-7
Also available as an eBook
ISBN 978-1-916-79757-4

Diana O'Neil asserts the moral right to be identified as the author of this work.

Designed and typeset by seagulls.net
Cover design by Jamie Keenan
Project management by Whitefox

Permissions

Epigraph and p. 100, ch. 7: 'For blood can nought but sin, and wars but sorrows yield.' From *The Faerie Queene* by Edmund Spenser. Public domain. P. 33, ch. 3: 'Rule, Britannia! Britannia rules the waves!' From the patriotic British song 'Rule, Britannia!' Words by James Thomson, music by Thomas Arne. Public domain. P. 36, ch. 3: 'Remember your mother, your family and your Kipling, and "you'll be a Man, my son."' From the poem 'If' by Rudyard Kipling. Public domain. P. 38, ch. 3: Lyrics from 'If England Wants a Hand, Well, Here It Is»' (1915) by Charles Vaude, sung by Harrison Latimer. © National Film and Sound Archive of Australia. Reprinted by permission. P. 83, ch. 6: Line from 'Jerusalem' by William Blake. Public domain. P. 91, ch. 6: Lyrics from 'Home! Sweet Home!' by John Howard Payne, adapted hymn with music by Henry Rowley Bishop. Public domain. P. 62, ch. 4 and p. 114, ch. 8: Excerpts from *War and Peace* by Leo Tolstoy. Translated by Constance Garnett. Public domain. P. 129, ch. 9: 'A Gleam of Sunshine' by Henry Wadsworth Longfellow. Public domain. P. 211, ch. 19: 'Ye Wearie Wayfarer' by Adam Lindsay Gordon. Public domain.

'For blood can nought but sin, and wars but sorrows yield.'

Edmund Spenser

This book is dedicated to:

my father, Lloyd, who taught me to love books,

my mother, Janet, who taught me to love words,

my son, Jack, who was the first to believe in me,

my daughter, Belle, who has always made me reach,

and to Toby, the love of my life.

CONTENTS

PROLOGUE

Jim Williams unwinds his fingers and withdraws his hand from his captain's desperate grip. His eyes then follow the laden, narrow stretcher and the grim-faced stretcher-bearers as they climb the wall of the shell hole at a jerky jog, navigating their way in the soft, torn-up soil. The bearers take quick, darting looks left and right, trying to ascertain the level of danger: they don't want to be sitting ducks. Then they're up and over the crater's lip, out of sight.

Jim Williams slumps. He sits in the dirt of the crater for a minute or so, leaning his forehead on his upright weapon, collecting the series of muddy, bloody images, working them into some kind of reasonable chain of events.

He mouths, 'He'll be right now … alright. The captain, he'll be alright.' It seems like a week ago, not just twenty-four hours, that the two had conversed in Ploegsteert Wood, both sound in body and mind, before the trial they'd just completed. They were preparing then, rather than mopping up.

The noise of sporadic, distant machine-gun and closer sniper fire around him is not helping to ease his rapid thoughts, calm his racing heartbeat, slow his hasty respirations. He closes his eyes and summons his fraying senses. The earth, the ground, is heaving and shuddering; every proprioceptive tool he has is awry; his balance is out of whack. He conjures from a fog of hesitation his father's wry smile. He wills himself to picture his mother and grandmother. He moves on to see his best friends: his red dog and his bay horse at home – so very far away. He pictures his sweet Charlotte Eva in Ypres and longs to be beside her. In his image of her, she is so still, solid, steady. Some soldiers confess that they can't recall the faces of wives or sweethearts. Not Jim. Charlotte Eva's face is there, right in front of him: a shy smile, blue eyes, fair. As he took his leave, not five days ago, she was sitting in a patch of sunlight, on a low stone wall, destruction all around her; but she, well, she was perfect. His determination is restored with the recollection. He must get back to her.

'Alright, alright, alright.'

He opens his eyes and looks around to work out where he's supposed to be. The crater is now empty of the soldiers: well, live soldiers. There are remnants of destroyed bodies. There's a torso in a ragged jacket, congealing blood pooling where the man's head ought to have been. There's a leg with tidy puttee and near-new boot still in place. There's a half-buried part of a head, brain exposed, scalp torn. Jim Williams doesn't want to stay to help clean up. He wants to get back to his mates: give them a hand to make sure the Hun are dead or on the run. The stretcher-bearers had headed toward what he believes is north-west; a safe bet, as that's where they came from. And the machine-gun fire and the individual shots seem to be from the east.

'Righto.'

Jim Williams gathers his greasy rifle, his tired limbs, his near-spent courage, and begins to make his way, stomping and sliding, stomping and sliding, up the hill the shell has created, in the same direction as the stretcher-bearers.

CHAPTER ONE

On a Sydney Monday in May – all sunshine and blue sky – I sat at a small, round, metallic table on the narrow footpath beside the entrance to the Neutral Bay ferry wharf. I had a short black, a croissant and a fountain pen in front of me, and a notebook was open on my knee; but I chose to watch the world go by, hustling and bustling to school, work, university, the city and beyond, on buses and ferries, in cars and on foot. I wondered what the names of the passers-by were, what it was they did for a living. *Do they think they live a good life?* I spent a lot of time wondering about other people because, if the truth be known, it kept me from realising my own shortcomings. On most other days, in the name of research, I moved around the lovelier parts of this city, stopping at cafés and bars, on verandas, at shopfronts, at tables or on sofas. What I saw, what I heard, was supposed to become my content. But I was a fake – I'd failed to progress my novel's manuscript.

On that morning, I might have delighted in the tinkly clink of the cables on the masts in the marina. I could have savoured the aroma of the sea – not the wild smell of the ocean, but of a tame, salty harbour – but I had another, more pressing engagement. There was a diverting parade of Sydney dogs busy with their morning walk, sniffing other dogs, trees and poles, their owners hovering, plastic bags at the ready. Big and small, bitsers and well-bred – a couple of off-lead dachshunds made me laugh out loud, with their pompous, marching gait. I matched the dog to the owner – a game I played.

'Tina! Tina!' a roly-poly woman in Lycra cried out. 'Yes, you too Barry! Come here!'

Tina and Barry? Who names their dachshunds Tina and Barry?

Yes, it was an entertainment, a distraction from my own mundanity. If only all the sights before me could translate into plots and fictional settings.

I had idled enough. I downed the remnants of my espresso, placed too many coins on the table and stood, shoving my notebook and pen into my bag.

'Thanks, Andy,' I called into the café's interior.

The owner waved back. 'Yeah, cheers!'

As I moved off to the ferry's jetty, I couldn't help but observe the unimpressive architecture – the 'heritage archway' – so trained was I to avoid my own dull inner monologue. The jetty entrance was a 1930s monstrosity, dark small bricks, stucco painted cream, clumsy styling, but typical of the northern suburbs, and highly thought of. There's not much built-history in Australia; anything 'old' is excessively respected. The walkway was chunky timber, greyed with weather, slippery when wet. There was water lapping, marine traffic sliding by, and eight other Sydney-siders studying phones, newspapers or each other as the ferry swung into view.

It was nine o'clock.

I sighed, my first of the day, as I waited for the ferry to chug into place.

I had dressed myself in Sydney-cool, mandatory hipster: Ray-Bans, chinos and deck shoes. (Told you I was a fake – but a well-dressed one.) My new place of employment, Jones-Jones-McKinnon – a mid-sized, successful advertising agency – sounded like a place where another person might be pleased to be employed. Call me a prideful cynic, but I had all kinds of misgivings. I doubted that this new job was what *I* ought to be doing. I dealt with my despondency by telling myself – fooling myself – *it's just for a year, just one year.*

I worked as a copywriter; well, a writer who intended to write copy – 'For just one year,' I reminded myself again and again, over and over, in what I strongly suspected was a sop to my fear of committing myself to something other than myself. I needed to make some money to pay my share of my children's costs, my two dear little daughters with their wide eyes and angelic smiles. These two beautiful burdens tore at my equanimity: how could I be a good mother while being a good self, a good 'me'?

The first had been born just on five years ago, after twenty-four agonising hours. Her glorious arrival was torture for me as my old self was torn from its eternal skeleton. I found myself raw, ferociously fixated on protecting this baby from all the imagined horrors that any new mother can conjure. The acute pain of these sensations changed over the years to become an agonising quotidian ache.

This one, my oldest girl, was named Charlotte, after my mother suggested it: she loved the sh-shing beginning sound and the snappy end to it. She had let me know that my father had always loved the name.

The younger child flung herself into the world three years ago, in a whirlwind of drama and fear, with an ambulance to herald her impending arrival and a couple of days in intensive care to allow everyone to calm down. She was named Persephone against my better judgement. I was worried she'd get 'Phoney' in the playground. My ex-husband, Charles, insisted on it and now we call her Persy.

I was not whole without them, and yet I was fraying at my edges. I couldn't place them in my pantheon: my fault, not theirs.

*

Onward and upward. I shrugged, steeled myself, stepping onto the yellow and green ferry, and I found my favourite spot, a wooden bench seat, outside, near the prow. The harbour was its usual splendid shades of green and blue, reassuring in its familiarity – I'd been criss-crossing the harbour all my life.

On this first day of my new job, a day of new beginnings, I could contemplate new endings – well, fairly recent endings such as the end of my marriage. I had divorced Charles six months before, and lo and behold, Life had caught up with me. How had I ever imagined I could continue my haphazard novel-writing life and support the girls in shared custody? It was a ridiculous delusion. As sad as it sounded, my entire marriage could be described as ludicrous from the outset. Churlish, I knew, but I'd never told Charles that he was right about my ridiculous escape plan to leave the world of work behind forever: I'd write a bestseller and make my fortune. Now I was paying the price: joining Jones-Jones-McKinnon, who were going to pay me to turn up five days a week and correct other people's spelling and grammar.

Explaining our separation to my mother, Clare, had been excruciating, made worse by the tension, the almost estrangement, between us. I'd called her by her first name for years, my somewhat unkind act to separate her from me. I didn't want to need her love.

'Clare, listen to me, Charles is a coloniser.' I leant forward in the chintzy armchair for emphasis. Clare's house, the one I grew up in, was her own parents' home; the same 'old ladies' furniture too.

'What? A coloniser? What do you mean?' she asked, head to one side. She's polite, my mother. She never challenged me; she truly couldn't understand me.

'Look, consciously or unconsciously, he identified a chink in my armour, and went for me like I was his latest project in his ever-determined fashion.' I got a bit melodramatic, waved my arms around. 'I know he is not malicious or malevolent, just opportunistic. He thought he could control me, effectively take over *me*, my life, as a partner, as the father of my children, and deliver a "desirable outcome" – his *despicable* words, not mine.'

'But, darling, that is not a bad thing in and of itself.' My mother managed to squeeze in a little of her pragmatism, but I was on a roll.

'He honestly believed that eventually I would want what he wanted, as much as he did. He believed he could persuade me to love the order, the sense, his vision, what he says he created for me. I wasn't persuaded.' By then I was crying, looking for my mother's undivided attention and acceptance – you know, as you do when you're miserable at a gut level. 'The grind of avoiding Charles is unbearable, Clare, though I miss Persy and Char every minute … every minute, Clare. It got to the point where I didn't want to go home – my home – because of Charles: here, there, everywhere, all up in my grill.'

'He seemed very nice about you wanting to be a novelist … and I thought it was terrific that his parents bought you that nice house.'

'Yeah, the one he got back for himself in the divorce!' I knew I sounded bitter – slightly crazed. It was a sore point, but totally illogical, as these disputes often are. The girls loved *his* house, and they were entitled to the stability Charles's ownership gave them. I had been able to buy a tiny flat in an area undergoing gentrification as a result of a generous settlement: I shouldn't have complained.

'And Charles is so happy to have the girls so you can spend your time wandering around the city and writing your book.'

That was a well-deserved dig. Charles had been doing the lion's share of caring for Charlotte and Persy, but in my raw state I couldn't bring myself to acknowledge this.

'Mum, I mean Clare, you're missing the point.' I was exasperated by her reasonableness. 'And anyway, he wasn't "very nice" … he attempted to humour me, big difference. He called it a *phase*.' How to explain this to my mother: Charles underestimated my resilience, my Teflon approach to colonisers.

'Well, darling, I know he was furious when you had the girls' birthdates tattooed on your shoulder. That was a bit over the top, as they say, on your part?'

'I was drunk, Clare, stinking drunk, and anyway … I like my tattoo.'

Charles had ignored me even more after the Great Tattooing Incident. He spent an increasing number of hours at his work. He was with a different ad agency – a rival of my new place of employment – as director of legal affairs, earning a great deal of money. His office there was ordered (his whereabouts were always immaculately neat), and he spent his days among hip people, who considered him an equal – clever, able, cool. His wife had not shared his co-workers' admiration and was considered truculent.

My shoulders slumped; I stared through tears and picked at the chintz material. My self-defence could only last so long. 'Clare, I think the children are OK. They seem to be going along nicely, with their time at our crèche, sleeping when told to, staring at the television when I need some peace and quiet. They are perfect little angels.' And I dissolved into sobs; sarcasm and guilt will do it every time.

'Oh dear. There, there. We'll work it out, sweetheart. Here's a tissue. I'll put the kettle on.'

It was my mother's answer for most things.

*

I was happy to get a little wet from the sea spray; the Harbour was gloriously choppy as my ferry trundled past the Botanical Gardens of the southern shoreline. I pulled my jacket around me: the breeze had freshened. The city grew on the ferry's approach to Circular Quay, past the Opera House, which always reminded me of when Charles and I met, on the front deck: a classic TV industry, alcohol/cocaine-fuelled bash on a balmy March night. There were too many drunks there, laughing loudly, dancing ferociously, singing – bellowing – in and out of tune. I was one of them. Charles hung around, cadged a lift to the after-party – he was as polite as ever. That was our first night together.

We met when nothing and no one could dent my inexcusable, arrogant confidence. I imagined Life's success would be mine, but I could not have told you what it looked like. I was twenty-three years old. He was tall, tanned, blond, a North Shore boy, with a smile that would win over the Devil. Honestly, I barely noticed he'd joined my slipstream, yet every time I turned around, he was there, until by the end of my

Master's, his presence was no longer a pleasant surprise: it became the norm. Charles finished his law degree the same year and it was everybody else's foregone conclusion that we marry. Like an idiot, I thought I had to make it a reality. I vaguely thought I might be happy, and perhaps I thought I wouldn't be unhappy.

We landed at the quay. Shouts, engines churning, water gurgling; I and fifty other city-working souls brushed shoulders as we shuffled off the boat. I dawdled up the hill a block and a half, to a steel and concrete tower.

In the cathedral-like foyer, I pushed the lift button heading for the death-defying twenty-second floor. Checking I was on time for my first day, I glanced at the smartwatch Charles gave me one Christmas, the kind you wear when exercising. The card had said 'To my darling wife! Now you can join me on my runs! X' (He loved to use exclamation marks – probably still does.) His runs consisted of stepping outside at six each weekday morning in a heavily branded outfit for a twenty-minute slow jog. Like a child, I undermined his wishes by lying in bed, covers over my head. I didn't give him the present he'd asked for that year and my hard heart took satisfaction at his disappointment.

The offices of Jones-Jones-McKinnon consisted of beige walls and smoky-green glass office dividers, with huge canvases of oil paint, blurring in primary and iridescent colours – Rothko imitations. I shivered as I swam in its cold, perfect modernity – though it was probably just that the air-conditioning was set way too high for my liking. I made a note to bring a jacket to work next day. How would I ever enjoy working in such a corporate hellhole? I was a *writer*.

I was installed in a large, sunlight-filled room – the Copy Room – which I would share with the other writers. Katia, the office manager – an older woman with an immaculate geometric haircut – settled me at a table far from the windows.

'So here's your e-diary, and voilà, you have your first meeting at 11.30. See, it's with the guys from BEER!, your biggest account – the big one for the agency, twenty-two per cent of revenue. You familiar with the brand?'

'Sure,' I lied. I was not into brand anything, but beer was the project, and BEER! was the cute, boutique sub-brand I would work on. The cynic in me, the anti-intellectual intellectual, wanted to groan.

Katia introduced me to the others. 'Tara, meet Peter, Johnny and Melissa, and our intern, Sam.' They nodded, smiled in a genuine way, murmured general greetings. 'They all have complicated surnames so I'll let them tell you those.'

'Ah, yes, I'm somewhat in the same boat,' I countered. 'My surname, it's Twigg-Patterson. I had a possibly pretentious great-grandmother, who didn't want to give up her maiden name because her father was something important in India, the British Raj and all that. It's been double-barrelled for three generations.'

This was the moment I usually got a blank look – turned out that most people didn't know much Empire history – but I ploughed on with my set script.

'I really ought to change it once and for all, but I never get around to it.'

I was fine with my double-barrelled name with or without much of a story to match it, but I must have been ripe for reconsidering what my name *meant*. For the first time as I met the team at JJMcK, I realised how little I knew about its origins. I'd fabricated a short-form palm-off over the years, but really, I was glib and ignorant of both the Twiggs' and the Pattersons' chronicle. Formerly, I would have thought, what did it matter if I didn't understand how my name came about? My superficiality must have been getting under my skin.

The others moved off to the office kitchen – the 'break-out' room – to get coffees for us all, but Melissa stayed behind and began the gossipy run-through of each of the team's foibles. I sighed again, internally this time.

'Johnny talks all the time … yak yak yak.' She made the hand motion with both hands. 'Peter never says a thing …'

When the rest of the team came back bearing a tray of espressos and lattes, they were in time to hear the last of Melissa's briefing.

'Oh, but I must tell you about Dom … you'll meet him this morning. He's the head of the client team, the brand manager of BEER!, Dominic Fitzgerald. He's handsome and dashing … and corrupting. A libertine. Look out for him; not judging, just saying …' she said. The rest of the group had chuckled, but none had disagreed. I was being schooled in the culture; it sounded like Dominic was the Pied Piper.

※

My first meeting was held in the boardroom – a huge expanse of immaculately shined oak and sixteen ergonomic chairs, fine art on the walls, discreet buttons commanding the entry and exit of big, big TV screens. All the BEER! team – agency and client – were there, so I could fade somewhat into the background of the eleven-person get-together. I just watched, analysing the players as an outsider.

At the meeting's end, in the hubbub of people collecting their notes and laptops, moving off into the general office area, there he was, bold as brass, the apparently infamous Dominic Fitzgerald. Melissa had been right about 'handsome'.

'Lunch, Tara?' Dominic had an aura; it invited enquiry. He beckoned to me – figuratively – with a raised eyebrow and a broad smile.

'Of course.' I wanted to know more about him, to see for myself his profligate ways.

'Right answer.' His arms were wide in candid delight.

※

Lunch was long. After a couple of hours of Sydney rock oysters, steak Fiorentina and citrus sorbets, Dominic announced that it was time to go back to work – for some. The minions that had accompanied Dominic and me were despatched in cabs back to their desks.

'But you, young lady,' Dominic had begun, and my smile crumpled. 'Oh, whoops,' he corrected himself, 'apologies … let me start over. You, clever and strong woman …' I had to laugh. 'Phew, got away with that … you and I will keep drinking. BEER! is JJMcK's biggest client, and I ought to get to know BEER!'s new copywriter. I've told your boss I'm briefing you this afternoon.'

At the bar, with its gleaming surfaces, deep armchairs and sofas, and the all-important Sydney view of the sea, we spent a long, boozy afternoon. I mostly listened; Dominic mostly talked. We talked about God and agreed to a shared form of aggressive atheism; we talked about history; we talked about movies, writers, and architecture. Dominic drank and drank and drank: beer after beer after beer. But he was an able drunk, continued with his sociable ways, his toothless flirting – a sheep in wolf's clothing, surely – and he remained polite to bar staff and other patrons. There was no shouting or giveaway stumbling.

The conversation turned to relationships, and mine particularly.

'So, Tara, you are married, partnered, celibate, etcetera, etcetera?' He leant in and I became more guarded.

'Relationships are a mystery to me.'

I half wanted to close down the topic, but as something of an oversharer I gave a precis of my absurd marriage and its inevitable denouement. 'Now I think of Charles as a parasite – most uncharitable, I know. Charles and I were finally over in one of those terrible kitchen arguments, the kids sleeping so it had to be in whispers, which makes it kind of bitter and mean. After five years of being together, I told him that I had made the most tragic mistake of my short life when I married him. That was it.'

Dominic sat back in his chair and regarded me most sympathetically. 'Sounds awful.'

'Yes, and harsh, but I don't regret it at all … except for my daughters. At five and three years old, they don't have any idea that their norm is not every child's norm. Their days and nights either at their father's or their mother's are just what happens, but they are beginning to realise they miss me when they are with Charles … and they miss Charles when with me.' I bit my lip. 'They're beginning to understand just what that might mean: years of divided loyalties – grief, I suppose.'

'Aw, come on, they'll be fine. Most of the children all over the world have far worse things to contend with. You mustn't dramatise it for them.'

I was increasingly worried as to what he might want from me after this long lunch: *will he try to kiss me? What will I do if he does?* I'd never really been able to read sexual attraction or indeed, it would seem, the difference between sexual attraction and developing friendship. *Perhaps they run on parallel tracks for a while and veer off if that be the decision of either party. How does anyone learn this stuff except by example?* I had no example to observe, critique or model; my family and friends gave me no road map. As for trial and error, my marriage was not something I'd recommend as an educational tool.

'And how about you, Dominic? What is your status? Girl-friend, wife, partner?'

'Ah, now you're talking. My Rachel. We've been together since we were kids. I adore her to bits. She's a much better person than I am, better at work stuff, better at people stuff … and she doesn't drink as much.' He guffawed. 'Don't know why she stays with me.' He didn't mean that bit.

He stood up and did the hand sign for the bill.

'Better get us back to the office, Tara, or we'll become the office gossip.' He winked and I felt very stupid. Time for the beer goggles to come off and get down to some work.

*

A couple of weeks later, I met Rachel.

'Sooo sorry. I just got caught up at work. One thing after another. And you're – obviously – Tara. I'm so glad to meet you.' Rachel begged forgiveness for being late, forgiveness that she knew would be granted having swept in, fashionably late, with an enviable elegance: tall, long-legged, striking; the others in the restaurant stared at her. She kissed me on both cheeks and settled herself like a graceful swan on a still pond and proceeded to take me in – almost making me squirm. 'I don't want to give you the wrong impression at our first dinner together … I'm normally very punctual. Dom's told me so much about you. I couldn't wait to meet you.'

'Ha!' Dominic leant in and kissed her on the forehead, then smiled. 'Hello, my lovely.'

The conversation was relaxed, and Rachel was easy to like, if a little suspicious. She seemed more emotionally independent than Dominic in the relationship, a condition both were content with. I was relieved that she was kindly dismissive of Dominic's blarney, which was effusive by the evening's end, fuelled by a few bottles of excellent wine.

'And now Dom must tell you the story of how we met,' Rachel announced when we'd ordered Vin Santo, biscotti and espressos. 'It's compulsory.'

'Oh, good grief, here we go.' Dominic laughed.

'But it's a fantastic story!' Rachel seemed to glow with the beauty and wonder of it. 'How could anybody not be overtaken by our story, the tale of two lucky children who found each other and held on to each other against the odds?'

'Well, alright then. When I was nine, after years of tonsil and ear infections, the doctor insisted I have my tonsils out. Mum left me at the hospital with a stack of books I never read, a bowl of fruit I didn't eat, and a Gameboy – I played *Tetris* for hours.

'I really tried not to cry – I was scared! – but I lost that fight. You know when they tell you when you're a kid, "Just a scratch now," before they put in an IV? What a crock! It really hurts. Anyway … the nice nurse held my hand, and I was only a little humiliated. It's hard to keep your cool when you're nine.

'After the operation, I became aware of my feet being touched. It was nice. Then a cool hand was on my cheek, and I had this sweet, pixie face looking at me.' Dominic, ever the sentimentalist, caught Rachel's eye, and had to halt for a moment. 'There's a bright light behind her head and the background noise of a ward, but the moment is quite … well, still. I just knew there was something fundamental happening. I had pain in my throat, neck, mouth; I was drowsy and hot, and vague, but something like an angel was hovering above me. Turns out, her name was Rachel; she was almost the same age and in hospital for the same thing. She told me it was only really painful for the first day, and anyway you get jelly and ice-cream, just like her mum said you do.'

At this point in the story, Dominic assumed his grand raconteur self I had come to know, a theatrical delivery with his hand on his heart and an enthralling voice, slightly quavering.

'The angel stayed with me' – he switched back to enter-tainer – 'and by dinner time we were sitting up together on my bed, eating all the green jelly and ice-cream a nine-year-old can eat before throwing up.'

Dominic waved his arms about in the excitement of the moment, to demonstrate their shared body language.

'She told me her stories, about her Labrador, Bertie – who was fat and naughty; her best friend Vera – who could do the splits; and her parents' antics – though she wasn't supposed to talk about that kind of stuff: the yelling and the throwing things.

'I was awestruck, dumbstruck … still am. I didn't ques-tion it for a minute … still don't. She giggled and kissed me when she left the hospital before I did. I cried like Bambi at the thought of being without her. And she said, "I'll see you soon, silly. My mum will organise it."'

Dom described how their childish chatter had become teen chatter and then adult chatter. Their childish mutual awe had become teen awe and then adult awe. They emerged to become adult individuals who took on the grown-up world together. Like a Venn diagram, their selves overlapped without drama or reserve, cemented in their partnership.

'I will never forget our meeting and never stop talking about it … just to annoy you,' Dominic teased Rachel.

'And I will always touch your feet to wake you.' She put her hand on his cheek and pecked him on his puckered mouth – quite the loveliest thing I had seen in an awfully long while. 'Go on, say it,' she said to him. Then to me, 'This is what he always says …'

'It's simple really, I just love you … but you *really* love me.'

All three of us laughed, with tears in our eyes. But perhaps my tears were more to do with my own shortcomings, my own failings, while witnessing this display of true love before me. Of course Dominic had never been interested in me, not for one second. Was I unlovable? Unloving? Or just a sad sack?

CHAPTER TWO

'I envy your luck at finding someone like Dominic. Where the bloody hell am I going to find someone who might love me so utterly?' I said, only half joking, while rearranging the heavy folds of my bright-white towelling robe. For my birthday, Rachel had brought me to a fancy spa, in a grand old building among giant trees, on a sunny Sunday in the Blue Mountains. As soon as I mentioned I loved a spa break to Dominic, it was a fait accompli. I suspected Rachel was buying my friendship, keeping me close, under surveillance. We had spent the long day lying about on soft couches, drinking herbal tea, and in between sessions of mud packs and massages we talked – mostly about her and Dominic's relationship.

'Ah, you've an outsider's view.' She shrugged. 'In all honesty, I sometimes wonder what I am doing with Dominic, this man-child. Sometimes he drives me bad-crazy with his antics, and then … almost as infuriatingly, he drives me equally good-crazy with his love. He's so lovely at family gatherings, my family being … well, cold. Where my family is concerned, the sentimentality that my parents and siblings seek … that kind of thing is beyond me, and natural to Dom. But occasionally he is really a pain, an embarrassment, so much so that I don't invite him to work functions now, after a couple of drunken incidents I'd rather forget. I can't get him to stop; the alcohol, it's a problem.' She took a sip of her aromatic camomile tea. Her sad eyes made me think that maybe she felt she'd revealed too much.

'It sounds like you're saying he's a bit of a burden to you,' I tried, reaching to understand.

'Well, yeah, sort of a burden – but more often than not he is the millstone that I love to have, to possess, to hold.' She smiled and looked directly at me. 'Can't you just hear how much therapy I've had!' She said it with a kind of sad drawl, self-parodying.

'Really?' I joked, both hands to both cheeks. 'Nooooo …'

Among laughter and escaping tears, she shared with me her well-held secrets. She said that she had never considered me – nor any other person – a threat to their relationship; she just *knew* Dominic was completely hers. She allowed us all to feel safe: Dominic and me as both work colleagues and friends, in a sort of sibling-esque creation of affection and easy-going functionality.

'Dom and I have a kind of almost absent-minded trust and dedication. I think of you and I, Tara, like happy cousins together.' She passed me a plate of crudités and hummus. 'Is that OK? The idea of cousins, I mean, not the hummus.'

Rachel burst out laughing and I joined in.

*

I had the children one hot summer's weekend and on the Saturday afternoon, while the three of us were splayed like starfish on my bed, snoozing and sweating, there was a knock at the door. There was Dominic, in sweaty tennis whites, having finished his pennant match at the local club, oozing health, apparently eager to meet the girls. I was a little surprised at the spontaneous visit, and part of me wondered if Rachel knew he was here.

'Where are they ... these two little kittens Tara keeps telling me about?' He barrelled into the flat, all vigour and energy and noise. The children woke, swaying and a little groggy, a tad overwhelmed by this enthusing giant of good things.

'What, these two? I thought they were kittens, not merely two cutie pies!' he prattled, smiling widely and spreading his arms.

They grasped my legs, unwilling for me to join the adult world too soon, holding me back for just a few minutes more.

'Now which one are you, Persy or Charlotte?' Dominic squatted down to their height, sought the eyeline.

'I'm Charlotte. She's Persy,' my older daughter said in a whisper, wide-eyed.

'And which one of you wants an icy pole ... or a gelato ... or a Bubble O' Bill?'

The fog of a hot afternoon nap dissipated, and with all of us chattering and asking questions and singing, we got the girls' shoes on. They ran after Dominic out the front door, down the stairs, over hot asphalt, to the corner shop, giggling and grabbing to hold his hands.

On the many times he saw the two girls after that first meeting, as men with no children often do, Dominic stirred my two to joyous hysteria, shouting with glee, with his pratfalls and animal noises. He brought them sheets of stickers and helped to plaster them all over my IKEA furniture. He brought face paint, and the result was hilarious and messy. He brought them toys, often way beyond their age group, but he persisted and, generous with his time, played with them for hours. Monopoly with a six- and a four-year-old made for a riotous afternoon.

There was nothing more lovely for me as a parent than to see my children coming to know and trust a good person – it was pure gold, but I couldn't help suspecting that Dominic wanted to have these children as his own. I didn't mean in a creepy way; it was as though he would be lonely without them.

*

On another hot day, we three adults and my children went for a swim at Balmoral Beach, a tame seaside family spot. It was a dreamy afternoon, all of us content and sleepy, and bringing only a touch of sunburn. In the dappled water and lapping wavelets, the girls had frolicked as only six- and four-year-olds can, and with Dominic's help, they had built a small village out of the wet sand.

We dropped the girls back at Charles's, said happy goodbyes, and adjourned to the pub nearest my place, the Oak Hotel. It had an unexceptional bar but was the watering hole of friends and colleagues, and we often ended up there, regardless of the

day or time. The hot evening produced the perfect temperature to sit under the giant oak in the courtyard, still in damp
bathers and beach T-shirts. We downed litres of soda water and
imbibed a great deal of rosé with ice. Maybe it was the exchange
of the girls with Charles that brought on the conversation about
Dominic and Rachel having children.

'Look, I'm thirty-nine, same as Dominic … and I've had a
wee bit too much to drink,' Rachel said with one of her generous smiles, reaching for the wine bottle to top up our glasses,
'so I can be blunt: I have no "ticking clock" as there might
be for another woman of my age. Good luck to them, but
I've buried any thought of having children, the very notion
is just too difficult to imagine. Bearing and raising children
is a foreign land. And I'm going to let it stay that way. It's too
hard to entertain.'

I wasn't going to break the silence that ensued, though
I was pretty sure my eyebrows shot up in surprise, so I took
a quick breath and held it. I simply couldn't understand her
point of view. I wasn't critical, just baffled.

'But what about me, Rachel?' Dom responded more
quietly than I'd ever heard him speak.

The yawning gap between Dominic and Rachel over
having kids was clearly one of the imbalances in their curiously perfect relationship. Though my speculation wasn't
worth much, given my apparent talent for blowing a marriage,
I guessed that every relationship had these conundrums;
indeed, I supposed that the measure of any relationship must

be the partners' ability to integrate disparate beliefs, to be pragmatic. Dominic and Rachel appeared to have what it took, so I was surprised by the tension in the conversation.

Dom turned to me. 'Since I was a small boy, I have been determined to have a large brood. I suppose you could see it as wanting to replicate myself, my ego in action. But it's more about my family, my ancestors, my friends – a sort of abstract procreativity.'

'So, it's all about you? Hmmm?' Rachel said it to be amusing but it fell flat.

'Let me get it out, Rach, I'd like Tara to hear my side.' He moved about on his chair, getting comfortable with his confession. 'Me and my siblings are very different people, but we hold close our upbringing; it grants us belief in each other and the world. We are a tight unit – attached – though naturally we argue, and occasionally one or the other blows up at a family function. Our father died miserable with cancerous pain a decade ago. The whole family were united in grief: we get strength from mourning, thinking about the past. We probably overinvest significance in our own lives and in each day. Maybe when you lose someone early on in your life who had brought you great joy, in desperate defiance of the Grim Reaper, you want to create new life.'

Rachel had been made silent, and I was stunned too by Dominic's eloquent insight. It was rare that he spoke about deep, important things. Neither Rachel nor I knew how to bring us back to the here and now, how to neutralise the atmosphere. Dominic spent a moment with a clouded face, then recovered with grace.

'So, where are we eating dinner? I'm starving.'

*

Once or twice that summer, I joined Dominic for his favourite pastime, tennis. Every now and then I'd give Dominic a surprise and take a game from him. When this happened, Dominic glowered from the other end of the court.

'Fuck, fuck, fuck,' he'd shout, his arms waving about; he was clearly tempted to smash his racquet. He made me laugh out loud, which further infuriated him.

'Look,' he bellowed, 'it's a game for gentlemen … I make an exception for your gender.'

'Well, thank you, kind sir. Your serve.'

He stormed toward the net. Time for a bit of mansplaining.

'My father and grandfather, and who knows? Maybe even before that … The Fitzgeralds play tennis and they play it well.'

That kind of talk made me crack up even more.

'Jesus, Dom, I can't take this very seriously: it's a private school wankers' game. I find it very entertaining that you should be so determined to win, but come on.'

My father had played a bit; indeed, my parents enjoyed their mixed doubles down at the local club – plus the gin and tonic and ciggy after the Saturday-afternoon tournament with the other reactionary conservatives. Full of fifteen-year-old, angst-ridden social awakening as I was, their guffaws and animation made me furious. This was at the club that I, of course, had refused to attend when I became a misanthropic teenager. I had refused to participate in this structured, happy-families, apparently bourgeois activity.

I let Dom win. I shouldn't have, but it meant so much to him.

*

On a quiet Monday morning, Dominic came into my office and leant against the shelving. I was reading banal ad copy with the most casual interest, pondering the legitimacy of starting sentences with 'And' or 'But' (or indeed, 'Or') and considering the possibility of criminal charges for the junior copywriter who had submitted this claptrap.

'You up for the industry awards tonight?' he began, his voice croaky with overuse. Dom and I rarely talked about the work we were both involved in, BEER! and JJMcK. We talked about the people and events around our work – not quite gossip. I liked to think it was more about unravelling personalities and motivation: a less severe form of, well, gossip.

'Yeah, sure. I'll see you there,' I replied, not lifting my eyes from the document I was reading.

'I've got a helluva hangover. Man, it's a several-Beroccas day.'

I raised my eyes, fixed them on my friend. Dominic rubbed his ruddy face in mock anguish but still wore his trademark big, white-teeth smile.

'I went to that party at Mario's. Unbelievable. Do you think those guys will get the Toyota account?' Dominic always needed my interpretation of the politics around us. He knew that my analysis was useful. In truth, I could read people –

read a room – better than Dominic, though Dominic had never thought of himself as less than clever in this way.

'Dominic, why do you drink so much? Why do you do this to yourself?'

For months now, I had witnessed this contradiction play out: here was a healthy, sane man doing his utmost to hurt himself. It was no good believing that he might not know how damaging his drinking could be. He was no fool. It was denial, avoidance, call it what you will. My growing fondness for my friend meant that his gradual decline into an alcoholic mist was painful to me … and to Rachel, as she'd made clear to me at the spa.

Dominic was not entirely sure if my question was a joke. 'That's rhetorical, right …? You're serious? Mate, I love it.'

A pause. I remained quiet; he'd answer eventually.

'Jeez, I don't know. Because I'm a functional alcoholic? But why?'

'Why.' I hadn't moved my focus.

'Well, I guess I like the feeling.' Dominic's face lost its smile.

'What feeling is that?'

'Um, kind of fuzzy,' he said, with a child's shrug. 'I like it when life's kinda fuzzy. It's fun, Tara, being pissed. Fun … Jeez, Tara, you sure can kill a good day.'

'Seriously, Dominic, if that's the best you can come up with to explain why you write yourself off so much … you've got to think this through.'

'Aw, fuck off. I don't have to explain anything to you.'

'No, Dominic, not to me … explain it to you, yourself. Explain to Dominic Fitzgerald just why you fuck with your health so … so vigorously and so often.'

An odd, slightly awkward silence between us was broken by Dominic, who plonked himself into the modern, uncomfortable, beige-coloured lounge chair near the window.

'Well, sure. I ought not to drink so much. You're right, but not entirely.'

Tapping the arm of the chair, he looked out over the hot, sun-drenched city, then started again, itemising on his fingers: 'My dad died when I was young, and my mum needs me. So, there's that.' He paused, took an audible breath. 'And I've never been as good as my brothers at anything. I don't know things about life … how to live it … and it can seem kind of empty. And I can't work out why I get so angry at little things. So, sure, I ought to understand it, but you know what?' He swung to face me fully. 'You can do things for no good or sensible reason, Tara. Look at me: I do dumb things just for the hell of it,' and Dominic started laughing, an infectious, affirming laugh that took in all the stupid things that crop up in everybody's lives: unexplainable, whimsical, nonsensical, infuriating, disarming. 'Maybe, Tara, you have to explain why you *don't* get stupidly drunk more often.' Both of us were laughing now. 'See, got you there.'

'No, you haven't, you dumb idiot …'

'Love you too, Tara!' Raising his right hand's middle finger, to give me a generous 'fuck you' gesture, Dominic stood and backed out of my office in good cheer, laughing like a madman.

A seed had been sown. Maybe he'd cut down a little. I hoped so.

*

One Friday afternoon, a classic, sub-tropical Sydney storm that had been brewing all day held off long enough for me and Dom to venture to our preferred small Balmain pub. The sun found its way between heavy, billowing thunderstorm clouds and streamed through the coloured-glass windows. We settled on having a couple of Peronis.

'So, what's happening this weekend, Tara?'

'Ah, I don't know. I asked Charles to have the kids so I could write, but so far, I can't get excited about spending a couple of days on the novel. I can't seem to generate any enthusiasm for it, especially now I'm working full-time.'

'Well, that's OK then, right? You're free, free as a bird.'

I gave him a withering look.

'What? Tell me,' he countered.

'Mmm … when the children are with Charles, I live in a kind of fake state. I can be a child – childlike – but it's superficial, temporary … and I suspect a slippery slope.'

Dom gave me the confused emoji face: one eyebrow raised, one lowered, mouth turned down, head tilted.

'Then, when they're with me I feel fake too, like I'm pretending to be a good mother. It's not just me; I've read it's a sort of domestic imposter syndrome and apparently it occurs in shared custody like I've got with Charles.'

As often happened when I shared something beyond Dom, I saw his thoughts cross his face in the pause that followed. He was no fool, but he often resisted having to consider matters too deeply – a kind of emotional languor.

Dom gave me a disinterested, 'whatever' kind of look. 'I gotta say I don't understand you.'

'I suppose it's the guilt I feel about Charlotte and Persy. Sure, I can laugh, have fun, be happy, but the point of it eludes me. I am hard-pressed to explain. And maybe it's more, perhaps a mood, a kind of anti-feeling. It's probably just a slow-moving, unavoidable low – the result of a fucked-up, failed marriage.' I felt myself warming to the topic, my arms describing a big space around me. 'Is this it? All there is? I've had the kids, now it's work till my deathbed? It's kind of empty.'

'Uh-huh.' Dominic nodded in an act of listening, while he checked out the rest of the room. Like a bad movie's coincidence, the air growled outside with deep-throated, ominous thunder.

'Wow, how's that thunder? It's really going to pour,' Dom observed. Was he trying to change the subject?

'I give myself all sorts of reasonable explanations,' I blustered on, looking at the marble-topped bar, 'but nobody, least of all me, wants to acknowledge that they may be, well, worthless. No, no, I'm being melodramatic. Maybe I am simply, merely, awfully ordinary. It seems a bit pathetic to acknowledge it. I mean, why should I matter?'

I glanced at Dom, wondering if I'd gone too far on the existential crisis, to check I wasn't boring him. I usually didn't dwell on it or get into any kind of funk over it. It was just a riptide, dragging me away from the certainty of shore. I couldn't control it and I didn't like it.

Lightning lit up the place, flickering for what seemed like ten seconds.

'That's rhetorical, right?' he said. 'So anyway, let's do something, Saturday or Sunday? The footy? That new Indian restaurant?'

Typical Dom. Moved on as though I hadn't just bared my soul. That was OK; I didn't mind that he didn't indulge my maudlin state. But I did not have the energy to join in the what-will-we-do-this-weekend? game.

'I don't know …' I chose to slump on my bar stool, perhaps a bit sulkily, staring at my glass.

'Why the fuck are you so miserable all the time?' Dominic play-pushed me. At least, I think it was in fun. I eyed his glass, which was already empty.

'I don't know … that I'm … miserable … *all* the time.'

'You alright, then? You seem … are you tired or something?'

'Well, I don't sleep really well at the moment.'

In truth, I woke most nights, sometime between three and four in the morning, not in a sweat, not with a pounding heart. I lay still, bored with myself, contemptuous of my own intro-spection. Sometimes I was still awake at dawn, and then I'd doze till the alarm went off. At least at that moment I knew what I must do: get up. I didn't want to raise my disquiet with Dominic, but I'd turned the key in the lock, opened the door, and it was starting to pour out.

Outside, the stupendous rain of the summer storm, like a grand waterwheel, sloshed out of the sky and deluged the asphalt and concrete. With a whoosh and roar of booming thunder, mirror-ball lightning cast shadows through the pub's windows and seemed to reduce the space between us.

'Look, it's nothing … really,' I said with a half-smile. Dominic wore a quizzical frown, and I chose to continue. 'Well, people of different times, in history, you know, seem to have had a better sense of purpose. So, what am *I* doing? What are *we* doing? What is *our* purpose? Where is the war we have to fight? The tsunami, the earthquake? Perhaps it is ridiculous, but I want to save someone, defend something, claim something, restore …' I petered out, defeated, but with a defensive grin now. 'Seriously, what's our emergency, Dominic? Our priority? I'm an adult, and I … we … don't contribute.'

'Jeez, you're serious.'

These were not the kind of considerations that challenged Dominic, but he sensed that I was somehow troubled; as a kind soul, he was moved enough to place a hand on my shoulder.

The rainwater bounced off the pavement outside, through the open doors and into the bar.

'I don't know … what is my "test"?' I dribbled on. 'How do I know I'm good enough? Is there anything I *must* do?'

I'd always thought that Dominic was not my intellectual equal, so I was almost talking to myself, posing my own internal conundrums, as I stirred the nuts in the bowl on the table between us. I didn't honestly believe Dominic could contribute much, but on this occasion it would seem I was determined to overshare. 'Sometimes I feel like I've got a big hole in my guts.'

Dominic shrugged, thoughtful for a moment. 'OK.' He sounded resolved, then catching the eye of the barman and raising two fingers, he added, 'Another round, thanks, mate.'

I dismissed the conversation as an unsuccessful fumble in my own dark place, sighed a little, gathered myself, sitting up straight. He turned back to me.

'Have I told you about my grandfather? Edward Fitzgerald. He went to both world wars. I don't know if he felt the need to prove anything but it's a damn good story. He was a real hero. I bet he never doubted himself or … you know, worried about anything.'

'To have fought in both world wars must have been doubly terrible. Did he come out of it OK?'

'Of course. He was a Fitzgerald.'

'Ha, ha, Dom. So, by that you're actually saying you are going to tell me the vanilla, family version … the shiny story. Have you confirmed any of the facts? Wouldn't he just tell you the nice, sanitised version?'

'Nah, Grandpa wouldn't have lied … I've never questioned his account.'

'I'm not saying he might have lied, just not told you the bad bits.' I brought him back to earth.

'I can't know the intimate details, but you know what I'm like … I'm the one who embroiders the details for the purposes of telling a good story,not him.' He paused for a moment, suddenly struck with a recollection. 'You know, once he nearly cried when I was talking to him about all this. He started to tell me about how he lost a friend … not because he died, but because he … Edward … was a failure. That was the word he used. He said he'd just wanted to be a hero, but he couldn't be. That was a sad moment. I guess he lost it for a minute. You know, kind of old man's reminiscent sadness.'

'Sounds pretty normal, pretty human. Everybody must regret something, have some remorse,' I blathered, caught unawares by Dominic's perception.

'Yeah, but this was my grandpa, so I just kept talking and pretended he wasn't upset. He pulled himself together. It was a bit scary, I guess. Wonder if I'd stuck with it, he might have explained what he meant.'

Dominic slapped the bar top as though he'd just had a good idea.

'Tell you what, do you want to do a bit of research into Edward's life? BEER! might want to do something around next Anzac Day; they said they're considering doing a campaign based on Australian soldiers who served in the First World War.'

'Well, I am a bit of a history nerd. I'll pretend I've adopted him as my grandpa and I'll see what I can turn up in the archives online … or, if you like, next time I'm in Canberra I'll have a scratch around at the War Memorial.'

'That would be very cool. Thank you, Tara. Really amazing.' He hugged me in his very fraternal way, ably assisted by a little too much alcohol. It felt warm, friendly and sincere.

We shared an Uber across the bridge, and when he jumped out at his place, he leant into the car door to say, 'Sorry that you're down in the dumps. How about Edward Fitzgerald though? Cool, huh?'

CHAPTER THREE

THE EARLY YEARS OF EDWARD FITZGERALD

'Oh, my dear.' Edward's bombastic and proud father stands in the bedroom in front of the fire's grate, arms akimbo, chest thrust outward, a grin as broad as can be. 'You are marvellous. Another fine son. Five!' he says to his wife, awash with a rush of overwhelming emotion and sentimentality in salty tears and urgency.

Edward's exhausted but joyful mother is propped up in the linen-clad matrimonial bed by numerous puffy pillows. She holds her sated newborn close as the sensuous tingle and luxurious rush of her abundant milk leaks into her bedding and flounced cotton nightclothes. Her head a little tilted, and with a tired but genuine smile, she nods ever so slightly to her husband.

'Marvellous,' he whispers, smacks his hands together, places the bundle of his new son into the crib, and turns the key in the door. He strips quickly, and pushes into this, his plentiful woman, among her blood and serous padding. She accepts his custody of her bruised womb with a quick involuntary gasp and then a small sigh of acquiescence. When he washes afterward, his satisfaction makes him blush with the magnitude of the pleasures in his possession.

The plush-cheeked, gurgling baby is bundled along the Manly seafront nearly every day of his infancy in an enormous baby carriage, at first by a nursemaid, then by his adoring nanny. The famous Norfolk Island pines lining the seafront are only as high as a man as yet, but the trees tower like giants for little Edward.

It is not long until his sturdy, chubby legs allow him to self-propel and he launches himself into mischief, trouble and good deeds alike. Now an engaging, curly-haired boy, with daring and dimples, Edward is admired by both the holidaymakers and the locals as he dashes up and down the beach, and in and out of the waves that expend themselves on the pristine sand.

Edward loves his mother especially. She is a cloud of scent, soft flesh and warm embraces, and he never tires of her hide-and-seek games, her reading to him, and her sharing of shaped chocolates with creamy mint centres.

'Mumma … Mumma! What fruit makes the best slippers?'

'Mmmmh? I don't know, sweetheart, what fruit makes the best slippers?'

'Banana peel!'

'Oh, what a clever little darling!' his mother trills at his eight-year-old riddling, bundles his head to her cleavage, strokes his back, cooing. She kisses her baby, her last child, on his red cheeks over and over, ruffles his thick, dark hair. 'Did you have a lovely day at school, darling?'

'I got all the answers in arithmetic. And we sang … very loud.' He bursts into song, 'Rule, Britannia! Britannia rules the waves!' and dances away from his adoring mother, yelling verse after tuneless verse of the Empire's vocational anthems.

His indulgent brothers, father and mother do nothing to quell his inherent joy. They feed his delight. Edward does not veer from the Victorian path of a privileged boy: reading tales of derring-do, dressing as a little sailor, and mock-marching to the mock-military band each Saturday afternoon at the local park's rotunda. He is safe, sleeps deeply, and is certain, just certain that life will always be 'splendid!' – a word he loves to use.

Good at all games, he thwacks cricket balls and tennis balls through hot summers, the fragrance of eucalypts and dust in his nostrils. The whomp of energising tackles in winter's rugby games keep him animated. But all year round, Edward loves horses, those of the household and of the neighbourhood. As a baby, he wriggled with elation as he rode almost every day, perched on the pommel in front of any of his brothers, who held him with genuine fraternal care, their still-smooth hands wrapped around his torso. When he could walk, he was seated behind, learning to move with the horse, leg position lengthening, his seat established. From five, he was on his own mount, a piebald Shetland pony, a mare named Beauty. All that year, he was quite a sight, in dishevelled clothes and with wild, overly long hair flopping, riding his thick-maned and -tailed mount. With a crowd of mismatched, wet and sandy dogs, dashing along the foreshore's road, there were broad smiles on all of their animal faces.

As a tall, thin twelve-year-old, he graduates to a sixteen-hand, chestnut thoroughbred, Kitchener; Edward has become a fine horseman. He hoots with joy when he hears the crash, bang, clink of any harnessing or shoeing that is taking place in any of the households along the tree-lined boulevard on which they live. If he hears a clank or a jingle or a certain kind of whinny from the neighbours' yards, he dashes toward the scintillating sound to participate. The families around the Fitzgeralds welcome him for the candid energy this happy, healthy boy brings, and they feed him currant buns and glasses of creamy milk as a reward for his assistance, and in the hope he'll come again.

Dogs, too, are his constant companions. The cook has a doppelganger in her plump, smooth-coated Jack Russell, Maisie, and this effusive terrier becomes Edward's best friend. Besides Maisie, he trains his mother's spaniel and his father's two retrievers to come to his exclusive call, to sit, to stay and roll over. He naps with the dogs on their blankets on hot afternoons in the shade, and in winter he smuggles one or another into his oak coach bed and snuggles up to the warmth of their shedding coats.

*

In 1913, the news is of international tensions and sabre-rattling. The alchemy of raw ambition and unchecked energy drives Edward to imagine that conflict means worldly adventure for the brave. He sees an advertisement calling for enrolment in the newly established Duntroon, Australia's nascent military college. He shows it to his father, who frowns.

'We had decided on you studying the law, young man. Your brothers are all making their mark in this way and you can follow.' But his father's firm hand on Edward's shoulder is all the encouragement the young man needs to proceed surreptitiously, and he continues to work on Pater and Mater for overt approval.

His parents are unsure whether to support him in his endeavours or not. There's change in the air, but it only makes them nervous.

'The college is new, not yet a place for gentlemen. It's no place for my little boy,' his mother wails, behind the closed doors of Pater's dark wood study.

'Yes, yes, my dear. I, too, am not certain whether a career in the army for a younger son will grant or deplete opportunity. It is difficult to know, but Edward … he's a jolly boy, who might thrive. Perhaps …'

They allow him to attend the exams, but Edward's mother half hopes, wringing her hands, fingering a lace-edged handkerchief, that he'll fail. She'll be a comfort to him – she imagines the scene of her largesse, drawing him into a restorative hug, cooing tender phrases – and this threat to her son's well-being will be put behind them.

For the first time in his short life, Edward works toward a defined outcome. He swots for the entrance exams, coached by a former teacher, using the published guide to the tests. He teaches himself how to focus and how to sit still at a desk for hours, going over and over rudimentary geography, history, physics, till his eyes weep with stinging tiredness and his neck aches, having little experience of sedentary days.

His wait for the letter of acceptance is not fraught: he is calm. With increasing self-awareness and self-confidence, Edward simply knows he will be accepted. He sees himself there at his imagined Duntroon – the welcome scratch of the uniform, the sweat of physical training, the camaraderie. He's sure it will be a matter of horsemanship and riding all day. He sleeps, converses with his family and friends with a confident certainty that might elude other seventeen-year-olds, and soon, in his emerald-green tweed suit and with a leather valise, he takes leave of his family to realise his dream. On the station platform, as he bends his head to kiss his mother on her powdered cheek, her mouth is in a miserable downward curve. This is it: the moment. His stomach is churning with butterflies; he can't wipe the smile from his face – even his mother's despondency does not give him a moment's pause. He comprehends for the first time that he is many inches taller than she, that he is growing away from her, from his childhood, from all that has bound him to the ordinary. He firmly grasps his father's and brothers' strong hands as he has been taught, and he is certain he is their equal – robust, lean, with a leader's posture and demeanour. His father, given to ostentation, delivers the notable send-off moment for them all by fixing his eyes, now ringed with crow's feet, on his son's. He proclaims:

'Remember your mother, your family and your Kipling, and "you'll be a Man, my son".' He kisses his youngest son on his forehead and turns away, snuffling into a flare of white kerchief.

*

The seemingly interminable journey does not diminish Edward's excitement as he travels to the college on the remote high plain. There are hours and hours on two trains that deliver him to Duntroon's closest station at the town of Queanbeyan, and then eight dusty miles by horse-drawn coach over rutted and rock-strewn roads. During a break in the last part of the journey, Edward moves away from the other travellers and walks to the top of a hill. He cocks his hand to his brow and, like a prospective buyer, surveys the plateau, an extensive series of dry sheep paddocks sweeping east and west for hundreds of miles. He looks to the south, where the plain rolls into the sharp ravine of the Murrumbidgee River at the base of the green-blue Brindabella Range.

'My land, my country,' he declares to his young self, puffing out his chest.

On the northern edge of the plain, there is one big farmhouse, the primary building of the young nation's first military college, Duntroon. Edward turns eighteen in his first weeks there. He is all stringy muscle, with not a skerrick of body fat. His deep-brown eyes under dark, defined eyebrows complete the picture of a direct young man with a striking visage. The constant Australian sun turns his skin a nutty brown as the trainees run up and down hills with full packs, and as they swim naked in the swirling Murrumbidgee River to cool off. There's a rope swing at the river that delivers Edward into the middle of the deep, brown water to the tune of a million cicadas. His exhilaration is heard in the yells of conquest he can't help but release as the wide arc carries him over the perpetual flow and he drops into the velvety cool.

'Didja see that?! I made it to the very middle. You should feel the current; it's incredible.' Edward plonks himself down beside one of his new friends, his training partner, Martin Brown. Martin is as thin as a whippet, sensitive and forever pushing his wire-rimmed glasses up over his nose. He's an insurance clerk from Hunters Hill in northern Sydney, a little older than Edward – twenty-two last birthday – and newly-wed.

'Oh, yeah, yeah, I saw.' He's folding and refolding the ribbons of eucalyptus leaves from the debris carpet of the gumtrees lining the bank, preoccupied.

'No … you didn't; you weren't even looking. Come on, you have a go.'

'I don't feel like it.' Martin's mouth is turned down; he shrugs.

'Martin, don't worry about … that man.' Ed whispers conspiratorially and places a hand on Martin's shoulder. He tilts his head to indicate a large, bare-chested man two hundred feet further along the bank. 'He can't hear us.'

'How can I not worry? He's the sergeant, our trainer, he's measuring my capabilities.'

At training the day before, Edward missed a target, then stumbled before the putative enemy. The sergeant yelled, 'Fitzgerald, you git, you stupid git. Here's your damn rifle. Do it again, and again, and again, till you can KILL some bastard.'

The big angry man then cocked the rifle, which that day carried live ammunition. The rifle was swung to point at Martin's feet and fired.

'That's what will happen if you bugger up. Your mate gets it.'

The noise shocked, a loud retort. The kicked-up dust rose like a cloud from the dry, clay ground. Martin froze in terror, and, beyond his control, his eyes swam with tears of visceral fear, bringing a storm of mockery from the instructor.

'Sir, yes, sir,' Edward interrupted, loud enough to drown out the instructor's jibes, a clear response and to halt the jeering, but not loud enough to challenge his authority. Ed's neck tightened, his shoulders becoming rigid. He did not look the instructor in the eye but quickly leapt to his feet from the dry grass patch where he had fallen. He took the shot again and it was a good one this time, but he couldn't yet release the lungful of air that he held hostage while the bully sneered. With his bayonet, he eviscerated a straw man hanging by the neck in a line of enemy scarecrows. Martin was left alone, the sergeant having lost interest; Ed had protected his mate.

'Look, that sergeant, he's just a bastard, there's no other word for it. It was a low act. Let's just forget the whole thing,'

Ed cajoles while shaking the leaves and ants from his clothes and pulling on his shorts over damp underwear. 'And anyway, let's head back; dinner's not far off, and I'm starving.'

That night in the mess, the gramophone is brought out, wound, and for the umpteenth time the young men hear the horn and drums herald the popular song of the time:

Comes a message o'er the ocean
A message to our sunny land
England calls Australia's soldiers
We must answer her command
If England wants a hand, well, here it is …

The last line repeats over and over again. It leaves the lads contemplative, sunk in a leather ottoman or on a chintz sofa, finishing their port, rustling the leaves of books or day-old newspapers. Martin and Ed are playing chequers, though Edward means to head to bed shortly. The most senior officer comes in grim-faced, serious.

'Very good, chaps. "Give me your ears", eh?' He's clearly nervous. 'A bit of news: orders require us at the front. Yes, I mean "over there". You'll all be given graduation certificates; you've all done very well in your endeavours.'

Silence hangs in the chilly air of anticipation.

'We leave in six days from Sydney Harbour. You've all got leave till then. Your paperwork is to be picked up from the office.'

Edward is first to find his voice. 'Three cheers for the king! Hip, hip … hooray! Hip, hip … hooray! Hip, hip … hooray!'

Glasses are raised, clinked; eyes meet. The ritual snaps their minds back to the immediate. They resume their professional face, an officer's sharpened acuity. A subdued hubbub starts up.

Martin Brown puts down his glass.

'Righto, then. See you in Sydney,' he says, and he leaves the room with a wave and a wink to Edward. No doubt, he is off to pack and be ready to leave as soon as possible, to see his young wife, say farewell to his family.

'Jolly good.'

'Oo-roo.'

One by one, the others make their exit, resigned, not yet overwhelmed, by the implications. One of them tries to hide his shaking hands, thrusting them deep into his pockets. Another tries to hide his eagerness; he wants to appear as a gentleman soldier, and he conjures a frown to cap his wide smile. Ed drags out the moment. He has a heaviness like a stone in his abdomen, not quite butterflies, not quite dread. Just for an instant, he longs for his mother's presence, the pang of a young man's yearning, gone quickly, and replaced with practical thoughts of packing and travel. He empties his glass of port, lifts the needle on the phonogram, tidies the newspapers on the table, refills his glass and resumes his seat for a little while. He's the last to leave the room.

*

They set out from Australia in June 1915. Many of them partic- ipate in the last months of the ill-fated Gallipoli campaign, where most of them die. Those who survive move on to the trenches of the European conflict. Edward, however, does not join his fellow graduates at Anzac Cove, nor does he proceed to France. Instead, he is selected and immediately attached to an emerging part of the British Army on Salisbury Plain, as a second lieutenant. He is on English soil for a crash course in their military ways. He is honoured at first to have been so recognised, seen as a potential leader of men. He offers his commitment to hard work and friendship to those around him. The English officers insult and ignore Edward in equal measure, and the soldiers are barely civil. Australians are viewed as gauche by the officers, who snub them, and second rate by the soldiers, who jeer. Edward is disappointed but not perturbed, isolated but not lonely.

What do they know about anything, anyway? Bunch of toffs.

By virtue of his constant requests, Ed is often allowed one or two days' time outside of the camp. He meets up with other Australians, men from the ranks and some officers too, and joins them on day trips and outings, sometimes to the coun- tryside, including Oxford, and even a weekend in Wales. He marvels at every little thing: the old buildings, the friendly people, the green vistas, the bare hills and snow-capped moun- tains. The viscous warm beer initially provokes an unexpected spit-out and a disgusted face, but the pies and peas warm him as comfort food ought.

On Salisbury Plain, the boom of the big guns across the Channel can be heard on still days or when the wind flows westward. Waiting to get started, Edward bides his time: he's worked hard to be where he is – trained, fit, able-bodied, poised on the edge of war. But after months and months of professional isolation, falling between administrations and being overlooked for active service in Europe, he is losing heart. He's heard the gossip about the disaster at Gallipoli and read the highfalutin words in the British newspaper accounts. He's seen the names of the dead: the listing included Martin Brown. He doesn't know what to do about that; he'd like to write to Martin's wife, send his condolences.

But like a fool, I never asked for his home address. I never thought …

On a warm day, when Edward wrestles with boredom as he counts pallets of new boots, a whippet-like superior officer with a pencil moustache and thinning, slicked-down hair strides toward him.

'You are to join Australia's Third Division, Fitzgerald. They should arrive any day now, God help us.' These last words are muttered. 'The Division, such as it is, will complete its training and fit-out here. You will assume a new role as lieutenant to … let me see,' he refers to the taupe sheets of paper in his hand, 'the 11th Machine Gun Company of the 43rd Battalion. Here, take it, your new orders.'

A brisk salute is acknowledged by the other. Ed can barely suppress a smile; like shedding a heavy coat, he is jubilant in his relief.

There's a quick connection when Ed meets his Australian commanding officer in September 1916. With a handshake of certainty and sustained eye contact in his moderately amused face, Alexander, Ed's new captain, a professional soldier, immediately takes the role as the older brother of the two.

'Just call me Alex when we're on our own, eh?'

On their first afternoon, as they get to know each other, they share a sherry and shortbread in Alex's tent. As an opener they spend half an hour discussing the latest rule change in the game of rugby – a diplomatic issue, as the Australian troops will play the English soldiers in the coming days.

Edward leans in, not wanting to be heard by Alex's batman. 'I say, it might be prudent to make our men aware that they may need to hold back their … their enthusiasm.'

Alex laughs. 'You've no idea how British you sound. The men won't pull their punches even if I told them to.'

Ed stares and blinks. 'Quite right too. You're right. Too much of the Poms has rubbed off on me. Oh, it is good to be with my countrymen again. Just to hear the Australian voice … does me good, sir, I mean Alex.'

Edward, used to being the younger sibling, remains the mischievous knave allowed by Alex's pragmatism and openness. After a year of cynicism from his British superiors, it's a release. The firm friendship complements both; they are cheered by each other. Alex's consistency restores Edward's natural optimism, eroded by months of English class politics, and Edward's sunny outlook smooths Alex's edginess. They work together well, sharing a dedication to the men in their charge. Edward develops; he grows his tendency to be effervescent, and it becomes a useful energy that bears fruit of the military kind.

*

Edward and Alex cadge a couple of days' leave in London. They arrive at Paddington Station, leaping from their carriage steps into the great covered cavern, home to a cacophony of steam escaping, voices shouting, doors banging, boots clomping over platforms. They are surprised by the number of uniformed men en masse, milling about, flowing from platform to platform. Some are entering the cool, dark interior, and some move outside to see the weak sunshine or take a breath of fresher air. Some are travelling with their units; some appear to be on leave. There are stretchers in a line placed along the length of the station. The solid stone exterior wall is the injured men's bedhead. As the two young men walk past the prostrate, their eyes dart to take in the human forms under the dark-green blankets. There is no sound coming from the mounds of damaged bodies and barely any movement. By choice, Ed does not dwell on the suffering; he is determined to enjoy his trip. He steels himself, his hands ball into fists, he looks straight ahead and strides to the exit.

Leaving the station, they head down the main thoroughfare. There are horse-drawn omnibuses, double-decker motorised vehicles, lorries and cars. Hundreds of pedestrians pay no attention to the various conveyances' right of way. There are workers in flat caps, women pulling flimsy shawls around their shoulders, neat women in fitted skirts and jackets, and a few dandy, older men in straw boaters who seem well past the age of a fighting British soldier.

'This is the place, eh, Alex? Look at this!' Edward's zeal bubbles to the surface, his arms outstretched such that frowning passers-by must avoid his exuberant gesture.

There is little colour in the dull streets, flags and bunting show wear and tear, some ragged, most dirty, drooping in the frequent, despondent rain. In his innocence, Edward finds the dogged energy of miserable resilience energising. To Ed, the grim faces indicate defiance and determination, not grinding deprivation. He is not sensitive to the nuance, the mounting waves of sorrow, the accretion of sadness.

As they make their way, Edward's gait loosens, relaxes, and he swaggers: he's a young man, hubristic, proud of his officer standing and his colonial, perhaps mongrel, status. He knows he's handsome and cuts a fine figure. His muscles are flexed, his posture assertive, as he and Alex walk the streets absorbing the life of the monster city, the largest and most populous place that the men have ever experienced.

They jump on a moving omnibus, and the conductor lets them travel for free with a wink. They make their way to Sloane Square where their designated officers' hotel, the Royal Court Hotel, is located. The French restaurant on the square has been recommended.

'We'll eat like kings, Al! And we can try the Frenchie coffee. Come on, let's sit outside. Here's a table.' Excited, Edward talks Alex into stopping there. In the British autumn, the two sit back – legs loose, arms over the adjoining chairs, caps tipped to the back of their heads – through the early afternoon, overcast but warm enough, watching the people pass by, like satisfied citizens of the world.

There's a theatre next to the restaurant, and the two buy a couple of seats for a musical. Edward loves a sing-along. That night at the show, he strokes the plush, crimson fabric of his seat – what a treat – and the band and performance has him entranced, tapping his foot, clapping his hands, laughing at the ribald jokes from the stage. He's never seen anything like it.

*

In the south-east corner of Sloane Square, there are cobble-stones in front of the train station, which resound with the clipping and clopping of the many work horses making deliveries in the wee hours. It's a delight to Edward to be woken in this way in the pre-dawn the following morning, and he takes a moment to think of home, of the horses, the dogs, his brothers, father and mother. He smiles, preferring on balance his current adventure, as he pushes back the bed covers and starts the day, which they will fill with sightseeing, strolling and admiring.

There's a small pedestrian island just outside the men's hotel, tucked into the mouth of the narrow Eaton Gate. At seven on their last evening of leave, daylight just gone, there are three young girls in slightly battered straw boaters, pinafores to their knees, scuffed and worn black leather boots, standing on that stone island as Alex and Edward step out of the foyer, jaunty with the prospect of a fine evening, and begin to cross the Square for their last London dinner, *entrecôte boeuf* and *frites*.

The tallest of the girls steps in front of them and pipes up, neck long and large eyes opened wide. 'Please, sirs, can you help us find our father? We believe he's in there.'

All three girls turn like a small flock of birds and point to the hotel's bar entrance.

Edward and Alex exchange a look above the girls' heads.

'Please … our mother sent us to fetch him.'

'Alright,' Alex volunteers, unable to resist the girls' sweetly put request, and he heads off back into the hotel while Edward makes conversation with the three. At ease with adults, the girls chitter-chat about the weather. Their hair is fashioned in rag curls, and the spirals bob around their small faces. Their pinafores are of navy serge, and they have thick stockings on their calves.

'Are you a soldja? My dadda is a soldja,' the smallest of the three tweets.

'Yes, littley, I am.'

'And what is your name?'

'Hush, Cleo, that's impolite.'

'No, no, not at all. My name is Edward. I am from Australia.'

'Australia?' The incredulity of the three girls brings a chuckle to Edward.

'Yes, Australia.'

The littlest speaks again: 'Our names are Boudicca, Titania and Cleopatra … Boo, Titty and Cleo.'

'Cleo, hush.' The oldest grabs the offender's ear and gives it a twist. 'Excuse my little sister, sir. Our mother asks us not to tell people our names. She says our father got carried away. He's a writer.'

'And here he comes.' Edward catches sight of a slight young man walking toward them with Alex, a cigarette hanging from the Brit's lip. He's weaving a little from the drink, uniform dishevelled, and grinning good-naturedly. The men chat and find enough in common for the Englishman to extend an invitation to supper, which is immediately accepted by the city's visitors.

At the small Chelsea basement home of the British officer, the evening is not without sadness and not without laughter. The Londoner is Robert, a journalist and author of one published volume of poetry.

'Fifty-three copies have been sold,' Robert says with a touching pride. He wears his heart on his sleeve.

His wife, Alice, gives the men a muted but genuine welcome. She has sad eyes and small red hands. Their home is three tiny rooms and a shared privy. The threadbare furniture is oversized, the crockery chipped, and the smell of the walls' damp is immediately obvious.

'A toast, my friends, a toast to the city – my city, my London,' Robert declares when they are settled. He slumps back into his armchair and groans. 'She is much diminished. The War, the cataclysm, is not even one hundred and fifty miles away from here, can you believe it? But London's decline is not caused by the sounds of artillery as it leaches across the Channel. Oh no. It is not the drunk and aggressive troops on leave. No, what causes the city's unease – *dis*-ease – is the thousands of injured and broken bodies arriving daily.'

Though anxious about the turn in the conversation – from fun to reality – Edward doesn't interrupt Robert's speech. He cocks his head as though in agreement, sniffs, lights a cigarette, but struggles to comprehend the image.

'No, it is the distraught and damaged men, distributed unceremoniously among the hospitals or homes, to the country or town centres. The pall of their mass agony accumulates. It lingers over all the inhabitants whether directly affected or not.'

Robert leans forward to the table between the men and reaches for his half-empty beer, takes a disconsolate sip. He wraps both hands around the glass and lowers it back onto the waxy wooden surface. He looks up at Alex, holds his gaze, then to Edward. A little dazed, solemn, he stares at Ed.

'An insidious wretchedness, like a viscous London fog, lies over my city. Birdsong was formerly omnipresent, now it is groaning, weeping, a lament that can be universally heard. The spirit of the Londoners *was* pugilistic but now is merely pained.'

Edward and Alex are reduced to silence by this poetic and theatrical speech, the alcohol sedating them. They murmur sounds of agreement, and nod and shake their heads.

'And we are all – the entire nation – literally and figuratively impoverished. Even with my officer's wage, we scarcely have enough to live on, and my beautiful wife and these magnificent children must return to Alice's parents' village on the morrow when I must return to the Somme.'

Alice moves closer to Robert, places a hand on his rounded shoulder. 'There, there; we will be fine. We will look after each other.'

'But, dear, I … I am afraid. I am fearful of injury, of death, of France, of the trenches, of this perverse warfare,' he confesses, blurting like a child, tears in his eyes.

Like a pietà, the children hold his hands, touch his face. The littlest is on his knee, her short, thin arms wound around his neck.

Bravely, Robert reaches for his resilience, perhaps to cheer his wife and children. 'Thank you, my little loved ones.' He wipes his face with the back of his hand. 'What do you say, gentlemen? I say, getting drunk is the best thing to do, and I will stay this way for as long as possible!'

Edward gets to his feet – already more than tipsy – and a toast is proposed, seconded, and glasses clink: 'To drinking until drunk!'

After many more bottles of warm, dark beer, then many glasses of warmer, darker port, the men sing Irish songs of oppression, though none of them have a drop of Irish blood in them. The melancholic times call for it. And when the streets are very quiet, at the time when the old tend to die, the two Australians walk mostly in silence with hands in pockets.

'I don't think we'll ever meet Robert, Alice and their girls again.' Edward fishes for some sort of clarity from Alex.

'You're right, but something there tonight, well, it's changed me a bit; something has been revealed by meeting them.'

'Sure, but I couldn't say what that was.'

'Perhaps … a sense of sorrow? Or … a glimpse of a counter reality?' Alex is better at articulating things that Edward can't hold in his hand, can't grasp.

'Ever the poet, Al. Well said.'

They return to the Royal Court Hotel to catch a few hours of shut-eye before the train must take them back to Salisbury Plain.

*

Edward shudders in his damp greatcoat, his cap pulled as low as it will go. He struggles to smoke a ragged cigarette while he stands on the forward deck of the whale-like ferry. The dim lights of Le Havre come closer and closer. The November night is cold and foggy, and the Channel flow has given the Company a sick-making crossing, the corkscrew motion making everybody queasy.

He observes the untidy disembarkation. The soldiers stagger a little on unsteady sea legs as they shrug their packs to their shoulders, pick up their weapons and shuffle toward the adjoining train halt. Most fall asleep even before the train leaves, but not Edward. As weary as he is, he is not at ease. The reality of the war is becoming clear.

In the wee hours, the train stops at the village billeting Edward's men for the night. The NCOs shout instructions and directions to the soldiers, who slouch and shamble away into the night. When his close supervision of the men's travel is no longer required, Edward walks down the main street, looking for and finding a crowded bar, more of an estaminet. The proprietors are doing an excellent trade selling the few items they have for inflated prices to the men who are moving either east or west – to or from the front line. Small, freckled red apples, French cigarettes, roasted chestnuts, packs of playing cards, small flat bottles of liquor: the items are displayed on the mirrored wall behind the bench.

Edward squeezes into a space at the marble bar.

'What's good?' he says to the English soldier beside him, whose uniform is muddied and unkempt.

The big man turns to take Edward in: his rank, his tidiness, his vigour. With his puttees and boots still neat and clean, in his untested uniform, Ed is clearly a new arrival.

'Anything,' is the unenthusiastic reply. It is difficult to hear as a great roar comes from the adjoining room. Edward glances in the direction it came from and sees a frowned-upon game of two-up. He ignores it; doesn't want to know.

Edward raises a finger to the barman.

'Uh, *merci*,' he ventures, and he receives a heavy, dirty shot glass filled to the brim with a golden-coloured, syrupy liqueur.

'Kess ker say?' Ed's Australian-French is enough for the barman and he gives the drink a name and adds what Edward presumes is a description. Something to do with berries? It slides down his throat, coating his mouth in a sugary tang, and at its end gives that perfect sting of alcohol he is looking for. His face makes it plain that a load is lifted: his shoulders relax, the space between his lower jaw and cheekbones becomes plumper and broad, his set mouth eases, the bumps between his brows are smoothed. He calls for another drink and another, seeking the gentle white noise of alcohol's wash.

The big man Ed first spoke to is standing a few feet away in a trio of other soldiers. To a man they need a bath and a shave. Their eyes are ringed with the crimson tinge of sustained apprehension. Their mouths are held in a tense, permanent sneer. They see him – an officer, an Australian, alone – downing his drinks, but they only glance in his direction; they're not brave enough to stare.

'So, fellas, where have you come from? Amiens, Armentières?' Edward breaks the impasse, glad to have the company, unconcerned, in his loneliness, by the lapse from reserve to familiarity. Only when Ed himself has had too many and his eyes are sufficiently glassy are the men at ease with Edward, enough to slap him on the back, call him a good bloke when he buys the next round, and the next.

*

'They're coming!' the cry sounds. The Third Division is now deep into the fight, rotating thousands of men through trench duties and then recovering behind the lines. There is no moon on this particular night, and the stars twinkle with a bright, white, cold light. It's just as cold at ground level. There'll be a hoarfrost in the morning.

'Sir, I can see pickelhaube spikes. There! There!'

The silhouettes of the raiders' helmets bob toward them along the access trenches, backlit by flares and yellow fires in no man's land.

'Prepare! Fix bayonets!' Some soldiers leap into activity; some freeze in fear. 'Move, move, move!'

It's Ed's first real contact, a close-quarters skirmish, and his mouth goes dry. His hands shake as they involuntarily rise to mimic surrender. Over the lip of the Australians' trench, right in front of Edward, come six, or ten – he loses count – mammoth creatures dressed in heavy folds of grey. These monsters have enclosed their skulls in grey, wool skull caps, knives emerging from the sheaths at their calves, knuckle dusters on both hands, mean faces and savage, threatening cries.

With a shudder across his body, Edward arches his back and his mouth drops open. He sees the Germans as animals, no less than beasts, not human. The threat is as clear as a clarion call: he scrabbles with the stud on his leather pouch and seizes the pistol from its holster. Fumbling, clicking, grasping, aiming, fire! The creature in front of him, face like a banshee, arms raised with a blade flashing in the dim light, not five feet away, crumples in a heap after a marionette's momentary flailing – like magic, like a dream – when the lead penetrates the large simian face at such close quarters. It is Ed's bullet that finds its mark, Ed's bullet that puts an end to this monstrosity, Ed's bullet that is victorious.

That man, he is dead, dead by my hand.

Pure joy fills Edward's heart, part relief, part pride, and part victory. He looks around; the raiders are being dealt with by his men, bludgeoning and slitting throats. He steps back from the fray, out of the fight, not quite sure what he should do next. Three, four minutes pass; he seesaws between ecstasy and horror. Ecstasy wins out and as soon as the attack is quelled, he's free to celebrate his success. He yells at all and no one, his head turning up and down the line of the trench, red-faced, eyes wide, head flung up, hopping from one leg to the other, and exclaiming to those around him, looking for congratulation.

'I got him, I bloody got him!' Like a boy playing cowboys and Indians.

The men around him are subdued. They're breathless, leaning against the wall of the trench, having fought – and won – a ghastly struggle, face-to-face with the fiends of their nightmares. They consider Ed with a blank stare.

That night he describes it for the assembled fellow officers in the dugout.

'It was a crack shot! I had to dig deep … but it was me or him; I took aim … carefully but not wasting a moment. I tell you, it was a close thing.'

What a warrior he feels, brave and fierce, telling and retelling the details, acting out the event, waiting for praise. He sees the rolled eyes, comprehends the downcast posture, but can't make sense of the muted response. Crestfallen, doubt creeps in like a tide; failure sneaks past the guards of self-confidence and pluck; misgiving arrives. In self-defence, with a shoulder shrug and a stony face, he must put it down to his fellow officers' weariness – it has been a troubling, long night.

Edward stores his first kill as a macabre curio, a slow-motion keepsake of sorts.

*

'Come on, fellas, get cracking. Gotta get this done.'

Edward's team have lost momentum. They've been sand-bagging for hours, shoring up the walls around a dugout entrance and along the top of a trench wall. Yesterday's barrage took out yards and yards of an important communications trench. It had to be mended.

The men get to their feet, slowly, stretching, stubbing out their cigarettes.

'There you go. Now, Quigley, will you hop up on that mound there, and we'll pass you the bags.'

As Quigley rises to his full height on the lip of the trench, a new bombing raid commences. The distant *thock* freezes them, widens their eyes, blanches the skin on their faces. They have seconds to register the danger they are in before Quigley's body is flung back toward the men below him among a mighty roar. The force of the explosion is enough to break Quigley's back as he lands on a ridge of pallets. The sound of the break, like the crack of a whip, can be heard even among the noise, by his mates around him.

It is the first death of a man from Edward's Company after four weeks at the front, an unusually long period to have not had any fatalities. As captain, it is Alex – not Ed – who duly makes a record in the unit diary and officially chronicles, in cool and distant terms, the demise of Private Thomas Joseph Quigley 'during enemy bombardment of our lines'. Edward does the honours at the graveside. He feels ripped in half – it was his instruction that sent Quigley to his death – but he says nothing. The spectre of Tommy at his death lingers – from neck to toe, his left side like minced meat, and an odd twist in his body that couldn't be straightened. Ed is able to get through the graveside ceremony though his speech is too brief and mumbled through gritted teeth. The hole in the dark earth is on the edge of a field, a group of silver birch to the east, and a narrow road to the west. There are more than twenty other mounds besides Quigley's in this makeshift graveyard.

'It is my painful duty to inform you,' he says out loud as an exorcism when he writes to Quigley's parents about the glory of their son's 'sacrificial' death.

Day after day, the mornings reveal deep, penetrating frosts where the drinking water barrels are sealed by inches of solid ice and rarely melted by midday. Light dustings of snow fall and drift in whorls on unexpected gusts; the snow in the early days brings a quietude, but later, in the white cold weeks that follow, it brings an ominous hush until broken by one side or the other when random shelling starts.

It occurs to Ed that the 'Hun' are equally as cold, as riddled with tickling lice, and similarly experiencing frostnip and infected wounds, disease and injuries. If the sun briefly emerges, Edward's exposed skin is warmed a little, and a rustle of leaves in one of the few remaining trees triggers a memory, a love of life, a recognition of Nature's largesse. At those fleeting moments, he sighs for the folly, the farce, the waste of time and energy.

Edward writes to his mother.

Dear Mater,

Things are a bit rough. I miss our Sunday roasts. I am well. All seems to be going to plan. Can't be much longer till I'm home.

Love to all.

Eddy x

He lingers on the X. Is it manly? Will his mother and father somehow know he's downhearted? He slumps as goosebumps rise all over him and he resists an anxiety that is fast becoming a familiar sensation.

✳

'Ed, look at me. What's troubling you?' Alex must whisper this personal exchange: none of the others in the dugout may hear. 'I need you to do this. We've got to get a prisoner from that bloody trench as soon as possible. The Huns have something going on in that sector and HQ want to know what it is.'

His hands behind his back, Edward toes a small lump of mud with his left foot while he gathers his thoughts. His cut-off gloves are not enough to quell the pain of distracting chilblains; he is shaking, as his layers of flannel, cotton, wool and worsted are not enough to keep him warm.

'Of course, of course, it's only that …' Unable to explain, he finishes there, and the moment passes as another officer calls to and diverts Alex. 'Very good, sir,' Edward chokes out the words to Alex's back as he moves away. He wants to make things right with Alex and calls out, 'For king and country.' It's a phrase that, as inspiration or consolation, is the usual liturgy offered at the conclusion of briefings. He'll carry out Alex's instructions. He stares at a puddle on the dirt floor of the dugout.

Edward has survived all his assigned small but lethal engagements, day after interminable day. But the other men of the Battalion are dying: disembowelled in close combat or by machine-gun fire; terminal fractures, through blood loss or because of smashed skulls, their brains fanned out around them. Some of them live through their ghastly gashes, their broken bones, their evisceration; their crying and howls of pain haunt those who remain. Edward is hungry all the time, thirsty, tired. The narrow wooden platforms for sleep crick his neck and hurt the hip he must lie on. His physical hardiness and obscure hope allow him a muted constancy, a sufficient belief in what the army is doing on this war-torn continent, in this sad place. Edward does not think very deeply about the cause and effect of what he does each day: matters will take care of themselves, over time, in some other place. But he is slowed by the relentless drear and awfulness.

Some two hours later, with six others, Edward crawls through the mud and foul water, over lumps of clay and dead men, in and out of craters, hyperaware, heart pounding, chest thrust forward. Their arrival is easily seen and heard: the Germans' defence of their trenches is efficient. There is a ghastly fight. Ed must wrestle with a man who is stronger than he. He smells the foul breath of his opponent on his cheeks, grapples with greasy skin, and stares at dying eyes as, with all the might he can summon, he pushes his bayonet past the enemy's tunic, past layers of clothing, past the skin with a little give, challenged for an instant by the live bone of the man's last rib, on, on, deeper to the Hun's liver.

He … I … we … are Edward's incoherent thoughts … *are both dying. Not a challenge, not fair. Just animals … kill the other before we ourselves are killed. Bags of blood and bone … we are just bags of blood and bone.*

Ed doesn't share his new paradigm with anyone else but tucks it away in the part of his brain that traps fear and regret.

Bags of blood and bone.

He doesn't wash the other man's debris off his face and hands for some days: he wants to wear the life he's taken. It's not a trophy, but a reverence.

Bags of blood and bone.

He and the dead man are one and the same, twinned.

The raid is a mess of gruelling hand-to-hand combat, but worst of all, no prisoner is taken and two of Ed's men are killed.

*

Whenever the unit is billeted at the rear for a few days, Edward chases wine, port, champagne, and he shares it with anyone close by: a fellow officer, but any enlisted man will do.

'Oh God … for Chrissake, can we talk about anything but shop?' Red-faced, slurring, he'll sleep deeply soon, passed out, prone and exhausted, unrousable like the dead around him. The quick, broad smile, a false swagger, a rehearsed cockiness is now a somewhat forced set-piece. The grind has eaten away at Edward's sunny outlook.

Edward is aware that one soldier helps him to his bunk, takes his boots off, turns him on his side to sleep it off. Not for the first time, it's Private Jim Williams keeping a caring eye on Lieutenant Fitzgerald. The other men dismiss Ed as hopeless.

'Dunno why you bother.'

'He's just a pisspot.'

'Useless as tits on a bull.'

'Ah, go easy, fellas. He'll come good,' Jim says to the worst of the detractors. 'He's just a bloke doing it tough.'

But Jim's generosity only highlights Edward's feelings of inadequacy. How dare this man humiliate him – all that matey hogwash. Williams must want some special treatment from Ed; why else would he act the good Samaritan? Edward's loneliness and feelings of isolation deepen.

*

The Boche increase their lethal activities. Snipers pick off the Australians one by one; constant bombardment annihilates teams of men; out-of-the-blue air raids decimate the troops; the visceral confrontation of trench-raiding parties continues. Edward persists. With painful, rounded shoulders and neck muscles knotted, he is mostly prominent bones in a loose tunic, and the only exposed skin – on hands and face – is the same colour as his boots. They're still in the Ypres area, moving in and around Ploegsteert; it's hardly a village or even an obvious settlement of any kind. A Tommy-built signpost heralds the entry to the former town: 'Plug Street'.

More than ever, the senior staff demands the unit's capabilities in the trenches. One day, bright with winter's cold light, though an associated Company relieves the group, one section of Edward's Company must remain in the trenches and take part in barrage fire. In the selection process, another officer draws the short straw and must stay on. Head down, mouth set, Edward walks to the rear – away from the noise, filth, cold, wounds, hacking coughs, stale cigarette smells, and the mix of piss, shit and blood underfoot – to safety, punished with the skulking feeling of agonising relief.

'Our guns were subject to heavy hostile fire but remained in action throughout,' Edward recites, flat-voiced, for Alex to record in the unit diary. Four men are injured, one of whom will 'die from wounds' four days later. Other men die because Ed has made himself safe. His neck becomes stiff and sore:

crushed muscles, cramped ligaments and sinews, irritable blood vessels, cascading lights in his vision.

*

After months in France and Belgium, the Company is 'resting in billets at Armentières'. For a lark, Edward insists that he and Alex have their portrait taken together. There's a kind of desperation to his plaintive request, as though there's something urgent to document, but he says to Al only, 'All the fellas are having it done.' The prints of their photos will be sent home to mothers, wives, loved ones.

Edward and Alex queue outside the stone building just off the main street, smoking cigarettes and laughing with the others in the line. Jim Williams is at the end of the row, waiting his turn, watching the horsing about among his comrades. Jim catches Ed's eye and winks at him in a good-natured way. Driven by his own embarrassment, Edward is angered: Jim has seen him at his worst, weak, pathetic, seen Ed's secret self; Jim is a threat to his authority. Ed fails to understand that nothing could be further from the truth.

'Here, you, Private Williams,' Edward shouts, 'is that insubordination? That wink, yes, that wink, Private. I'll thank you to piss off. Yes, I mean it, back to your billet. Go on!'

'Easy,' is all Alex can whisper to Ed, turning away slightly to hide his intervention.

'Yes, go on, fuck off.' Edward can't still his anxiety, his face flushing, hands sweating. 'Bloody cheek,' he murmurs as Jim leaves the courtyard.

The line of men has fallen silent and stays quiet until Edward and Alex enter the studio. A guarded susurration starts up and in whispers they discuss the unreasonable outburst from Edward, a little disturbed, unsettled.

On entering the studio, Edward and Alex are slightly embarrassed by their venture, and Ed, overwrought, especially after his eruption, acts like a boy, tries joshing his friend. He delivers playful punches and grins like Wonderland's cat.

'How's this then, eh?' says Edward, wide-eyed, as Alex hangs back.

'Er, how do you want to do this?' Alex rubs his nose, red and runny from the damp, cool air. Then, with something of a sad smile on his face, he tugs his crumpled jacket downwards and straight.

'Come on, Al. You take the chair, go on.'

With jerky, nervous hand movements, Edward directs – coerces – his friend a little longer, and it is concluded: as the more senior, Alex will sit in a casual pose on the wicker armchair provided by the photographer. Edward will stand – not quite lounging – behind the chair to Alex's left, his right hand on Alex's left shoulder. Edward chooses to have a cigarette in his left hand, which, through force of habit, is turned in at an angle. The mud is still present on their boots though they tried to scrape it off. Their recently washed faces have the shadows of the not-quite-clean. Their caps hide their greasy, grimy hair – and the lice hide themselves. The backdrop is a painted canvas of Roman columns and pedestals bearing grand vases of indeterminate but blousy flowers. Edward's captured smile is fixed, broad and toothy; but if someone wants to truly *see* him, his eyes are a giveaway: overly open, pupils dilated.

The men arrange to have copies of the photo sent to their families.

'Oh, they'll like that, eh, Alex?' Edward is bashful, wistful, suddenly teary; his bottom lip misbehaves. 'Us … here … together … now.'

'Yes, yes, they will.' Alex pretends not to notice Edward's discomfort. Perhaps it's best not to draw attention to it.

*

The temperature rises ever so slightly. It is undoubtedly spring; there are tiny buds on the rare, remaining shrubs and trees. Edward and Alex can sit comfortably on a couple of upturned logs in front of Alex's tent. There's a lacklustre small fire smouldering and both have a mug of black coffee. They talk freely in the quiet of the rear.

'Look, thanks for recommending me to Headquarters. Secondment in a liaison capacity is perfect, though I'll see less of you, my friend.' Ed's gratitude is palpable; he leans forward. He doesn't like to admit – even to himself – just how much he needed this transfer away from the front. 'But I'll be visiting the Company a lot with reports and orders and such. Have you heard the latest … about the next engagement?'

'I doubt you're supposed to tell me much, Ed,' says Alex with a wink, 'but go on.'

'Well' – they put their heads together – 'every senior officer in the area has been asked to ready their various charges, attend briefings, inspect and report back on the lot: health, fitness, equipment. Alex, they're reporting on their readiness for a massive engagement.'

Alex nods and shrugs, stirs the ashes. It is not news to him. It won't be a long wait for orders. He predicts early summer as the moment they will move.

'Well, keep me updated, won't you?' Alex claps Edward on the back. 'You know, I could eat a horse. Let's get some of Cookie's bread and jam.'

*

In early June 1917, final orders are received for many thousands of men to move into Ploegsteert Wood, near the town of Messines, six or so miles from Ypres. As he learns the extent of the planned battle, Edward experiences gut-wrenching dread. Acid burns his gullet, his eyes sting, his neck no longer easily bends or turns, so rigid has it become. The men of his original unit are more than friends, they're mates; and Alex is a brother, one of the sources of his own life force. The danger is very real for all of them; he's now witnessed hundreds of times how easy it is for a man to be broken, to die. His internal conflict is constant: his public, capable persona versus a hidden, terrified mortal. His rare snatches of sleep plunge him into deep caverns of exhaustion, and then are broken by surges of all-consuming fear. He dreams of drowning among macerated corpses, churning in the briny, dumping waves that fall onto Manly Beach near his home. In his nightmare, he struggles and squirms in the swell; his mother is on the sand, unaware. On waking, he calls out a word that those around him can't figure out, and he jumps to his feet in a sweat, dopey, swaying, breathing fast, puffing little clouds of fog in the miserable dugouts or billet rooms.

A significant battle has been planned. It might change the course of the war – and Edward Fitzgerald's life – one way or another.

CHAPTER FOUR

YPRES

'So, it's the one-hundred-year Battle of Messines commemoration next week, Mumma. Have you seen all the bunting at the square? Are you going to take part?' Charlotte wrangled her long, blonde hair into a high ponytail with the insouciance of a thoroughly loved only child. At twenty-two years of age, she was as pretty as a new day.

Charlotte and Ingrid sat in their tiny courtyard at the rear of their home, which was tucked behind Ingrid's pharmacy premises. The French doors from their kitchenette were open, and the early-summer Ypres air embraced them, while the scent of jasmine was in the air.

'What? Oh no, I find those First World War ceremonies too … twee? It's just for tourists, Char.' Ingrid watched her daughter tucking into her breakfast, in awe of the child she'd created. 'You look very well today, sweetheart. Has your headache passed?'

'I quite like the events … and I know you *love* the bands. All that *oompah, oompah,*' Charlotte chortled. 'Come on, it will be *fun*. We could go together. Come with me to the Gate on one of the music nights. *Please*.' Charlotte's emphasis reflected an exuberance she brought to everything in her life. Her blue eyes and her skin shone. She was cheeky and irreverent, and she delighted in ridiculing her mother's staid ways.

'It's not supposed to be fun, for heaven's sake … that is what I mean about it being for the tourists. It's a commemoration, silly, not a party.' Ingrid was a stickler for historical truths. 'And anyway, I thought you had to work. Isn't the hotel fully booked? Is it mostly the English?'

'God, yes, I'd *conveniently* forgotten I have to work. Can you pass me the eggs? And don't let me forget that I'll need some *more* paracetamol to get through the next few days. I'll help myself from the shop: I know which drawer. I think it's work that gives me the headaches.' Charlotte flipped her hand in the air. 'All the guests want the *real* history, and apparently, I embody the *real* Belgium. Very draining.'

'Well, you probably do … represent Belgium, being a native, the latest of countless generations living right here in Ypres. You want some salmon too?' Ingrid passed her the painted plate, then leant back in her chair, putting her hands behind her head, and looked up into the blue sky above them, sighing with contentedness. It was so good to have her daughter back home; they'd lost touch during the last year, Charlotte's final year away at university. The days had just got away from them until it was just a quick phone call once a week.

'Yes, please, and is there more coffee? Thanks, Mumma. I had a *terrible* nightmare last night … I dreamt of my death.'

'What …?' Ingrid paused while Charlotte continued to wolf down eggs, smoked salmon and strips of fresh, dark sourdough bread. 'Your *death*?' Ingrid tried but failed to keep the anxiety out of her voice.

'Have I *frightened* you, Mumma?' Ingrid gave a quick nod and Charlotte patted her mother's knee, wearing an indulgent smile, and her charm bracelets jangled. 'Too morbid? I don't mean to be. I'm desperate to share the nightmare with you – not the dreadful details, but it made me realise I have not said important, "grown-up" things to you, as I should have. It made me think that *everybody's* time is running out, including mine.'

Charlotte's gaze dropped to the flagstones at the rear of the flower-filled courtyard where a lone sparrow hopped about, scouting for crumbs from the breakfast table.

'Firstly, I love you, Mumma. You have been a *wonderful* guide and companion to me, and if I ever get to have children – though my nightmare would have it otherwise – I'll model my mothering on yours.'

Ingrid clasped her hands in her lap. 'Darling, this is all a bit gloomy. Tell me you're OK … not depressed or anything like that. I like the sentiments, but it is horrifying to think you're saying this because of your dream. It was just a nightmare.'

'I'm completely fine, Mumma. Only these headaches that I keep getting, they're annoying.'

'I've told you to go to the doctor; why not? They'll check you over and make sure everything's fine.'

'Oh no, it's nothing. Maybe I need glasses or something. Can I carry on? Is that OK? I've still got things to offload onto you.' Charlotte gave a hoot. 'Ha! Sorry, Mumma. This was not meant to be torture. I just want to say a few things.'

'OK. I'm listening … but just for the record, not enjoying it.' Ingrid gave a lop-sided grin.

'OK. Secondly, I want you to know I don't really mind dying. This is not to say I *want* to. Only that its inevitability is not scary, and I acknowledge that it's going to happen one day.' Charlotte saw her mother's face crumple in distress and took her hand. 'Maybe the long, sad history of Belgium has invaded my bones. The Ypres curse, you know. Suffering and death are always a strong possibility for any of us. Tragic Belgium!' She was only half joking. 'I don't know … I guess the culture of this country means we all think about it more than perhaps other nationalities.'

It was quiet between them. Ingrid was admiring her daughter for her bravery: to consider these things at such a young age and in such a mellow way. Charlotte seemed to be gathering her thoughts for the next admission.

'I know some people are filled with fear that they'll miss out, a feeling that death will rob them of a glorious life. That's not my thinking. I believe that my life, even up till only now, has been great, excellent, perfect. And that's pretty good compared to so many. Death is going to be OK.'

'Oh, darling, please, let's stop this conversation. You're only twenty-two. You've got the rest of your life ahead of you.'

'No, Mumma, let me get it out. If I die before you, don't grieve. I'm happy. I have always been happy, and I think I'll be happy enough to die. So go on, have a full life after I go – if you live longer than me.'

Charlotte took a sip of her coffee and maundered on.

'It's strange, I always thought that I might play some kind of significant role in other people's lives. One of them must be you. I hope that by the time I die, I will have completed this role, in your life and in the others' lives – whoever they may be. I guess if I don't, that will be my only regret. I recently read something by Leo Tolstoy, which I rather like: "Seize the moments of happiness, love and be loved." That is how I intend to live my life.'

Ingrid rose and found the box of tissues on the oak dresser in the kitchen. 'Here, darling.'

'Mumma. I meant every word,' Charlotte muffled as she swiped at her nose.

'I know you do; you're a wonderful daughter. Just try very hard not to die before me,' Ingrid laughed through her tears, '… please.'

'Oh, Mumma! I'm so sorry that I've frightened you. I'm not going to die anytime soon. I'm as fit as a fiddle, healthy as … I don't know what.' Charlotte embraced her mother. 'You know dreams are not predictors of the future. They are just metaphors and similes; they force the unconscious mind to reflect. And that is what I've done. The dream forced me to consider how much I owe you and how much I love you. That's all … really, Mumma.'

They heard the townhall clock strike the hour. 'Christ! Is that the time? I've got to get going.' Charlotte raced indoors and up the stairs to get her things for her day's shift at the hotel.

*

After their breakfast, Ingrid sat on a little longer in the sunny courtyard, uneasy, though why, she could not say. She heard Charlotte leave for her shift at the hotel, shouting a cheery 'See you later.' Ingrid sighed and rose to tidy the house and prepare for work. However, on this particular morning, even by imposing neatness on the small rooms that she and her daughter shared, she could not rid herself of what she felt haunted by: her story, her mother's, her grandmother's, her great-grandmother's – Belgium's history. The Ypres curse. Maybe generational trauma. Like a metronome, death after death, tragedy after tragedy, grief after grief. Now her child, her baby girl, walked in the world independently, subject to hurt, vulnerable to pain.

Ingrid's mother and Charlotte's grandmother, Charlotte Marie, was born in Ypres in 1918. She had died at sixty in 1978 while Ingrid was training to become a nurse in Paris.

Young Charlotte and Charlotte Marie had never met, but the slipware plates with the blue borders that Ingrid now cleared from the table, dusted in breakfast's crumbs and wearing bright-yellow egg debris, had come from Charlotte Marie's farmhouse kitchen. Using them, handling them, telling of their origin – that was some kind of continuity between the generations, wasn't it? A sort of protective hoodoo?

Ingrid had been told all her mother's stories while sitting on her knee as a girl. Charlotte Marie's expressive face had illustrated the pain of every tale, the minor key.

'My mother, Charlotte Eva, died while giving birth to me,' Charlotte Marie had revealed to her young daughter. 'My father was deemed "unknown" … that's what they said in those days.' Her mouth had turned down. 'I felt the shame,' she whispered.

'But, thank God, we were raised by mostly kind, almost silent nuns … they could sneak up on you when you didn't want to be caught out,' Charlotte Marie said with a chuckle, 'and forty or so other orphans and I played in the rubble, slept in the alcoves of the bombed churches, cold and hungry. Oh, we were a ragtag bunch. Over a few months, we moved to the cellars of the warehouses and the public buildings that had been sheared to street level.' She had wiped the tip of her reddened nose using the discoloured handkerchief bordered by the off-white lace she'd tatted some years before.

'Ah, I remember we lived on watery soup from huge barrels … they were steel cans, the words "US Government" written on their sides. We were glad for it, mark my words. Oh, and big chunks of dark bread … not sure where they came from, which big town could have made all that bread for so many mouths. After a while, small bakeries … just a few bricks, piled higgledy-piggledy … set themselves up in the rubble. They were the first … the first sign that life was returning. Oh my, the cold winters following Armistice … all that mud.'

Ingrid had listened carefully, hungry to know her mother, this strange alien who seemed to understand everything, everyone, how the world went around. The account left the indelible impression that her mother was indefatigable, and so Ingrid must be too: hardy, enduring, resilient.

Have I told enough of the stories to Charlotte? Does she understand the importance of survival, pushing through?

Ingrid ran the hot water into the sink, squirting detergent, washing the breakfast dishes. She thought of her father, Eugene Jan, a dairyman. He made his own cheese from his herd that grazed among the shell indentations surrounding Ypres, near Ploegsteert Wood. In Eugene's lifetime, the sharp, dirt edges of the pock-marked landscape became rounded, and the craters' murky bottoms became shallower. Eugene had been twelve years younger than Charlotte Marie, too young to fight in the Second World War, but not too young to be able to ignore the heartbreak around him. Eugene learnt that stealing from soldiers meant survival for the family – but stealing from the German soldiers gave great pleasure.

A nasty prize from Eugene's foraging was a Luger, wrapped in a Nazi flag and hidden upstairs at the back of the oak wardrobe. The forbidding atmosphere of the contraband weighed on Ingrid's mind as she moved through the rooms below. Quite suddenly, in this week before the Battle of Messines commemoration, Ingrid wanted to get rid of it, get it out of her house.

Why have I not done so before? The place can't be a sanctuary, a place of peace, until it's gone.

Perhaps triggered by Charlotte's talk of her death, a reminder of the Ypres curse that had plagued her family for generations, these urgent thoughts, new to Ingrid, compelled her up the narrow timber stairs to the tall cupboard on the landing. She pulled down a wooden box and unwrapped the wax material around the gun.

'How the hell do I get rid of this thing?' This Ingrid said out loud; alone, it sounded oddly noisy. She stared at the Luger for a minute, then re-wrapped it and stowed it back where she'd found it. She feared she'd be judged – both for keeping it this long, and for getting rid of it. And what would Charlotte think?

Later. I'll deal with it later.

Ingrid's mother, Charlotte Marie, had not conceived a child for many years of marriage, not until Eugene's emphysema had taken almost all the breath from his lungs. He

survived until baby Ingrid was two months old and then he
had died from respiratory failure in the farmhouse kitchen,
lying on the cold flagstone floor. Ingrid could imagine the
scene as she swept her own flagstones: the shadow of a man
she knew only from one photo and hearsay.

'I held his hand while he died,' Charlotte Marie had told
Ingrid, while she herself lay on her deathbed. 'I said to him
that I was glad of our time together. That was it, my dear. Not
very grand, but at least I could give him some comfort.'

Her mother's death had aroused Ingrid's sense of duty
rather than anguish. The grief she'd practised all her life
seemed sufficient, enough even for this new tragedy. Ingrid
took three months' leave from her nursing course and sold the
farm. She'd not miss it – the 1950s house, the fields, the barn
– examples of the region's rebuilding after the last world war.
The new structures were not places in which a heart could
find a true home. They were cold dwellings, concrete, pale
brick; they were built phoenix-like, but steeped in woe and
heartache. Every sod turned to place or re-place foundations,
every drained swampy field or planted crop, had torn another
corpse from the topsoil, another half-stripped skeleton, more
rotting uniforms, bullet casings, unexploded ordnance.

Ingrid, like many other Belgians, experienced unresolva-
ble dissonance: tough, ragged mental scars of the last hundred
years. There was no forgiving, no forgetting, no conciliation.
There was, however, the next day and the next; a largely

predictable, quotidian life to be had. After her mother's death and after the farm was gone, Ingrid moved on with her life with a dull determination: she had to make a future for herself.

As for so many other Belgian households, Ingrid's had omnipresent photos, portraits, community memorials, evoking the silhouettes of men and women missing from their lives. Downstairs again, sneaking another coffee before her professional day began, Ingrid took a moment, leant on the table edge, and stared at the dresser. She considered every memento there: large and small photos in modern frames, a nosegay of dried flowers from some distant wedding, an antique fob watch, a display box of medals, embroidered homilies, postcards, a painted ceramic crucifix with rosary beads draped over it.

Is it time to get rid of them … for Charlotte's sake? A fresh start.

One of the black-and-white photographs was of Ingrid in her nurse's uniform, wearing the awkward smile of surprise and caught mid-stride. A colleague had snapped her on her way to an afternoon shift in the old-style training hospital. There was dappling on the building behind her, the sun wandering between leaves on summery air. Ingrid remembered this time in Paris as coloured by doubt. Was she liberated by her mother's death or trapped by it? She was away from 'home', Ypres and its surrounding near-empty, pocket-sized fields, but her absence gave her no relief from the sadness that had permeated her earlier life; she carried it with her. For four years, in her unforgiving, starched uniform, she walked the dingy Nightingale wards and cold corridors, day and night – soothed, tended, cared – in a fog of cool detachment. Her eyes ached from study, she battled to remain attentive in lectures, her feet were lumpen from the work. Throughout, she wondered if this was how she atoned for some ubiquitous sins: those unattributable, invisible sins that *must* have caused the curse of Ypres that had dominated her family's fortunes.

*

When Ingrid met and married Charlotte's father it was, she had thought to herself, just what she was supposed to do; the experience was not exceptional or wonderful or adventurous. He was a pharmacist in Ypres, dull but safe. When Charlotte, their only child, was four years old with bobbing, golden curls, mother and daughter had watched from the front step as the husband, the father, left the marriage to live with a young woman who had assisted him in the pharmacy.

'Bye bye, Papa. Bye bye, Elena.' And casually, before replacing her thumb firmly in her Cupid's-bow mouth, she had asked Ingrid: 'Mumma, where are they going?'

He and the young woman were killed in a head-on collision one year later.

Serves them right had been Ingrid's private reaction, a bitter grunt: she didn't shed a tear. *Hope they rot in hell.*

Ingrid and Charlotte had inherited the premises and the thriving pharmacy business, including the six rooms behind and above the shop where the two women now lived. Their pharmacy home was on Menenstraat, which ran from the Grote Markt leading to the Menin Gate, the busiest retail area of Ypres.

The day outside was muggy, too humid for comfort; there would be a storm later. As Ingrid swept the steps of the shop before opening, noting the grey clouds above her, she looked up and down the road.

Menenstraat, leading many thousands of young soldiers to their miserable death. Hundreds of thousands of feet marching to desolation. Now it's covered in advertising, idiotic bunting and flags.

With a gut-wrenching surge, the urge to weep over-whelmed her. She pushed tears away with the back of her hand, chiding herself for her foolishness. She couldn't shake this crushing dread. Why now was the usually repressed feeling of doom present? Only days before, Ingrid had been so delighted to have young Charlotte back from Brussels, where she had attended the university for four years. Charlotte had studied business, and they'd talked about the two of them working together in the shop. First, she was completing one last summer working at the hotel, where she'd had such a happy time in the preceding summers. Ingrid adored her daughter; sometimes she feared she loved her too much. Charlotte was the only relative she still saw and as Ingrid didn't have many friends, nor a husband, nor a particular companion, Charlotte was her focus.

Ingrid closed the door that separated the domicile from the pharmacy and moved to the shop's front door to switch the neon sign from closed to open. She tried to shake her fear, stretching her arms above her head, circling her shoulders, rolling her head. To Ingrid, the Ypres curse that doomed its population to tragedy had never ceased: the loss of young men in the war, Charlotte Eva's death in childbirth, Charlotte Marie's hardship as an orphan and her husband's early death, the betrayal and death of Ingrid's own husband. How would young Charlotte fare? Ingrid had little trust in the world unfolding favourably; how could she protect her own daughter?

CHAPTER FIVE

CANBERRA, SYDNEY, HOBART

Life carried on. I dressed, ate, slept, played – I lived.

At day care, my daughters executed weird, spidery drawings where stringy-limbed Mummy and Daddy appeared as aliens, and a psychedelic-yellow sun beamed down on a flowered landscape.

My ex-husband continued to stare daggers at me when we met to exchange our little hostages.

Work was dull, but I was distracted by it.

Sydney delivered on its siren-like promise: 'Relax! Among all this sunshine and bonhomie, you won't even notice the troubles of others.' The hypnosis was almost complete – sipping, say, chilled Pinot Grigio on a balcony high on the cliffs above Bondi Beach – anyone could imagine that Paradise is found. In the pit of my stomach, gnawing doubt remained.

Not long after Dominic told me his grandfather's story, I had to travel to Canberra for JJMcK. I was there to help a production company prepare for a photoshoot in the bushland of the Brindabella Range, where the city of Canberra meets the Great Dividing Range. The shoot would take place at a swimming hole, on the leaf- and bark-littered banks of the Murrumbidgee River – a fine example of a typical Australian waterway: small, unreliable, and often disappointing. BEER! was to get a new ad campaign to boost its market share. I had written a shot list adhering to the brand and progressing the product story – such as it was. It was hard for me to be enthusiastic, engaged even, for a beer designed by marketers, produced by a multinational, and that tasted awful, full of sweeteners and chemical preservatives.

Driving down the highway in the fancy rented car, tapping the steering wheel, the air con chilling my skin, I argued with myself for the millionth time about the pros and cons of my current occupation: my imagined raison d'être was at cross purposes with my reality. I worked each day for someone else's profit, selling a product I didn't even like. But I wanted to write my novel, complete my big project. I knew writing for myself was a deliberate distraction from the world around me; I also knew it was my process of distillation. It brought me contentedness. I might never be a bestseller, that much I'd accept, but to not do it at all was a denial. Writing for myself was an itch I didn't scratch. When I came home from work every day, after the girls were in bed, I knew I ought to continue my own projects; instead, I watched TV and read other people's books. Splayed on the couch, on my third glass of wine, I felt I was lazy; insufferably torpid and slothful. It was an uncomfortable recognition. But, I reasoned with myself at one hundred and twenty kilometres an hour, sliding by the articulated lorries and vans, whooshing past despondent eucalypts dirty with dust, I should stay in this job for the money, the certainty, the lie.

On the first afternoon of my trip, Canberra turned on its sunshine and clarity. The dome of blue was persuasive: maybe life was beautiful, maybe *my* life was beautiful. Around the roundabouts and down the avenues, glimpses of kangaroos and parkscapes full of cockatoo drama filled a Canberra visitor with a sense of health and vitality. After a couple of hours of review with the production team's photographers, I was free to do as I had promised Dominic – go to the Australian War Memorial archives centre and search through the records of his grandfather, have a bit of a dig around, see if there was anything of interest there.

I would have done the research without Dominic's insistence. Edward Fitzgerald's story had lodged within me; it clung on like an earworm, an eyeworm – phrases and images. I imagined Edward's upbringing and how it might have felt to put on that uniform. I dreamt bits and pieces of it at night, what he must have experienced – the loss of innocence, the physical hardship and exhaustion. The archives promised to deliver the tale further, shift it from phantasm to reality. I thought I'd see some significant documents, perhaps some artefacts, and that would help settle the tale in my mind. I wanted to own a little piece of it, make it mine somehow. The story idea thrilled me: could Edward be my protagonist, my hero?

I entered through the grand main doors. There, two sculpted lions, guarding the small entrance foyer, stopped me in my tracks. I'd never noticed them on previous visits. They were of limestone and a little over a metre in height from their curled and clawed paws to the top of their tousled-haired heads. I was compelled to touch a paw and noted that the residual shine on it suggested that many others had been likewise lured to do so, maybe as many as millions of finger-tips over the years, leaving remnants of DNA and wonder. A volunteer guide noticed my attention and joined me.

'Do you know the story of the lions?'

My blank look only encouraged the volunteer to launch into his spiel.

'No? Well, they're from Belgium, donated by the mayor of a city called Ypres, commonly called Wipers in the First World War … a bit of a joke, you know. They were at the entrance to the town and were damaged by German bombs and literally pushed to one side for the duration. After it was all over, the mayor thought it would be a nice gift to Australia as so many Australians were stationed there and, well, fought from there for Belgium. They've been in Australia since 1938 … the lions, that is.' A happy, gummy smile underpinned his enthusiasm for his topic.

I acknowledged the story, thanked the guide, and we both moved on. At the stolid, timber reception desk stood a bevy of smiling museum assistants. I didn't take up their spoken offer of guiding; I knew where I wanted to be. I'd been here before: I loved museums, galleries, and especially archives – any place that held memories, mementoes, narrative voices, any amphora of the past. I felt bigger, better, more included, whole, if I spent time in places such as the Memorial, read a little, observed a bit.

As I made my way across the foyer to the archives, the marble steps of the internal flight of stairs clattered with the footfall of the noisy school kids on their civics excursions. In the archives room, I settled to the task, selecting a screen and keyboard, getting comfortable on the institutional chair. I spent a few minutes familiarising myself with the menus and databases. I got a hit straightaway. Pages and pages of information were listed pertaining to Edward Fitzgerald: his service record, an archived manuscript, entries in various books, photographs, unit diaries. I was staggered by the discovery, excited by the possibilities, and started to wade through the files, agog, making notes for Dominic.

The nominal roll – the list of those in Edward's original Company – was the sixth document I selected to read, and it unfolded on the screen in a font a little too small to read, but when enlarged, the first name on the list was 'Twigg-Patterson, Alexander, Captain; 25yo; Profession on enlistment, Soldier; Next of kin, Mother, Mrs J. Twigg-Patterson, Kew, Victoria.'

I couldn't move my eyes. I read it over and over. I froze: cognitive dissonance. I had looked for Fitzgerald and I saw *my* surname, Twigg-Patterson. It couldn't be. Could it? My mind was racing. Was this *my* grandfather? Great-uncle, perhaps? He must be related and very closely, as no other family had that infuriating surname.

Two names below Twigg-Patterson, there it was, the name I was searching for: 'Fitzgerald, Edward, Lieutenant; 20yo; Profession on enlistment, Soldier; Next of kin, Father, Mr Edward Fitzgerald, Manly, New South Wales.'

Alexander and Edward, they were comrades? Friends, like me and Dom? Soldiers together?

I had never heard mention of any family member's role in the First World War. My grandfather, this Alex Twigg-Patterson, must have died well before my birth and my father, James, had said nothing about him as far as I could remember. I had never asked while I'd had the opportunity. James, now dead, was no longer any kind of source. When James was ill, dying slowly and emanating disappointment, I was too occupied by my own teen feelings of mortality to consider my father's past. It was then I began to call him by his Christian name.

Standing at the printer just outside the archive centre, alone among the crowds of visitors to the War Memorial, I printed reams of documents with a sense of urgency. I felt cheated, as though a secret had been kept from me: my grandfather was significant … to me, to others. It was important that I knew, and someone should have told me. Perhaps then I would understand what I had to do, who to become. These documents were my own Enigma code. Thoughts ran through my mind as I wondered whether there was a story here, a writing project, even. Why had no one told me about him?

I had to tell Dominic about this extraordinary coincidence. But first, I had to find out more.

Gathering the papers, I charged out of the research centre, took the stairs two at a time, past the Menin Gate lions, rushed through the exit. Breathless, standing on the wide, stone terrace, looking down Anzac Parade with its hundred huge gum trees that shrank with diminishing distance, under the cloudless, sub-alpine blue sky, I dialled my mother, Clare. She might know some detail.

'Ma, you there?'

'Yes, darling. How nice to hear from you. I was just thinking how much I was looking forward to seeing you. How are those lovely girls?' A calm trill, and I could hear her budgerigars in the background.

'Ma, what do you know about Alexander Twigg-Patterson?'

I heard her sip from her ubiquitous cup of tea. 'What … you mean your grandfather?'

'Yes, of course, I mean my grandfather … my grandfather, is that him? … Wait, do you mean there is another Alexander Twigg-Patterson?'

'No, darling, don't jump down my neck. I haven't heard from you in weeks and now … well, you sound upset.'

'Well, Clare, I am upset. Who the bloody hell is Alexander Twigg-Patterson? Is he my grandfather? Did he fight in the First World War? In France?' A pause. 'How could you and Dad fail to tell me about this? It's important.' It had never occurred to me that James might have been one of the children of the 1920s or 1930s – a baby born *entre deux guerres* – with a father perhaps stunted by the horrors of war, the heritage of the First World War.

'Yes, darling. Calm down. Yes, Alexander, he was your grandfather and, yes, he did fight, um, somewhere in Belgium. Look, where are you? Come over, and I can tell you the bits and pieces I remember about it. I'm not sure I know the full story. I don't know that your dad even knew the full story.'

'I'm in Canberra … for work. I can't come over just now. Did you ever meet him?'

'No, no, more's the pity. I gathered he was a nice old chap. I remember your father saying that Alex had a terrible cough, a chronic cough. Perhaps that was a legacy of the war?' Clare hesitated, diplomatically not wanting to further alienate her daughter from her father. 'Your dad didn't like to talk about the past, his family.'

*

I raided Clare's archival boxes on my return from Canberra and at the bottom of an old suitcase I found a cache of old photos I'd never seen before.

On the evening when I told Dom about our – their – connection, there was one picture that he and I lingered over for hours.

'This is the one I treasure most. See, it is of the two of them, Alex Twigg-Patterson and Edward Fitzgerald.' I felt myself choking up but soldiered on. 'This is a studio shot, one of the tens of thousands of similar photos taken of the troops in France and Belgium. There's no specific identification, but I know this one was taken in France. There are so many similar *cartes* in collections around the world, it's not hard to research a particular studio and photographer.'

Dominic held the old photograph, turning it over in his hands. 'It's incredible.'

I nodded. 'How amazing is that? There they are, captured forever – friends, colleagues, partners – near Armentières, in early 1917. They look happy to me; maybe it's a youthful sense of immortality – remember, they were in their early twenties then. But they're certainly glowing with friendship and maybe the benefits of hardship too – the cold, the marching, the adventure. But that is my interpretation. For all I know, it might have been the complete opposite.'

It had been, of course, as much of a surprise to Dominic that our grandfathers soldiered side by side. He was subdued by the revelation, made more thoughtful than he usually was. That evening his big body took up more room than it ought in my small living room, in my small armchair. In his characteristic way, he'd already knocked over a beer and a lampshade just getting settled. He was always a strong presence in my flat, but that night his company felt more genuine than ever before, like he belonged beside me, a lifelong friend, as he held the studio photo between his big hands and looked at it almost longingly.

'Perhaps we are more like them than we can imagine,' he ventured in a husky voice. 'I mean, we're friends … and they were. We're not that much older than them.'

'Sure, the genes are all there. But we've grown up in such different times, different education, different foods even.' I shrugged; it was an inadequate response, but I didn't know quite how to help him express the unfamiliar feeling he was experiencing: confusion, exposition, conflict, joy?

'We look a bit like them. Both of us look a bit like our grandfathers. That's very … um, cool.' He looked up at me from the photo, seeking confirmation or verification. His eyes were wide and his mouth was working overtime. His hesitant voice suggested he was struggling to process the coincidence in some orderly fashion. 'We really have to find out more. Are you going to do more research? That would be great.'

'It's huge, isn't it?' I nodded, wanting to let him know I felt the same.

'Yeah, huge. And really … nice.'

Rachel had sat still and quiet throughout the conversation. I caught a slightly anxious look on her face when she saw Dominic so obviously moved by the photographs.

'What do you think, Rachel?' I pushed, curious and wanting to include her.

She developed a frown. 'Well, all good, I mean, it's exciting and well … extraordinary. I guess …' She faltered. 'I guess I am worried that if you dig into this stuff,' she rushed, 'you can find not just good things but things you don't want to know.'

'OK, yeah, I agree, but isn't it important, better to know … "the good, the bad, the ugly"?' I smiled.

'I don't know. Hey, Dom, you love and admire your grandpa so much now. What happens if what you find out about him reveals that he wasn't so great?'

'Oh, that won't happen.'

'Well, let's consider the worst possible outcome.' Rachel was on a roll, not angry but determined to protect Dom's equanimity in relation to his heritage. 'Right now, Edward's a hero to you … gee, didn't you hold his hand as he died?' She took a sip of her wine, frowned. 'So, what if, say, you discover he was found guilty of … murder? If he's a paedophile? Or a failure? What if he disappoints you? What then?'

Dominic was silent for a moment, considering, and I let the valid thought settle in me too.

'I reckon,' Dom pronounced, 'I think I ought to know the whole of it. He tried to tell me something important all those years ago. I would like to know … no, I'd be honoured to know, what it was.' He took Rachel's hand and said, 'It'll be OK, Rachel, you'll see.'

At the end of the evening, when he was leaving, Dom hugged me – not the norm.

'Thanks, mate. Thanks for letting me know about all this. I feel like I know him – Edward – better. I kinda like him better. That's a gift.' He gave me his big smile, the one that made the world a better place, and when I closed the door behind him, I smiled with the pleasure of our newly cemented bond.

Something about Dom's reaction, perhaps holding a mirror up to my own, gave me the first hint of urgency. It was the beginning of a quest. Not satisfied with knowing the historic factual details of Alex's life, I began to want more. I picked up each of the images that were lying on the table from first known date to last. They had lost their simple charm, and set up a yearning: How did Alex feel? What did he think about this or that? What made him anxious, angry, happy?

There was a group picture, taken in Brisbane. It must have been snapped as the soldiers arrived to take their places in Alex's newly formed Company; they came from all around Queensland, New South Wales and even Victoria. The soldiers shared a steady stare into the camera. Front and centre was Alex, the only one with a soldierly bearing, in the full and official uniform of the AIF and with appropriate captain's adornment. The photo showed an ingenuousness among the soldiers. Could a photograph capture gullibility?

At that time, these young men had only their imagined glories, none of the deathly and murderous loss-of-innocence experiences soon to be had. In spidery handwriting, perhaps added at the time or much later, the caption read 'A, Brisbane, 1916, with his unit'.

The last photo in my timeline was of Alex in 1958. He was standing in a vegetable patch beside a flourishing rosemary bush. He was in a drooping cardigan over a flannel shirt, its collar caught under the knitted wool. The sun was over his right shoulder and though the detail of his face was lost, he seemed sad. In the note that accompanied this photo from a cousin of my father, I read: 'This was taken in Manly, a couple of years before Alex died, I think. Not sure. Can't imagine why he's in the garden. I don't remember him being much of a gardener, but I didn't really know him well.'

What happened to Alex after the photo of his troop forming – Brisbane, 1916 – and this one in his garden – Manly, 1958? It was getting to me. His worries, preoccupations; his indulgences, celebrations. I needed to stand in his shoes, to glimpse his world.

I'll put it to Dom, I thought as I checked in on my sleeping daughters, tucking their blankets around their small shoulders, pushing their fine hair off their soft faces. *We should go to the site of the Battle of Messines*. A resolution of sorts, and I went to bed.

*

I spent every spare moment of the next month interviewing, reading and researching the life of my grandfather, Alexander Twigg-Patterson. It was the most incredible story, and about a man I was directly related to. I had designed the cover art in my mind and could already picture it on the tables at the front of all the major bookshops. My abandoned novel seemed dry and insular in comparison. I felt sure that, once I had all the research ticked off, this book would write itself. What could be more perfect than the memoir of a war hero written by his granddaughter?

His unit's diary became one of the most important resources for me. The diary was digitised and easily accessed, only a couple of clicks away, but I chose to travel to the War Memorial again and again to study it thoroughly, to have the physical diary in my hands. The first page with the first official entry, dated 5 June 1916, was slightly discoloured with age, crispy thick paper – authentic: its existence a confirmation that the past is ever-present. At the base of that page, there was his signature, 'Captain A. Twigg-Patterson', approving the day's account of his new unit for the first time. My eyes filled with tears. It was a link, a tangible link. It was irrefutable evidence of him and me, together somehow, a connection. The penmanship of his signature reflected my own: the same 'P' in Patterson – a bonding, bold flair – and a little childish dash across the pair of 't's.

I was getting to know Alexander Twigg-Patterson. I had gathered his story, the chronicles and narrative around and about him, all the stories that made him; and now I would take a trip to *find* him.

*

To know Alex better, one essential interview for me was with James's sister, my Aunt Mary, who was in her late seventies. She was sufficiently robust to be living alone in a tiny weatherboard worker's cottage, one of those that line the hilly streets of south Hobart. I spent the weekend there, learning how to gently interrogate an elderly woman about her long-gone father. I was hopeless at asking open-ended questions and listening to their answers, always trying to jump ahead.

Mary was a short woman, with a fluff of soft, wavy, white hair. A little dumpy and overly sedentary, she had a twinkle in her blue eyes and cheeks like down pillows. She had the same gentle smile that I had seen in the photos of Alex, and the same square chin.

'Tell me, Aunty Mary,' I had to use the title she insisted upon, although we had never much bothered with titles in my family, 'was he like an officer with you kids? You know, did he order you around? Was he violent? Did he shout?'

Mary looked askance. 'You've got it all wrong, dear. He was the gentlest of fathers. I am terribly lucky to have had such a loving dad.'

'But surely … he was eventually a major! He regularly took charge of thousands of men … their lives. He orchestrated a massive movement of troops, significant engagement with the enemy ... and you're saying that you didn't see any of that?'

'Well, that's all news to me,' Mary said quietly, dusting imagined crumbs from her lap, looking a little tired from the force of her niece's enthusiasm.

'What, he didn't tell you anything about serving in the First AIF?'

'You mean the First World War?' Mary offered. I nodded, brightening; now we were getting somewhere. 'A little, not much.' Then she chuckled. 'But he did tell me all about his childhood and growing up.'

Through the afternoon, Mary told me all the child-hood and family stories that she could think of, all of which described only a kind, calm and moderate man with not an ounce of discernible regret or envy or hard feelings. Even in Alex's post-war life, it seemed there was no bravado, booze, aggression, hubris; no depression, drama or heartache. She confirmed that Alex always had a 'weak chest', a chronic cough, numerous bouts of bronchitis and several of pneumonia. She laughed when she recounted the many times she'd sit and talk to him while he sat at the kitchen table, towel over his head and an earthenware bowl full of steaming boiling water. The water contained an aromatic tincture that gave him some relief.

'It turned the water brown and smelled ... greasy. I'll never forget that smell. I think I must have been worried about my father as we sat there. It's a haunting memory, not a happy one. Do you think it was the gas that did it to him? That injured him so?'

'I'm not sure, Aunty Mary. I suppose no one can be sure.'

I loved Mary's tale of my grandfather's life, but she had little to offer where I was most interested: I wanted to understand the effect of the war on Alex. There was no doubt Mary knew her father well, but her gaps were the parts I thought essential to my knowing him entirely. Perhaps you couldn't know anyone entirely, alive or dead. Perhaps we stockpiled, marshalled, the parts we held as more important than others, those that suited our convictions. It suited us – those who remained – to include only that side of a person we wanted to consider.

To hear Mary tell it, Alex was a benign character, nothing particularly special before the war, not what one would imagine of a man who played such a leadership role as Alex did. Surely there was something more to be discovered here. I asked, 'Would you like me to tell you what I've found out so far about his time with the AIF in the First World War?'

Mary took a moment, puckered her mouth, frowned a little. 'Only the good things. I don't want to have to grieve the side of my father I haven't known. Is it cowardly of me?'

'No, I don't think so.'

My turn to take a breath, to pause and consider: what to leave out, what to leave in. What does a daughter want to know about her long-dead father? Should she know everything, some things or nothing of great importance? I decided to dwell on the highpoints of Alex's career. I only touched on his hardships because, after all, they were significant. I kept my eyes on her face to see if it was too much, and if I'd seen a hint of hesitation there, I would have halted immediately. I made sure to emphasise that he rose to great heights through excellence, was well regarded and liked.

After my twenty-minute download, Mary considered my information, looked out the window, studied the floor.

'Well … I never. I think that calls for another cup of tea.' And she rose from her rather deep chair and moved into the adjoining kitchen. I heard her put the electric kettle on, swirl the tea leaves from the last pot into the sink. I followed her.

'Are you OK, Aunty Mary?'

'Nothing that a cup of tea and a shortbread won't cure.' How sweetly she resolved her own reservations with a simple, commonplace activity – the eternal tea-making. Her small smile relieved me of my guilt at disturbing her peace.

On the Sunday evening, I said goodbye and thanked her in the little sitting room, telling her I'd wait outside for the taxi that would take me to the airport, the flight back to Sydney, back to work.

'I think this is what having a grandma must feel like, Aunty Mary.' Overwhelmed with regret at my selfishness, a lifetime of misplaced priorities, I drew her to me and hugged her long and hard, ashamed that I'd not earlier sought to understand this splendid, generous person – who, as I was starting to discover, was a *part* of me.

She extracted her short, rotund body from my overly emotional grasp and patted my arm. 'Oh, get along with you, dear. Look after your daughters, be a good girl for your mother, and come and see me again very soon.'

*

My mother gathered more photographs that still existed among the collections of my father's distant relatives: a project for her, and of great benefit to me. When I took possession of them, I stared for hours at the face that was uncannily my own. The slightly downward sloping eyes, the gentle smile and a smirk in some of the photos I saw as similar to myself. There was one of Alex looking spiffing in his uniform on a very fine horse, and one with three others dressed to the nines in a shiny car, perhaps on an outing, maybe a picnic. One official shot appeared to be a group of eight staff officers taken toward the end of the war, seated precisely – like a sports team – clean and tidy livery, neutral expressions. The site of this photo appeared to be a courtyard of a French manor house; the wall behind the sitters was made of large stones hung with ivy and dotted with moss. There sat Alex, third from the left in the front row, a slightly quizzical look on his long face. From the distance of one hundred years, Alex looked at me, his granddaughter, as if to say, 'Really, I have no idea how I came to be here, here among these others.'

None of the photos were properly captioned but the various relatives had an inkling about where they were taken, with whom. The smattering of information that had been shared with Clare, who noted the details for me, may have been correct; there were various clues as to the location and the date of the images, which sometimes supported long-held assumptions, those Chinese whispers of long-dead antecedents. The origin of most of the pictures remained obscured and uncertain.

After Aunty Mary had shared so much with me, and as the photographs arrived, I learnt much more about Alex's life. Through institutions, organisations, relatives – and relatives of relatives – I found information, details, letters brittle with age, and private journals filled with secrets and dreams. I had awkward conversations with people I hardly knew or had just met, and I heard of quite a different Alex to the one I had originally conjured. Sometimes it felt like spying, prying into a decent man's life, poking around in dark corners. Sometimes it felt like I was reaching out and grasping his long-fingered hands.

CHAPTER SIX

THE EARLY YEARS OF ALEXANDER TWIGG-PATTERSON

Born in Melbourne, 1891, Alex is the oldest of three boys and one girl. He has a fleshy, vain Australian-born Englishman for a father, also named Alexander, who with his pigeon-chest thrust forward and his red-tinged, flamboyant Prussian moustache just so, he'd place a foot on the fireplace ledge and lecture the room.

'I regard Federation as entirely appropriate for a nation so deserving of its Commonwealth status, especially through our British bonds. After all, we are strictly speaking Britons, aren't we?' He'd throw his shoulders back and look into the middle distance as though surveying a Lake District panorama instead of a dingy Melbourne parlour. 'Who doesn't dream of returning Home? To walk "In England's green and pleasant land" if even for a short period.' Alexander Senior is smug with decency and properness in his small universe around the millpond that is Port Phillip Bay: 'So much more refined than Sydney Harbour.'

The family live in a small timber cottage, bought outright with his wife's inheritance, though as is appropriate for the times, the title is in the name of Alexander Senior. The home is found in a respectable suburb. It has a front garden of roses, and a bricked backyard with a clothesline, privy, woodshed and aromatic peppercorn tree.

For a mother, Alex has Jean, a short and unyielding Scot, with a small, tight mouth and jutting jaw. She has a permanent squint because of what may be myopia, or perhaps it is caused by a meanness – both pecuniary and emotional. Jean is responsible for the extended surname: Twigg-Patterson. She would only agree to marry Alexander Senior if she retained her maiden name as part of their married surname and for the children's surname. So entirely devoted to her much-decorated father, Twigg of the British Army, she will *not* let the name perish. The fiery stubbornness of Jean's youth becomes a querulousness, a petulant pursuit of her will, and she harries her children from the day they are born with lectures and tirades concerning manners and the correct behaviour expected of young gentlemen and ladies. The children learn to accommodate the rants – not with particularly good humour, but with a steely, silent fortitude. The boys of the family protect their individuality; but the shy and round-shouldered daughter is ultimately lost to Jean's demands.

The only breathing creatures in the world Jean truly loves is a succession of fat Pekingese dogs, all named Poppsie, distinguished one from another by their ever-so-slightly different tan-and-black coats. All the Poppsies yap and nip their way through the years of family life; they are hirsute gremlins inhabiting the underworld of Twigg-Patterson feet and ankles.

Jean's firstborn, Alex, is a long, thin baby dragged into the world after a forty-eight-hour labour, with a high-forceps delivery, Jean obstinately refusing ether. She would endure; and so she did. For several minutes after his hair-raising delivery, the babe is declared 'flat' by the two midwives attending: a slow heartbeat, failure to breath, a dusky purplish colour. With brisk action from one of the midwives, who is as tenacious as Jean, the baby is scuffed, rubbed and soon forced from his womb-like state into the world of oxygen, noise and scratchy, cold sheets on the baby's bassinet.

Over the years, Alex toddles and then strides among the increasing number of his siblings. He is a leader to his brothers and sister; he intervenes and adjudicates where necessary, never punishes nor authorises revenge. Even-tempered, calm, somewhat separate from the rest, Alex becomes a person with the best of human qualities. Before his early school years, his head of fine hair is made up of blond, soft curls, and Jean keeps it at shoulder length as is appropriate for his time. It darkens to a light brown and straightens over the years and is cut very short around the neck, longer on top when his schooldays begin. His ears stick out but that suits his lean face and neck; he has a gentle smile and a burbling chuckle, neither of which run to mockery; his blue eyes are crystal clear and when he catches and holds the eye of one of his family members or friends, it is a pleasing moment for them. His skin tans easily in the summer time and he is the first to rise for a walk, a running game, or to free a seat for an elder.

Perhaps because of the Scots influence, as they grow up, the Twigg-Patterson children can stand back a little and err on the side of their emerging national identity. That the capital of Australia is Melbourne, at least for a time, is a sound choice according to Alex and his brothers and sister, but increasingly they relate to the idea of a united Australia, an admirable notion, heroic, grand. Alex and his siblings become aware of the world beyond their home in the first decade of the twenti-eth century, a time of haughty pride for other post-colonials; but pride is a sin in the Presbyterian Twigg-Patterson house-hold so the children must channel their burgeoning sense of self to foster 'duty', which their mother allows as honourable.

✳

'Alex, old chap, shall we walk together while the others return home?'

Alexander Senior speaks in an aside to his oldest son. The man looks tired; his eyes are a little wide; he blinks too often. The boy, sixteen years old now, is wary and a little afraid of the departure from convention. There has never been a time that his father has suggested a private tête-à-tête. A 'man to man' is inconceivable.

The outing on this precipitous day has started as a family excursion, a pleasant jaunt, travelling by tram, taking tea at the kiosk, seated beneath the blooming wisteria, sparrows darting among the chairs and tables, enjoying any aberrant crumbs.

As father and son walk at a slow pace, side by side; both have their hands gripped behind their upright backs. They walk on the Tan, the ring road around the capacious, grassy, tree-filled Royal Botanic Gardens. It is a carriageway where the wealthy of Melbourne exercise their thoroughbreds and Welsh ponies, or circumnavigate the gardens seated in their carriages. Those of the slightly down-at-heel-yet-aspiring middle-classes of Melbourne, such as the Twigg-Pattersons, take the air with a dignified stroll, careful to avoid the hooves and wheels, stepping over the droppings and puddles as might occur.

'Things have not progressed well this year; indeed, the firm is in a spot of bother,' Alexander Senior begins. 'Time you left school, earned a living. Understand what I'm getting at?'

Alex remains silent, not at all sure what his father is fishing for.

'Things, financial things, are not what … they should be.'

More delay.

'You're old enough. It's time, do you understand?'

A pair of chestnut hunters trot by. A trio of hounds pace beside them. A scatter of noisy, dry leaves tumble along the carriageway.

'Well, there you are then. You'll join a bank, I imagine.'

The two progress. The breeze is just strong enough to threaten Alexander's hat and he raises his right hand to steady it.

'A bank then, sir?' The tops of the oak and poplar trees shimmy, this way and that.

'Yes, a bank, very good.'

A few minutes of walking in silence brings them to the tram stop at the gardens' gates. There, under the timber shelter, they meet the rest of the family seated on the benches, enjoying each other's company – Alex's two brothers and his sister. The exclusive exchange comes to a halt and is not commented upon, though with stutters mid-story, sidelong looks and nervous movement, the rest of the family makes it clear they sense some irregularity.

That night while everyone sleeps, Alexander Senior leaves the home, runs away from debt, embezzlement and a mistress. A small scandal and great shame ensue. None of the siblings speak of their true feelings on the matter even to each other, and resentment toward a father who is too cowardly to face his plight is buried deep in their Victorian subconscious.

*

The brothers and sister – Alex, Raoul, Leslie and Eila Twigg-Patterson – are serious young people during the first decade of the new century. Their Scots upbringing is without frivolity and now they very much need to make their own way in the world. Alex begins a career in a bank, as a teller – starched high collar and hair middle-parted – and is followed in a similarly dull clerical pursuit by his brothers as soon as they turn fifteen. Raoul and Leslie both become clerks in the burgeoning industry of electricity supply, and the three brothers travel together each day by tram to Melbourne's somewhat dusty centre, to their offices of dark wood and marble columns.

*

'I say! Good show!' Raoul grabs his brother's hand to shake it when he sees Alex in his new military uniform. 'What on earth will Mother say?'

It's a sunny Sunday morning, in the kitchen, after church. Their mother is taking tea with the minister; the brothers left straight after the service, and Eila was sent home to prepare the Sunday roast – a leg of lamb, then a shortcrust apple pie.

'Just wait till Mother gets home,' Eila pipes up, a little fearful of the repercussions, the rag-curls of her Sunday hairdo shivering, 'though you look smashing, Alex.'

'I'll simply explain to Mother. I'm twenty years old now, old enough to decide to leave the bank. It's risky perhaps – but the decision has come to me slowly, and it's sensible.' Alex fills the enamel cup on the sink from the tank tap and takes a sip. He looks out the window at the yard: it's gently raining and sombre-grey. 'You know, and Mother knows, I've never felt at ease as a teller. The bank's safe and well paid, of course. But it's … it's *too* easy. The work has no purpose and, indoors all day. I have to fight the boredom … the inertia.'

Leslie is leaning against the dresser, hands in pockets, head tilted. 'You'll be living somewhere else, I suppose?'

Alex nodded. 'Into barracks, on St Kilda Road.'

'But you'll leave us behind!' A whining comes from Eila.

Smiling now, he turns back to his siblings. 'I searched for something else and found order and honour as opposed to the menial, the pernickety. I've joined the Commonwealth Military Forces – the CMF!'

'You must be dreaming. The military is hard. You'll be dying to get back to the bank.' Leslie – the realist – finds it hard to celebrate Alex's decision. 'More importantly, this household needs your wages.'

'I've signed on for five years, and I've actually increased my wages and will of course continue to send it all to Mother.'

'Mother will still be furious,' Raoul, something of a clown, chips in, laughing, and claps his hands with glee.

His mother does not speak to Alex for a week – huffs and puffs like a hen in a dust bath – not because of the move itself, but she is furious that he did not ask her permission before making his decision. Little does she know that her children are amused by her sending anyone to Coventry. It happens frequently, either to one of the siblings, a neighbour, or a fellow worshipper at their church: no one is exempt from Jean's silent rage, and no one is much traumatised by it either.

*

Alex proves to be good at soldiering. A natural horseman, yet at ease with mechanical devices, he is perfect for history's moment. Alex specialises in artillery. The way the machines work fascinates him; his appetite for more information, explanation, and access to their greasy steel pieces, drives him to professional dedication and success. He revels in the practical, problem-solving exercises that are posed during his training, and he puts to good use his long, thin fingers, twiddling nuts and bolts, securing a pipe's collar, twisting and turning a wooden-handled monkey wrench with focus, his pursed mouth giving way to his tongue-tip fixed in concentration to his upper lip.

Mentored, favoured, the growing young man is promoted, quickly and deservedly. He suits his uniform, a light-brown gaberdine tunic, corduroy breeches and service cap, and it becomes an extension of his identity, his next layer of skin. His lean physique is bolstered by the shape the uniform brings, and the physical training fills out his thin frame. Calisthenics are in vogue: an Australian invention spawned on the goldfields, and now spreading widely through suburban and country-town fellowships with meetings held in town and church halls. With the hoops and Indian clubs, Alex adopts the practice. He views the responsibility of maintaining strength and fitness as a manly duty, an obligation, and is satisfied – but not proud (oh no, that would never do) – of the growing muscles he sees in the mirror. The budding pairs of pectorals, biceps, triceps and deltoids are worked on daily, and his body becomes capable of hard work and long days.

With no inclination for a social life, Alex only makes time away from soldiering to visit and care for his mother. All three brothers contribute to their mother's and sister's living expenses. Eila is considered their mother's companion, and the two women remain in genteel poverty, captured by their gendered status, in their single-storey, single-fronted terrace, a respectable distance and uphill from the working men's cottages. Outside the parlour window, the trams clang and rattle, but much of the noise is sufficiently muted, except for the metal-on-metal squeal as the trams round the right-angled corner at a nearby intersection. When Eila hears it, she clasps her small hands together in her Swiss cotton-covered lap, and gathers her Christian patience for this long, sacrificial life. Surely, it's soon time for the comfort and reliability of afternoon tea?

*

When war breaks out in 1914, the CMF allows the second-ment of their experienced professional soldiers as trainers to the Australian Imperial Force, the national response that will support Britain in the war against the Austro-Hungarian forces. The AIF is almost entirely made up of volunteers and Alex is found suitable to train the mix of men who come forward and sign up. He spends a year, quietly and deter-minedly, instructing men of all sorts in artillery warfare, in the ways of guns and cannons, small and large.

By the end of 1915, the outlook for the Allies is grim. The situation in Gallipoli and Europe is dire. The CMF releases almost all its men to the AIF including Alex. He is promoted to captain and asked to lead the 11th Machine Gun Company of the 43rd Battalion, with the Third Division. The Company is a force of almost two hundred men, and he is to mould them into a coherent group that can travel, train, set up, and fight whenever and wherever they are told.

On the eve of his leaving Melbourne to join his men in Queensland, Alex dines with his mother, sister and brothers. There is sherry in the parlour, and as it is chilly in the evenings of Melbourne's April, there is a small, somewhat struggling fire in the metal grate. Alex is in uniform; Eila is teary.

'Really, young lady, control yourself,' Jean admonishes her daughter with a hiss, and Eila dabs her cheeks with a now-damp, fine-lawn handkerchief.

'He'll be fine,' Raoul reassures.

'Back in no time,' says Leslie.

Eila gives a weak smile; her brothers are such dears.

A toast is proposed, 'To God and country', and the glasses tinkle as the brothers and sister catch each other's eyes. As Alex leaves to get the last tram back to barracks, there are handshakes between the brothers and a slightly stiff, ladylike embrace from Eila. With a hand on each of his cheeks, Jean draws Alex's head down to her height, and kisses him ceremoniously on the forehead, setting Eila off again, weeping a little louder this time.

*

Alex's Company is first assembled in Brisbane. There, in that hot, unsophisticated Queensland town, Alex is billeted in the manse of the local church of a sparsely populated outer suburb called Kenmore. The well-meaning and censorious Reverend Brown, his profoundly deaf wife and their adopted daughter, nineteen-year-old Lottie, make him welcome during his two-month stay: awkwardly, politely and in a most Christian fashion.

The dutiful Reverend Brown is pale-skinned, has damp hands, and his red nostrils run. Distracted, Alex tries not to stare but finds himself watching, waiting for the clear liquid drip to drop.

The reverend's stout wife wears a piqued look that confirms her isolated state: she was so affected by rubella as a child that not a single noise penetrates her ears. She does not speak but occasionally makes an abrupt sound to direct domestic proceedings. She uses simple hand signals too, mostly to stop or slow any social activity. She is the moral conscience of any room. Like a hawk, she watches the comings and goings, dalliances and separations, of the household. Contrary to the emerging conventions of the hot and humid climate, she has not yet moved beyond Queen Victoria's culture of mourning and wears heavy, black fabric dresses, black lace headwear, and jet jewellery. It does not surprise Alex that sweat-beads line her upper lip.

Lottie is very obviously not of the reverend's stock: rosy-cheeked; a fast, gap-toothed smile; and when not in her adoptive mother's company, she shows off her expressive hands, displaying a vigorous nature. Alex is affected; perhaps because of his family's muted enthusiasms, he is susceptible to liveliness, open to vitality. He blushes when she is seated beside him, and stammers in response to her parlour-safe questions.

There is no coincidental opportunity to be alone with Lottie, and Alex does not attempt to create one; indeed, he cannot imagine that they might embrace, let alone kiss – he has no experience of that kind. With Lottie hovering in his consciousness, he dreams fleshy scenarios and, with a quiet grunt, he comes on waking in the early morning. What Alex has done for his own pleasure over the years is considered by him as 'accidental', not deliberate, thus not a sin. In his teen years, he did not plan to tend to himself, but it happened – rarely – in such a sleepy state that Alex could exempt himself from wantonness.

One night, an evening of entertainment is planned, but it must end early for the reverend needs a good night's sleep. On the morrow, he will leave in his pony trap before sunrise to visit the outer reaches of his parish in good time. As the Reverend Brown plays the upright piano, Lottie sings 'Home! Sweet Home!' Her chest rises and falls, breasts straining to be free of their tight bodice, all the while facing in Alex's direction with – some might say – cow eyes.

'Mid pleasures and palaces though we may roam,
Be it ever so humble, there's no place like home!
A charm from the skies seems to hallow us there
Which, seek through the world, is ne'er met elsewhere.
Home! Home! Sweet, sweet home!
There's no place like home, there's no place like home!'

Alex believes his is true love, and what else could this picture of loveliness have on *her* mind? He discovers yearning.

The reverend's wife sees it all and is irritated to know she is powerless to curb Lottie's lust. She can only set her mouth even tighter than before, her narrow lips in a horizontal line. She's never liked Lottie, an immodest hussy, but has been obliged to care for the orphaned girl because of her husband's expectations.

This simple man is her prey, she thinks to herself of Alex. *More fool he.*

The reverend's call to prayer brings the evening to a close, and Lottie manoeuvres the seating to ensure that it is Alex's hand she holds in the prayer circle. As the reverend drones a blessing on the present company, the household, the king, the soldiers defending humanity against German butchery, the members of his congregation – blessing at great length many, many worthy entities – Alex's temperature is rising. When Lottie bumps into him as they place the chairs back against the wall, it is an electrifying brush with Beauty, Nature, a nymph, a fairy princess. As she leaves the room, she turns to smile over her shoulder at Alex, a strand of her brown hair loose from her French roll.

'Good night, Captain Twigg-Patterson.'

'Good night, Miss Lottie.'

Alex does not sleep well, and after hearing the pony's clip-clop as the Reverend Brown leaves the stable, he lies motionless, listening for birdsong to ascertain the hour. A click of his door opening, a murmur of nightgown, and Lottie is beside him, the faint pre-dawn light allowing him to make out the shape of her features. They are still just for a moment and Lottie is the first to move, squirming out of her nightdress. Alex surrenders: all his nervousness is converted to adrenalin as she pushes his nightshirt up and off. Any reservation is gone with the cool skin of Lottie's hand moving over his torso, his behind, reaching between his legs. The dynamic shifts and Alex, without conscious consideration, takes part. The gratification of love or lust – or both – is complete.

Spent, he considers her loveliness without guilt. He decides, *She must be the one for me, forever.*

'Lottie,' he whispers, 'you are so sweet, so very, very sweet. Shall we be engaged? You are a dear little thing.' He knows no romantic poetry of love to whisper in her ear as their bodies cool – no Donne or Shakespeare's sonnets have ever featured in his education. He makes do.

Lottie smiles. 'And you, you are my hero, Alex.' She moves her legs and pelvis, caught up in their shed clothing, and awkwardly pulls him from her, conscious that – well, the girls have told her – by leaving his thing in her after, you know, she may get with child. She's not sure that it's particularly reliable information, but may as well pay heed, just in case. Her breasts bump against Alex's hairless chest, and a new frisson stirs in him, believing Lottie's movement is affectionate, rather than practical.

'Lottie? What do you say? Shall we tell the reverend that we want to marry?'

'Um … alright.' She had only sought the dare, the conquest, something to whisper to her friends. She wanted to be something special – not to Alex necessarily, though that was nice – but to be something special to someone, someone the other girls would think was wonderful.

The hesitation in her voice brings Alex part of the long way back to reality.

'Er, Lottie? Did I do something wrong? We love each other – look, we just did … well …' Alex has no language for the deed. It is something he has never discussed with anyone else, ever. At school the other boys had used words like 'fucking', even 'rooting', which seemed rather harsh for Alex's sensibilities. His fellow officers might refer to 'an interesting night out with a young lady' or even 'humpy-rumpy' to Alex's great discomfort. He couldn't use any of those terms here and now with Lottie. That would be down-right impolite.

This conundrum reminds him of the extent of his igno-rance: the possibility that the act was not right; the possibility that Lottie did not have a similar life-changing experience; the possibility that he was mistaken about … the meaning of … He still doesn't have the vocabulary.

Alex moves to lie on his back and covers himself with the linen sheet, like Adam sensing the serpent's presence. For the first time, he becomes aware of Lottie's body odour, her armpits and crotch, pungent and yet alluring.

'Do you … do you want to keep it a secret, Lottie?' Embold-ened, one hand moves to cover his heart, and the other moves to Lottie's thigh in a hunt for more.

'Yes, Alex, that might be best. You write to me from over there and I'll write too, and when this is all over, we'll meet up again?'

Alex considers the proposal, rather less than he had thought was possible for them moments before.

'But because we have … don't we … ought not we …?'

'No … maybe … it's just between you and I, and, well, we'll treasure it, and I'll treasure my memories of you, and it is very special, but we'll keep it as our secret, won't we?' Nervous now, running on, out of her depth, Lottie begins to glimpse the enormity of what she's stirred up, what she has woken in him. It was meant to be a bit of fun. What if he tells the reverend?

Alex feels something like promise fade inside him: a disappointing discovery that what was so extraordinarily beautiful could be wasted. Was the act not miraculous … the very basis of life itself? He tucks away his doubt. His sad resolve brings out the polite gentleman in him, and he averts his eyes from Lottie's form for as long as it takes for her to rearrange her nightdress.

With some element of propriety restored, Lottie turns her electric smile to Alex again, and in the dawn light she blows him a silent kiss as she leaves. And with that airy kiss, Alex wavers and discovers stubborn sentimentality within himself. He determines to *love* and *marry* Lottie because he ought to, and he's pleased with his resolve. But there's a place in his abdomen that is empty of that purpose and in a corner of his mind he suspects he'd not protest the point.

He floats into a deep sleep, but only briefly. His soldierly internal clock wakes him at 0600, and he finds he is hard again with the memory of Lottie's soft, plump thighs where they meet her Mound of Venus, but to act on his vivid vision is somehow disrespectful to her and he leaves his bed believing any celebration of his newly discovered manhood is unbecoming.

Saddling his horse, and then on the road at a trot, watching the countryside wake to another hot Brisbane day, Alex is tense with the contradictions of the two would-be lovers. His heart beats faster with a daylight recognition – there's prowess and shame, pride and guilt. When he dismounts in front of the timber shack – temporary headquarters of his Company – there is only a snappy salute and the start of a captain's day, no remnant of his fleshy encounter.

Is it contrariness, revenge or a defence? If he has sinned, caused the loss of his innocence, and if he must be cast out from Paradise – with or without Eve – he will have it on his terms. Alex arranges sleeping quarters for himself at the men's camp. He writes to the reverend thanking him for his Christian generosity and explaining it's best for Alex to be in close contact with his troops from now on. His letter ends with a request: 'please extend my thanks and regards to your wife and daughter for their charming hospitality'.

Lottie is relegated to a rare, remote, dreamlike memory, neither missed nor dismissed.

CHAPTER SEVEN

ALEX AT WAR

Alex's Company leaves Brisbane for Sydney by train, and then by converted cruise ship from Sydney Harbour for Europe in mid-1916 – not with the carefree, adventurous attitudes of those troops that had sailed in 1914, nor even those who headed off in 1915 with their earnest conviction and a sense of duty. There is a muted awareness of the trouble ahead and just what is being left behind.

With the entire Third Division, the Company arrives at its first official, longer-term destination – England – and assembles on Salisbury Plain. Alex is allocated a new lieutenant, one who will be an aid to integration and liaison having spent some time with the English army. He sees this young man walk toward him and senses that this man will be an asset to his leadership. Alex breathes a sigh of relief. Lieutenant Edward Fitzgerald, his second-in-charge, will become a close companion and colleague.

'Gidday … sir,' Edward says with a slightly sloppy salute.

'Yes, good day to you, too,' is Alex's relaxed response with an equally casual salute.

A look, a handshake and a mutual nod are all it takes, and the friendship follows.

To Alex, Edward is a blessed man who radiates good will and optimism. The two soon talk in shorthand, work in unison, and respond to each other with a smile and a laugh. For Alex's entire young adult life he has supervised and cared for younger men, plus his mother and sister. Like a puppy, Edward wants only to please and seeks pleasure: he rolls with the challenges and military absurdities; he laughs when things go pear-shaped. Alex can shed some of the apprehension raised by his own self-commissioned responsibilities. It is therapeutic for Edward, too, that Alex is steady and stable, a man who points out the good and the right of things, a man to say 'stop' when it's warranted, and 'go' when it's safe.

But Alex remains something of a loner. As an officer, he is allowed to take a local farmer's trap and pony to see Stonehenge: it's so close to their camp on Salisbury Plain, but hundreds of generations and thousands of miles from an Australian's experience. He goes by himself, wanting a little time from his officer self, and finds it cathartic, wandering among the monoliths and wondering about those who placed them there. He's chilled by a cool afternoon wind penetrating his jacket; the gusts find space to infiltrate around his buttoned collar.

Is it the breeze that gives me these goosebumps? Or am I haunted by my predecessors?

He smiles at the thought, and squats to cheat the wind of its triumph. He is balanced on haunches, with his back to the stone, and looks through the late-summer light, across the bright green fields to the stands of dark green trees. Starlings, larks and finches bob in among the tufts of luscious grass and flit in and out of the hawthorn hedges. English birds sing with pretty melodies, so different to the raucous squawk of kookaburra, cockatoo, galah. He is all alone at the site and returns to the camp sated. It does him good to be alone – bar the wraiths of the Neolithic – even for a couple of hours.

*

In November 1916, Alex finds himself quietly pleased to be addressing his two hundred-plus men, standing on a chair, arms akimbo, in the mess hall at a hastily convened get-together.

'Well, it seems we're off.'

The men cheer, loud and long. They've been frustrated by what they feel is wasting time. They're bored, pent up.

'Now don't get overexcited. Settle down, settle down. I want you to be the soldiers you've trained to be …'

Alex wants to give them a pep talk, inspire them, but the men burst out afresh, cheering cheekily, irreverent. They know this officer can take a joke.

'Yes, yes, very helpful, very helpful indeed,' Alex responds with a smile. 'After your lunch here, I want you to prepare your packs for moving on, finish up and send any letters for home.'

An excited murmur rips through the crowd.

'Tomorrow morning at 0600, we will entrain for the coast to meet our seagoing transport, which will take us across the Channel to France.'

Noisy hoots and even noisier cheers follow, almost drowning out Alex.

'This is it, men! We're off to teach the Boche a lesson!'

There's too much noise to continue, but Alex gives in to a laugh, and yells, 'Dismissed!' He knows the men are ready – as ready as they'll ever be.

When his supervision of the logistics is complete, Alex writes a letter to his mother – formal as usual, and saying one thing, but meaning another:

Dear Mother

I received your letter of 7th May. Thank you for your kind thoughts and good wishes. While I am fulfilled in my current position, it is enormously satisfying to receive news from my dear family.

Please send my best to Eila and fond regards to Leslie and Raoul. It sounds as though the boys' dedication to their work as you describe is beneficial to both employer and employee! Even if any referendum on conscription is successful, you need not fret for them; presumably they will remain safe in their pursuits in Melbourne. They will not be called upon to serve overseas; their duty is fulfilled by maintaining Australian industry.

In the next few days, we will move on from our base here in England. It has been rather lovely – so green with gentle hills to roam about on in our off-duty hours. We might have known our departure was imminent as yesterday the king inspected the Third Division. What an honour! He was also giving out medals following the battles at a place called Pozières, and during this ceremony I was able to catch his eye for a moment. He appears to be a great gentleman. He is smaller than I had imagined; certainly, his horse is quite small for a thoroughbred. The horse is a beauty, a dark chestnut.

I have made some good friends among my fellow officers, particularly a chap from New South Wales by the name of Edward Fitzgerald. I shall bring him home to meet you, Mother, when we can return to Australia.

My troops are fine young men too. I can only hope to serve them well.

This has been a long letter! Please share it with my dear brothers and sister. Give Poppsie a pat for me. (I imagine her at your feet while you read this.)

Your loving son

Alex

*

'What do you think, eh? Are you going to be able to do it when required? Kill a man?' Alex asks Edward as the troop train rattles from the French port of Le Havre to the town nearest their first camp. The question is now asked in earnest.

In a freezing wind, with grey skies and gritty, icy rain, Alex's men left the English port of Southampton and crossed the choppy Channel in *La Marguerite*. Most of the troops remained on deck for the journey of several hours. They figured out that if they felt woozy on deck in the very fresh air, it must have been worse below in the fug and stench of hundreds of poorly washed men, who are dressed in less-than-clean clothes and live on a diet of coarse-tobacco cigarettes and sugary tea.

Now as the train crawls across the dark countryside, the officers are in first class, their service caps at jaunty angles or despatched to the wire racks above their heads. They lounge on the capacious leather seats, read or chat quietly. The troops are in third, more closely packed on wooden bench seats, more raucous, some singing, some snoring, tunics awry, puttees loose. At least they are warm and dry.

'Of course. Don't be ridiculous.' Edward snorts, his courage questioned.

'I'm not being ridiculous. You know we've been briefed on the issue: soldiers of all armies are shooting high, low, wide. Anywhere but to kill.' As a professional soldier Alex has thought about the killing of another human being and rehearsed it during his training more frequently and formally compared to Edward, but it troubles him more than his friend.

'Ha! Then I might be the only real soldier out there.' Edward is amused at the irony of great armies facing off, but the individual soldier not wanting to engage. Alex ignores his bravado.

'You know, the vast majority of casualties are being caused by artillery these days. I can't believe the sheer number of shells being used; it's staggering. It seems very few of us look into the eyes of our enemy in battle.' Alex has brought the conversation back to earth.

'What about those god-awful trench raid stories? Mad Boche hacking at the unsuspecting, with their painted faces, knuckle dusters and blades. Animals,' Edward blusters, waving his half-eaten apple for emphasis.

'Ah, they're just men like us, Ed. And I'll wager they're regarded as heroes when they get back to their hidey holes.' Made serious by the paradox, the gap between the propaganda and the reality, Alex looks down at the hands in his lap: will they soon be covered in blood? Things that have been hypothetical till now are becoming real.

'Yes, well, it's bloody well uncivilised,' says Edward, and it's Alex's turn to chuckle.

'Too late to protest that now. War, my friend, is the breakdown of civilisation. As Spenser said, "For blood can nought but sin, and wars but sorrows yield." Or something like that.'

'Oh God, you're going all philosophical, all bloody poetical, on me. Pass the brandy.'

Alex catches and holds his breath a moment and decides he should say something to Ed about his drinking, his pursuit of alcohol.

'You might want to ease up on the brandy … and the rest of it, my friend.'

Edward shoots Alex a look of alarm, which turns to shame. He quickly collects himself. 'What? What are you saying?'

'I'm worried about you.'

'Oh, bollocks. I'm fine.' Edward cranes his head to look out the dirty window.

Alex plucks at his trouser crease and determines not to pursue the matter; maybe it's better to have peace between them.

*

With a nod, Alex acknowledges the civilians he sees on the quick march from the train station to the No. 2 Rest Camp – the first camp for Alex's Company on French soil.

'*Bonjour, bonjour. Nous sommes soldats australienne.*'

He hopes his awkward French, a bit of a lop-sided smile and an informal wave will suffice, but the lack of response or an accusing glare makes him doubt it. The route takes them through villages that are still intact, as the fighting is beyond this back area. Small shops, cafés and bars are open, but many other places are boarded up with rough, hand-painted signs declaring there is nothing left inside. There are a few towns-people on the streets who do not greet the soldiers: too tired, too cynical, and sometimes too frightened. Who can assure them that these soldiers won't steal from them, won't destroy their homes, kill their livestock? It seems like every group of armed men that arrives leaves with something that isn't theirs.

In the weeks that follow, Alex and his men move in and out of action, in the trenches, erecting or dismantling tents, working with supplies and ammunition, building huts or lean-tos. Alex feels the cold – the penetrative, devilish cold – of this, his first European winter: hands and feet are scarlet and itchy with chilblains, his bones – even his teeth – ache, his ears are bright ruby-red. The frigid air seems to better conduct the sounds of the distant shelling and gunfire. The sharp cracks and the basso profundo booms make up the white noise in these winter's days. The soldiers acquire and barter unusual items to supplement their uniforms in the quest to stay warm. Scarves, balaclavas, gloves, jumpers, jackets, vests of all colours and patterns, are purchased – or stolen – from the French civilians. Alex's batman finds Alex an oversized, knitted beret – replete with frayed pom-pom – too clownish for an officer to wear anywhere but to bed. The clothing is worn in a ragtag manner; the soldiers' formerly universal look is gone. It takes days, not weeks, for all items to turn a shade of khaki from the dirt, the mud, the squalor of tens of thousands of men massed together.

The soldiers are always hungry, always empty. The tumbling, churning, gnawing sensation in Alex's belly is a background condition, a constant presence, slightly sinister, a reminder of his vulnerability. He learns to rise slowly as light-headedness becomes the norm. Behind the lines, food becomes the focus. Hot meals are discussed in advance, during and after service. The cooking contraptions – wood-fire stoves and ovens – are brought along on their own carriage, dragged by one strong horse. A carriage of supplies follows, with the cooks and assistants guarding the contents. As the carriages go by, ever on the move to reach their daily destination, groups of soldiers pass them or are passed. Barbs and comments fly.

'What's for tea?'

'More horse stew.'

'Hurry up … I'm bloody starving.'

'Keep your shirt on!'

'I'll have a cuppa, thanks, mate.'

'What I wouldn't do for a bit of me ma's fruit cake.'

For the men, a brew-up among a small group barely curbs the longing for food or for home, but gives them something to do. The occupation, the purpose and the result are appreciated in a world of uncertainty. A steaming mug of black tea, dark as stout, is a comfort, and if they're lucky, a couple of lumps of sugar makes sitting in an informal circle with a couple of mates a pleasure. And a brew-up provides Alex with an opportunity: he finds he can sit with them, in good-natured conversation, if there's a mug of tea in his hands.

'Cold, eh?'

The weather is always a safe topic to open with, a chance to exclaim.

'Brass monkeys, eh, sir?'

'What? Oh, I see. Mmm, brass monkeys. Very good.' He blushes.

'Won't be long till spring, sir,' a kind trooper helps the captain out.

'Quite, quite. Well, must get on.' When he gets to his feet, he's convinced his men seem chuffed at his presence, or at the very least pleased that he made some kind of effort.

*

At the front line, what were mere lines on a map now materialise for Alex as zigzagging trenches, and place names on the map are revealed as flattened villages. As days go by, both sides win a little, lose a little; the Australians are subject to a thorough shelling. His Company soon discovers the whereabouts of their co-forces, New Zealanders, some under muddy canvas sheets suspended by tent poles and surrounded by sandbag walls; some crouched in shallow earth hollows scraped from the trench's side. Alex's men relieve the Kiwi soldiers, who are desperate for a break.

'What took you so long, ya fuckers?' The lined faces are like gargoyles.

''Bout bloody time.' Caked in mud, the whites of their eyes are emphasised.

'Steady on there, fellas,' Alex placates. 'We're all doing our best, fighting the same enemy, eh, fellas?'

Each day on waking he rehearses lines that might ease tension and fear: enquiries after a man's minor injury; a funny story about a rat in the officers' mess; or simply a wish for better weather – yes, there's always the weather. All his men are green, but some of the older ones have a bit of life experience, better to accept danger, to put this into some kind of perspective. Some talk about 'fate', some of revenge. No one mentions sacrifice except the padres, and few of the men listen to the prayers or sermons.

Some groups are sent on trench raids with bayonets in place, or reconnaissance forays in search of intelligence, or to provide support for other teams with enfilading fire. Alex's men disprove the naysayers who feared that these soldiers – latecomers – would not be the extraordinary fighters that the earlier divisions had proved to be, tested as they were at Gallipoli and in Egypt.

In the trenches, the troops learn to catnap with piercing and irregular noise, in interminable drizzle and with the stench of rotting flesh like acid in their sinuses. At the front, there is no hot food for days on end, and rock-hard biscuits are broken up and dunked in tin cups of tea if they can get it, or in the murky, donkey-borne drinking water, all swallowed with alternating mouthfuls of bully beef from tin cans. Every now and then a young soldier is commissioned to carry a crate of apples along the trench – a bit of fresh food at last. The Germans can hear the celebrations. Alex doesn't know whether to shut them up or cheer them on as the men sing ditties to the tune of 'Loch Lomond', and the tuneless voices drift over no man's land:

I'll take the tripod
And you take the gun
And you'll be in action before me
And if you get shot
I'll take the bleedin' lot
And I'll eat your rations
In the morning.

On Christmas Day, 1916, those at the front each receive an Eccles cake; Alex sees tears on the cheeks of his most ferocious fighter as the big man picks out each currant individually to savour the sweet experience.

Alex records the first death for his Company, his first loss, which he takes to heart. Certain he's responsible, he holds the loss in his chest like a clenched fist, and it sits there, heavy, intrusive. The dead man is Thomas Joseph Quigley. Alex can't attend the burial ceremony as he must be at a briefing at headquarters. To focus at the meeting, he puts on his brave face. He wears his professional persona, his mental 'uniform', and banishes thoughts of the ceremony taking place. On his return, he asks Edward – who has done the burial honours on Alex's behalf – for the details.

'How'd it go, Ed?'

'Oh, you know, fine. Sad and all that.'

'It is … really … Quigley … good lad. You've written to the family? Want me to do it?'

'No, no. All done.'

*

Their laborious work continues. It never seems to end. There are days when the enemy delivers an intense bombardment and the men shelter, suspended, for the hours of the attack's duration. There are weeks of work parties for trench or communication lines maintenance, and they are shot at, either by sniper or machine gun. All day, every day they fire on the enemy: harassing fire, covering fire, indirect fire. Living in trenches, repelling enemy attacks, eating poor-quality food: Alex now only ever sleeps in snatches. More of his men are wounded, more are killed.

*

At the daily officers' meeting, Alex is at pains to let the group know of every one of the losses.

'By now, you've all heard about MacIntosh and Hardy? Killed three days ago in an enemy raid on our front-line trench.'

The meeting is quiet for a moment. All eyes stare at the small flame struggling in the brazier in front of them. Alex continues, 'Before they could even fix bayonets, the enemy slit their throats.'

'They were buried yesterday, sir. The ground is so frozen it took all day to dig deep enough,' the second lieutenant offers. 'We chalked their nicknames on the crosses: Raincoat and Hardly.'

A sad laugh from all eight in the circle. They are not used to their charges dying at all, let alone in such a terrible way.

'Raincoat and Hardly?' Alex sighs and shakes his head, a small smile. Black humour is important to get them through. 'Alright, moving on, we need a discussion as to how to keep the gunlocks from seizing: the oil normally used on the guns is freezing. These extraordinary conditions, this bloody ... wretched, bone-breaching, all-pervading, icy cold is buggering with our weapons. Any ideas?'

There is not much to say. No one knows the answer, no one knows what might work.

'Then I'll ask Headquarters; see what they've got to say.' Alex shuffles the paper spread on his knees, takes his time, staging a moment. 'I have good news too. We are to be relieved.'

'Oh, good show.'

'About time too.'

'Thank God.'

'We'll retire to Armentières in forty-eight hours … sleep, eat, bathe, then sleep some more … but only for as long as it takes to prepare to move to a new sector … two weeks, perhaps.'

To a man, they sit up, lean forward; someone stokes the fire and adds more wood. One proposes to make tea. Cigarettes and hipflasks are offered around. All wear a smile, and colour suffuses their formerly dull, grey faces. Alex declares the meeting closed.

*

Day after day, Alex finds his clerk or a junior officer, and together they sit or stand, lean against a wall or crouch in a cleared trench area. While hunched over a temporary table, seated on an upturned wooden crate, wearing gloves with the fingers cut off, they fill the pages of the unit diary, listing the names of the wounded and killed: they're coming in quick profusion now.

Documenting the men's activity, the unit's diary is a book of jeopardy, logged in the understated army-style language that Alex has been trained to use. In monotone, he records the arduous and constant nature of the threat. He is too tired to enhance the account – there are no flowery adjectives or adverbs – and he feels too flat to consider his current circumstances or his former life in any coherent way. His family's needs, Lottie's sensual gift, the aesthetic of Australia with its eucalypts and ancient dust: these things do not enter his mind. It is one foot in front of another, hour after hour, day after day, night after night. Alex has been responsible for his men in the front line for four months now. He cannot rest, he cannot dream. Alex snatches his few hours of pre-dawn sleep using his version of counting sheep. He nods off to an imagined sound heard only in his head: a rhythmic dirt-scraping, shovelling of grave diggers. The pretence brings him peace; the illusion that the bodies of his dead men are being cared for.

The diary entries for April 1917 document an escalation of enemy activity, particularly in an increase of aircrafts flying over the front line, often engaged in machine-gun fire. The men on the ground are fascinated, particularly Edward, who is always the first to point out the shape in the clear or cloud-pocked sky, and Alex, shaking his head, watches bemused as it brings about a levity among the men. With his boyish enthu-siasm, Edward shouts and dances about while the other men whistle and applaud the men and planes overhead, whether they be friend or foe.

'What do you think about that, hey! Those planes … so damn … exciting!' raves Edward. 'A wonder! A marvel!'

Only Alex sees the paradox: the contraptions lift the spir-its of those put in great danger by their very existence. He keeps the observation to himself.

*

In May, Alex sits in the second tier of seating around the big table in the magnificent Château de Bertangles, near Amiens, headquarters of Australia's General Monash. The tenor of conversation among the most senior officers is a bubbling dynamic. The verbal exchanges are swift, movement is rapid, people pacing, entering and leaving the room quickly. Papers are piled high, maps spread on tables and pinned to upright stands. Triangles of paste sandwiches, fruitcake and scones are on offer and are eaten rapidly while standing. Teacups rattle in their saucers and the teapot is renewed constantly. There is an energy that, no mistake, can only be described as optimistic. Alex is there to confirm the readiness – or otherwise – of the artillery in relation to an attack to take place soon. Witnessing the many planning sessions, he is privy to the thought-processes of General Monash. He likes Monash's quiet but authoritative style – the cut of his jib, so to speak. Alex is certain that Monash represents a new way of approaching this bloody and bloody awful war. This thickset older man, with his trademark full moustache, is determined that not a single detail will be left unconsidered in preparing for the next big bash.

Plans are made and remade; maps drawn and redrawn; orders drafted and redrafted. In early June 1917, Alex and his men – with several thousand others – move into Ploegsteert Wood and its surrounds for the Battle of Messines.

CHAPTER EIGHT

'Funny name.'

With an awkward laugh, Edward Fitzgerald cuffs his friend on the side of his head, knocking the officer's cap askew. It falls to the ground, revealing Alex's thick thatch of auburn hair, cut short back and sides as is required.

'What … *my* name? My surname?' says Alex, turning. 'Oh, you mean the wood? Ploegsteert Wood?' He's a little annoyed: he and Edward may be friends, but it is an over-familiar gesture from a lieutenant to his captain – tonight, of all nights. And is that a whiff of alcohol on Edward's breath?

'The fellas call it "Plug Street",' says Edward, oblivious.

Alex rakes his fingers through his hair, reaches to the damp, rough grass for his cap, and draws it down firmly; his ears are pushed out a little.

'Where did you spring from, Ed? I thought your group wasn't coming into the wood until jump-off.'

'Oh, I thought I'd surprise you … check you turned up for the big show.' Now Edward's expanded toothy smile makes apparent his big, white teeth in the dim night light.

They are speaking, as instructed, in whispers, having been given orders to 'go dark' until further notice – no fires, cigarettes or conversation above a measured hiss. As the cooling night falls on 6 June 1917, thousands of Australian troops have moved quietly – as quietly as an army can move – from the neighbouring villages and camps, up to Ploegsteert Wood in southern Belgium. The troops are aware and comforted to know that a New Zealand division are to the north of their position, up and around Hill 63. The troops are also aware that the British division is beyond the New Zealanders: less comforting, but that prejudice may just be the rub of the ever-growing chip on the shoulders of the Australian soldiers. Now they wait for whatever will come to each of them in the next twenty-four hours. Both Edward and Alex know the encounter may be grim and it will be big. Edward as a lieutenant and Alex as a captain are privy to the anthill activity that has preoccupied their superiors for weeks now. These two men know that this engagement is a significant battle; it may bring something positive to the Allies. It could be a turning point.

Best not to give it much thought. One day at a time. One step at a time.

As they sit in the dark wood, on a waxed-canvas groundsheet, Edward pulls out a hipflask. He swigs first and hands it to Alex, who sniffs it, tilts his head, questioning.

'Brandy, Al; it's not great, but the best I could find.'

Alex takes a quick, small pull, and makes a smacking noise in response to the crack and zing of the rough alcohol in his mouth.

'My God, how many of us are there?' Edward looks around in the moonlight, as though noticing for the first time that they are surrounded by the men. 'Cheers.' He takes a second swig and tucks the flask away.

'Just around us, hereabouts, you mean? Well, our 11th Brigade, a couple of thousand, I reckon, but in total … perhaps most of the Third Division.'

'And remind me … when's jump-off? I forget.'

With a roll of his eyes, Alex replies, 'Oh, Ed, you know damn well … 0320.' Alex checks his wristwatch. 'And it's almost eleven.'

He's nervous, thinks Alex, startled by this truth. *And perhaps … tipsy, on this night, of all nights.*

Over the past few hours, in groups of eight and nine, men have been making their way in and around the somewhat cleared area where Edward and Alex sit. These troops find a spot that suits them and then squat or lean on packs, assisting one another in getting comfortable. There's a fierceness, a tension in the air while the men continue to stream into the wood. The soldiers' bravado of eight hours ago, voiced in their briefings with cheers, is almost gone, and the cheek of their marching song that regulated their tramp into the general area is no longer such a hoot:

Mademoiselle from Armentières, parley vous?
Mademoiselle from Armentières, parley vous?
Mademoiselle from Armentières, hasn't been fucked for forty years,
Hinky dinky, par-ley vous!

The men are subdued yet edgy, watchful but not anxious, waiting. They smell of damp woollen tunics, and the aroma of bodies not often washed, in underclothes worn for weeks at a time. The odour has become a comforting fug, a sensory authentication of their survival: they're alive. The smell is tolerable; the lice less so. From young to old, their faces are set in a solemn attitude; some sitting, some standing, a few chatting quietly. Edward and Alex can hear snippets of their conversations.

'Got a fag, mate?' says a burly soldier in a husky voice. 'Ta.' He takes the makings and starts to roll his own. 'Name's Bullen. I'm from Booligal. Where are you from, hey?'

'Melbourne. Well, that's where I grew up.' The speaker is young, not a whisker on his face, let alone a crease.

The older man squints, close to the young man's face. 'Grew up, you say? Huh, you've got a ways to go yet, boy.'

A sergeant hisses, 'Keep it down,' then swings around to address a trio close by also exchanging whispers. 'Shut your fuckin' gob, would ya?' He makes more noise than his comrades.

The soldiers share any food they've acquired in the last few days as they've rotated through the surrounding villages and towns, south and west of the front line, including Armentières and Ypres: bread and cheese, of course, but apples and olives too. They chase their picnic food with water from their individual canteens.

Alex discreetly deep-breathes the wood's scent of damp earth, with its fragrance of pine and rotting leaves. He is taking stock, centring himself. His sense of purpose overrides any fear and the magnificence of Ploegsteert Wood lends him strength. In childhood, on weekly walks in Melbourne's Botanical Gardens, he learnt the names of the European trees. It gives him great pleasure to privately identify the old and tall Flanders trees: oaks, poplars, pines, elms and cypresses. He thinks of them tussling and jostling together in all weathers to retain their place in the wood, spreading by seed and suckers. The shrubs and saplings are not as easily identified, especially on this dark night, but because of them Alex and his men find the undergrowth a little difficult to move through. There are scrawny tufts of grasses and indeterminate just-green hedge plants, and the uneven floor of the wood is littered with big and small branches, recently fallen or in various states of decay. There is rustling and flapping intermittently above the soldiers' heads; the birds are unsettled by the human presence. The occasional tickling of insects on Alex's uncovered skin, on his face or hands, is only the briefest of distractions.

'It's cold tonight, eh?' says Edward to Alex, rubbing his hands together, blowing on them. 'And it's supposed to be summer.' The cool of the dirt is seeping through the bottom of Edward's boots, across the knitted barrier of his thick woollen socks, the chill travelling, upward, blood- and bone-borne.

'Ah, well, at least we've got a bit of moonlight.' Alex can make out the soldiers reading a scrap of a shared newspaper, handed from man to man, perhaps an account of a victory or loss, perhaps some news from home. Others read a well-thumbed letter or study a photo portrait. The stars are obscured by the moonlight and the light cloud, but on the ground, cigarettes glow. They're lit end to end in cupped hands and are held with the ember turned into the men's palms, hidden from the enemy. With each drag, the orange light is a brief, fierce glow – a small, bright heart in a chest of finger-ribs. Wafts of cigarette smoke give away the small groups of men ignoring the instruction not to smoke, an instruction given by Alex without much conviction: it is impossible to police.

Alex is responsible for settling his Company. These men, in his charge, are as much a part of him – an extension of him – as the long bones of his limbs. He earns their regard and they earn his: a truly symbiotic respect. As much as they want him to lead them well, he wants them in the best state of mind and as physically able as is possible. In this army of volunteers, regard and respect are not blind to capability. He acknowledges the several sergeants and lance corporals, who ably assist him with his task, with a nod or raised hand.

Sergeant Parker approaches Alex and Edward. 'My men, they're all here, sirs.'

'Very good, Parker. I heard you were short of water. Did you manage to rectify that?'

'Yes, sir. We're set to go.'

'Well done. Stand ready.' Alex's reply sees Parker return to a huddle a stone's throw away.

A private approaches Edward and Alex, and squats to speak to them. He is a big man. His tin hat is a familiar shape silhouetted against the low light, and his features are blurred. It's an unusual act: officers and privates don't chat.

'How ya going, fellas? Got everything you need? Water?' asks the private.

'Yes, fine, thank you.' An edge of displeasure from Edward. He remembers the man. Williams, who wouldn't let him be, trying to bring the men's attention to Edward's confusion after Quigley died. Williams, pestering him at Armentières when he and Alex waited to have their studio shot taken. Might this soldier – the one who's been privy to Edward's weaknesses – be taking yet another liberty? He and Edward have had words in the past, and Edward wants to believe him to be imper- tinent. He inclines his head to consider the possibility. He is mindful that Alex has warned him against overreacting where this soldier is concerned.

'Look, where should you be, Private? Which section are you with?' says Edward.

'Oh, I'm just moving around, checking everyone is feeling ready for it. Thought I'd see if we're all alright.' His body is quite still like a monumental bronze, a sculpture of Atlas, and his voice is a slow, warm, deep drawl.

Alex observes the man's solid form as the soldier hunkers down, squats to Alex and Edward's level, becomes a protective wall, a barrier to the excesses beyond. In this light, in this place, he could be an illusion, a mythological figure of Alex's imagination.

'I've seen you among the men, Private. You're good with them. Have you considered working toward a promotion?' Alex has noticed his quiet ways, posture and gestures of solidarity in and around the camps and on long marches. This big man is a natural leader, an instinctive and important part of any team.

'Sir, you know, I just can't see it. I think I'm best right where I am, with me mates.' The private's reply is a velvety growl. 'No offence though, it's an honour to have it suggested of me. I mean, this,' he waves his arm from left to right, 'feels big, don't you reckon? Bigger than all of us.' The soldier drops his voice to a hypnotic whisper. 'Like we're greater than the sum of our parts.' He pauses, looks down, draws the fingers of his right hand over the soil at his feet. 'You know, most of the men ask each other all the time, "What will you do when the war's over?" I think dreams keep us going. What about you, sir?'

The question is directed to Alex. He is surprised but not offended by the boldness of the man.

'You mean … what will I do after the war?' Alex says with an almost-shrug. 'I honestly don't know. And you?'

The big man hesitates before answering.

'I reckon I'll do as Tolstoy recommended. Pretty good advice when he said, "Seize the moments of happiness, love and be loved!"'

There is a further pause in the conversation. Annoyed, Edward says, 'Seriously, Tolstoy? Good grief. I think you'd best move back to your position …'

'A fine idea,' Alex says with a soft laugh. 'You know Tolstoy?' He can see the white of the big man's eyes and his teeth in a smile by the moonlight but not much else of his face.

'Well, not personally.' The soldier raises his eyebrows for unseen emphasis. 'That's a joke, sir.'

'Did you mean to say Tolstoy?' Edward sounds bemused. 'You're a bush philosopher, eh …? Quite the intellectual.'

'My grandfather had a fine library, and he let me have the run of it. I was lucky.'

'But perhaps it's best you rejoin your assigned group, Private?' Edward is determined to close down this exchange.

'Yeah, righto, if you think so. I'm off then. Best of luck and see you on the other side and all that. Let's give these Huns a hiding, eh?'

Still squatting, the private extends his hand to Alex; another unusual, indeed, unheard-of gesture between ranks. And after a heartbeat, Alex grasps it, holding it for a moment longer than entirely necessary. There is a comforting steadiness to the private's shape and his deliberate, enveloping handshake of warm, dry skin. The handshake over, the sturdy limbs that have enabled the private's stable crouch raise his form again, bringing him to standing. This everyday physical movement is executed with grace. Alex rises to standing too.

'Thanks for your concern, Private. What's your name?'

The private is standing with a lanky ease, hands on hips; he quietly states his name.

'Cheerio then,' he says, and he evaporates into the dark of the forest.

Inexplicably, Alex wants – desires – this man's strength to remain beside him. His arm moves to stop him, to hold him in the radius of their little clearing – too slow.

'Did you catch his name, Ed? I think it was Williams. Was it Jim Williams?' Alex crouches again next to Edward. Though not given to flights of fancy, Alex is strangely affected by the encounter. His eyes search the gloaming for the receding form, to requisition its strength.

'Yes, Williams, something like that. Don't know what he's on about. Tolstoy!' Edward shakes his head. 'He needs to get back to his group.'

'You seem to have it in for this particular soldier, Ed. I remember the man. Is it something I should …'

'No, no. He's an … upstart. You know the kind of …'

Still sitting, Edward plucks at some strands of long grass beside his crossed legs. 'Listen, just so you know, I won't be joining you out there.'

Alex turns to face Edward. 'What? What do you mean?'

'I've received orders to transfer to Intelligence till the end of June.'

'Oh … righto.'

'I applied months ago. I forgot to tell you, sorry. Then it came through just yesterday.'

Alex looks down, considering the news. He is curious to find that he is hurt. He considers Edward a friend, a colleague. Now this: a significant show, and Edward will be in the rear, at the back of the action, safe and sound? And he *chooses* to leave the men? Alex realises that Edward has artfully, though not without good sense, manoeuvred his way into a role that sees his own promotion and preservation. He will be important to senior military staff and kept behind the lines.

But Alex is a self-contained man. He positions the news in the category of entirely surmountable: there must be something positive about it. He will be glad for his friend; he'll figure out how to do that as soon as he can think beyond this imminent encounter.

Alex claps Ed on the back. 'Well, I'm happy for you. We'll meet again after the battle in Messines.'

Edward looks at the ground and whispers, 'Thanks, Alex. In truth, I feel a bit, well … you know … I should be with you and the men, and …'

But Alex is already rising; he brushes a couple of leaves from his uniform, ready to move on.

'I'll be off then, Alex. See you tomorrow, I reckon.' Hesitation is reflected in Edward's face. Adrenalin is mobilising his jerky thinking and jumpy actions.

The two friends shake hands. They lock eyes for a moment of brotherliness, solidarity.

The night-time air is empty enough for the waiting men to hear the clear sound of commencement – the *thock, thock, thock* of shells leaving the enemy's guns. In the moments before the ordnance arrives, Captain Alexander Twigg-Patterson and Lieutenant Edward Fitzgerald witness their soldiers turn into moonlit, monochrome statues, frozen in their casual attitudes.

Then, when the first beyond-loud, reverberating explosions occur, the men instinctively fall to the ground, seeking the solid earth's protection. Within minutes, the two officers hear all around them the shouts of agony, of desperation, and the military quest for silence among the men is over.

The soldiers have experienced intense bombardment already, the terror, the resignation, the anger. There have been seven full days of crashing, deafening, infuriating explosions all around them: churning guts, banging hearts, contorting faces with ill-disguised fear. The determined Germans know full well the Allies are there in the wood and beyond; they can see the build-up from their trenches and with their binoculars atop the Messines church spire. Their biplanes soar over the British lines, allowing a bird's-eye view of the activity. During these days preceding the battle, some of the early shells find their targets. A direct hit to the ammunition dumps of the British ensures bedlam on a massive scale. Injuries and the death-toll increase on each of the seven days.

Phhht. Phhht. Phhht. These shells are a mix of explosives and phosgene gas.

'Masks, masks, masks! Get your masks on!' shout the sergeants – not that the men need to be hurried along. The scramble is on for their only form of protection. The soldiers can smell the gas, and they know that it will burn their exposed skin, causing sheets of it to bubble, peel, ooze and scar; and they know that if they breathe too much, too deeply, it will decimate the lining of their lungs. Edward's seen the contorted corpses and he's seen the survivors suffering in the camp hospitals. He turns to identify the best line for an exit from the area, then swings back to shout above the hubbub.

'Cheers, then,' he shouts at Alex. A great lurch in his stomach, more regret than fear. He doesn't want to leave Alex … but needs must.

Edward pulls his mask down over his face and makes his way, crouching, to the rear. He heads for one of the several established tracks through the wood that leads to the command staff, found in a large, khaki tent a mile or so from the far edge of the trees, on farming land usually filled with crops, pigs, chickens and cows that has been worked by Belgian families for hundreds of years. The tent has three long trestle tables covered in maps and sheafs of papers, orders and summaries. There are inkwells, pens and lead pencils, wooden trunks, canvas cases, deckchairs and three-legged stools. Serious men in neat uniforms will gather and disperse, gather and disperse, in twos and threes through the next twenty-four hours, conducting the orchestra of mayhem taking place in the several miles in front of them. Edward seeks the most senior officer's ear to let him know the status of the men in the wood. He catches the eye of the portly figure he's looking for.

'How are your chaps faring, Fitzgerald?' the more senior officer, an Englishman, starts.

'On schedule, sah!' A little of Edward's British Army experience leaches back into his pronunciation. Ready to swallow his pride, he knows a little toadying will go a long way. His salute is sharp.

'Very good, Fitzgerald.' The older man is sweating; is it nerves or illness? He dabs a voluminous handkerchief to his forehead and the back of his fleshy neck. 'You and your countrymen will soon experience your first major battle, a big test for such a small nation and with so little experience. Let's hope you can put on a good show, eh?'

Edward retains a blank expression.

'The bloody useless French army is spent, exhausted.' The man is almost talking to himself; his brow creases and his mouth softens. He looks off through the flap of the tent, beyond, across the field to Ploegsteert Wood. 'The Belgian citizens are beaten. And now that we have persuaded our governments to accept our proposal of reaching the Belgian coastline ... sweeping the German troops before us ... we'll take their naval ports – and end this damnable war.' Recovering his military self, his chevron moustache curls with his rodent smile and he rubs his damp hands together. 'This particular battle, we'll take all this area' – his right hand wafts over the battle plan map on the table beside him – 'the first part of our plan.'

CHAPTER NINE

Sydney's Chinatown provides great yum cha, and Dominic, Rachel and I were part of a group of friends who often met up there. We met on the Sunday morning following our discussion of our grandfathers' photographs. After ranting about how awful the idea of eating chickens' feet was to him, Dominic told the table about our grandfathers. Among pork buns and rice done in so many different ways, our friends were universally astounded at the serendipity of the discovery, and Dom was proud to relate the tale of my research before handing the line of conversation over to me.

'Yep, all true. The War Memorial archives are wonderful. But, Dom, don't you reckon we should go there?'

'What, me? Canberra? Not likely; the most boring place on earth.' Dom was entertaining the crowd as usual.

'No, Belgium. Ypres, Messines – it's called Mesen now – Hill 60.' I toyed with my chopsticks, stalling perhaps. 'I reckon we would be able to feel … what happened there … feel what our grandfathers felt.'

'Wouldn't that be kind of like chasing ghosts?' said Rachel, not unkindly, as she reached for a prawn dumpling. 'I think I'd find it a bit confronting.'

I shrugged. 'It feels right to me. I'm not sure I can really find out what it was like for them unless I go there, sit with it, sit with the story … there.'

'Why not?' Dom piped up, staring at me, teacup in hand, with an unreadable expression and raised eyebrows.

'Why not indeed. We'd need to get organised, Dominic, if we're going to get there in time for the centenary.'

'The what?'

'It was on 7 June 1917, when the big battle took place, when Alex got injured, and after which Edward appeared to take a change of direction. It's a hundred years ago in two months' time. We could go while there's a lull at work, between post-production and sign-off. I've checked the schedule and I've asked Charles if he'll take the girls.'

I bit my lip and swallowed the surge of guilt and anxiety at leaving the girls behind, not doing my share, not loving them as I should – and Charles hadn't even said yes yet.

A big smile overtook Dominic's face. 'You're on.' And he turned to Rachel, a query on his face.

'Not for me,' Rachel countered, holding her palm up. 'I'll keep the home fires burning, thank you very much. And P.S., Dom, you goose … you don't even have a passport.'

In retrospect, I think Dominic was simply full of bravado that morning. He had not thought it through and had no idea what he was looking for. At this point, a trip to Europe was a lark, a jape to him, a road trip. I doubt he could've found Mesen on a map. But though the word 'journey' had become a cliché, it applied here. Dominic and I were going on a *journey* in all the many and probably overstretched meanings of the word.

*

'Look, do you really want to come? I can go by myself, you know.'

Several weeks later, I'd pushed the arrangements through, several times almost rejecting Dominic's enthusiastic participation because of his infuriating inability to execute simple requests: get a passport, confirm what days he was available to fly, get his international driving licence. Things that I completed immediately took Dominic weeks, and that was with my constant reminders.

'Yes. I really want to come.' His voice insistent, up an octave, and without much conviction, he would pretend to be hurt by my criticism. 'Jesus, mate, just give me a day or two. Keep your shirt on.'

'Well, so long as you're not coming just to keep me company … or, God forbid, to look after me. You've got to come for your own reasons.'

'As if! I'm not your fucking mother,' hooted Dominic with his infuriating good humour. 'This trip will cement my bond with the man; I will see the links, relive the moments. And surely, by some kind of telekinetic, time-travelling osmosis, at least some of the finer qualities of my grandfather will graft themselves onto my own self. What do you reckon?'

Though said in jest, I suspected Dominic did feel this way. He loved the idea of Edward, loved the tales, the medals, the glory.

At last, on a grey day of high, dense clouds, we found ourselves in Sydney's Qantas lounge, the enormous steel birds tethered outside the big windows, loading, unloading. We had a couple of glasses of champagne, and Charlie Bean's book, *Anzac to Amiens*, peeped out of my daypack, the bible for First World War tragics such as myself – I had read every word of it, twice through.

'Well, Dominic, we're off.'

'Yeah … cheers.' A clink of glasses. 'You're very formal today, Tara.'

'It's significant, a significant day. We're going to find out where we come from, who we are, what we will be. I'm still amazed at the coincidence of our grandfathers knowing each other. What are the odds!'

'Actually, I've been thinking about it and the odds aren't that amazing.' Dom burst my bubble like this frequently, especially when he'd been drinking. He had been so touched when I told him about our links – astounded, excited, keen to know more – but at the moment of our departure, it was as though he'd sobered up and was protecting himself from any hurt or dissembling that I or this trip might bring about.

'You're going to tell me that it wasn't a complete freak of history that we met *and* that our grandfathers were in the same unit! Here it comes: you're going to pull some numerical shit on me.'

And he did.

'We – and our parents – are: one, Anglo; two, university-educated; three, comfortably middle-class; four, of a similar age; and five, Australia is a really small place, Sydney a tiny town – was then, is now. It is not that surprising that we know each other.'

'Ah, there's no romance in that answer.' I raised my glass. 'Here's to coincidence, serendipity and … and …' I took a considerable swig.

*

Driving into the north of France and then into the west of Belgium, the landscape was flat, neat and bleak. There were few forests and few grand buildings to enhance the acres of seemingly homogenous fields that stretched beside the kilometres of well-organised highways and interchanges. While Dominic snoozed under his airline eye mask, soothed by the suspension of our hire car, I considered how easy it was for armies, for invaders, to overrun the area, just as had occurred so many times through history. By actually coming here, I'd already had insights that a reading room or an archive centre simply couldn't give, for all their astonishing plethora of documents and digital files: a sense of the place. Presence was the essential ingredient, the bit that my imagination needed to be able to truly *see* the past, to know my grandfather, to write this memoir. I smiled with no one else to see it.

I hadn't looked at the Tripadvisor photos when I booked a hotel in Ypres online a few weeks before leaving Australia.

I'd had mental images of ivy-covered, dark brick walls, mossy paths, grottos – an Australian's virginal view of European accommodation. When we pulled into the car park, the place was a little disappointing. Cream brick, aluminium window frames, gravelled and concrete paths, populated by tidy European tourists replete with Birkenstocks and fancy camera bags.

Dominic, roused by the absence of movement, glared sleepily at the building. 'Doesn't seem very fucking historic.' There was that bubble-bursting again.

'No … remember that almost the entire town has been rebuilt *twice* in the last century.'

'Oh, yeah. I'm hungry,' he said. So that discussion was over.

Gauzy curtains gentled the light from the tall floor-to-ceiling windows in the reception area. The young woman who greeted us resembled every stereotype of a northern European beauty: long, straight blonde hair; light, clear blue eyes; a quiet smile, baring a wide gap in her white front teeth. Her staff badge revealed her name as Charlotte. She was tall and lean with a casual way of moving, as though she was cruising rather than walking. I was struck straight away by her direct attitude, her bearing: open, friendly, honest.

After a couple of questions Charlotte quickly understood why we were in Ypres. She let us know that at any one time there were hundreds of Australians – and British, French, all the world it seemed – in the district seeking similar experiences, and that the hotel offered several services to help tourists navigate the area.

'I've met a lot of Australians, young and old,' she said to put us at ease. 'Do you need help with your search?'

Though her English was perfect, the sound of her formal conversation was engaging: I looked forward to her saying something else; it was pretty to my unsophisticated ear, lilting, sing-song.

'The hotel has a researcher and library to assist; I can book tours and I can advise on many things.'

'No. I think we're good, thanks.' I was the first to regain my manners from our jetlagged state of mind. 'We mean to go to the Menin Gate Ceremony tonight. Eight o'clock, right?'

Charlotte nodded.

She told us that she had been working at the hotel for a few years now, through the summers, starting as a chamber maid and then at the reception desk. Most of the staff lived in a wing adjoining the hotel, eating the fine food from the hotel's five-star kitchens, allowed to use the pool and the bar within reason. The owners were honest burghers, people who could list generations of their Ypres families.

'It is a good job, a good life,' Charlotte said as she gave us an access card each for our rooms, which were next to each other. 'By the way, most of us staff drink at the little brewery halfway down the avenue, to your right as you leave the hotel. You can't miss it. You should join us one night.' Charlotte seemed genuine in her invitation, and Dominic and I agreed to try the bar.

'My daughter's name is Charlotte too,' I said. It took a couple of seconds for her to process this, then her face lit up and we bonded, casually, in that ancient way that women do.

Dominic was more interested in the free peppermints on the counter. Men really missed out sometimes.

*

'So, here's the tourist briefing, Dom.' I read from my guide book: '"The nightly Last Post Ceremony has taken place at the Menin Gate every night since 1928, only interrupted by WW2." It has nothing to do with the centenary celebrations, but is a must-see as far as I am concerned. OK?'

'Sure, sure, sure. I'm your partner in crime. Let's go. And then we're going out for a drink and dinner, right?'

We walked along Menenstraat in the early evening, with hundreds of other people all streaming toward the city's edge. When we arrived, it was crowded with thousands of mostly British tourists. Among hundreds of selfie sticks, camera flashes, rustling jackets, day backpacks and jostling groups keen on remaining in a comforting clutch, Dom and I found ourselves on the edge of the crowd, unsure as to where the ceremony actually took place. As we made our way through, the sound of bagpipes was heard coming from the town square and the chatty crowd became quiet. I got goosebumps – distant bagpipes are eerie. As the pipes neared, we found the edge of a low brick wall to boost us sufficiently to see the group of offi-cials in the very centre of the brick structure. The Belgians, like the French, loved the tricolour silk sashes and heavy gold mayoral chains: there were six men decked out in this sartorial splendour, wearing serious ceremonial expressions.

The Gate was a solid arch, the width of two car lanes and two footpaths, and three storeys high. During the day, the townspeople used it as a way of accessing the oldest part of the town; it was originally an opening through the solid-earth ramparts of the city, a formal and grand gateway of medieval brick within the banks of ancient dirt. In 1914, the Gate was flattened and the earth churned, rendering it impassable. There was nothing like it in Australia and it was completely beyond our comprehension, but rather than be wowed by its immensity, its age, its significance, we were busy coping with the crowd. Along with some one thousand other tourists, we had come to pay homage. For each visiting person that homage was different. Some, like us, had antecedents who were stationed in the area in the First World War, some had heard the myths and legends, some wanted to experience the sense that they could communicate with their ancestors one hundred years on.

The lights came up on the structure as the daylight faded. The enormity of the building mimicked the enormity of the loss, and small swallows flitted in and out of the arches. The crowd settled; there were a few moments of respectful silence. Not many of us could hear the official speeches: there were just too many visitors to meaningfully access the event, to hear the poetry's magic, conjuring the pathos of more than fifty thousand missing dead men in just this patch of Belgium. Their body parts and stories were scattered in a few hundred square kilometres around this edifice.

As the crowd broke up at the ceremony's conclusion, there was a nervous trill, anxious laughter, a shriek or two; those not used to sombre reflection hurried back to a normal state of mind, that of the superficial and comfortable. We heard random comments:

'Glad that's over.'

'Können wir jetzt zum Hotel zurück?'

'That was creepy.'

'Deirdre did say it was boring. I don't know why we came.'

There was also:

'Je ne peux pas m'arrêter de pleurer.'

Subdued, we made our way back to the town square and chose a restaurant for dinner, settling for an outdoor table; being June, it was not too cold among the braziers. This café was tucked into the corner of the Grote Markt, the main square of the town. It was snug beside the external archways on the short side of the Lakenhalle, the original medieval warehouse and trading centre, almost entirely destroyed by 1918, now rebuilt as a facsimile. At a nearby table, we spotted Charlotte reading a book with a glass of wine and a cheese platter. I wondered if she would welcome our intrusions, a couple of jetlagged tourists, into her evening. Then Dominic nudged me and I stepped forward.

'Peut-être, vous venez ici, avec nous?' I ventured boldly in deplorable French. 'Let us buy you a drink?'

Charlotte's big, encouraging smile showed us that she didn't just come to sit with us dutifully, but for the pleasure of meeting new people. We ordered beer and wine and downed them quickly. Dominic waved happily at the waiter for more. Relaxing back into the lounge chairs, the smoothing effects of alcohol relieved the discomfort of the Gate ceremony, gently shoehorning us back to a place of laughter and stories.

'Tell me, Charlotte, do you know much about the Battle of Messines? Our grandfathers were both there.'

'Of course. The hotel books tours to Ploegsteert Wood. It is very popular. The anniversary is in two days.' She was back to her professional self.

'We plan to go to Ploegsteert Wood, a hundred years to the day the troops moved up into the wood before reaching the jump-off point.'

'You mean the sixth … on Tuesday? On the morning of the seventh was when they went into battle.' Charlotte paused, her head tilted to one side. 'It's a sad story. I find it … confusing … that you will make yourself sad, going there … to look for your grandfathers?'

'But we've got to do it though,' Dominic chimed in, crouching over his beer, twirling the coaster. 'I mean, we have to be there, see it through. It is like my grandfather … Edward was his name … he's trying to tell me something.'

Charlotte smiled gently and ventured, 'I don't know if many Belgians share your feelings. Many of us think of our history of troubles as a curse … the Ypres curse.' She gave a small shrug, then quickly pushed her fingers through her hair. 'Perhaps because we live with it all our lives, and the sadness … it is just part of our world. Belgians never forget it, but we don't look for it.'

There was a moment of quiet between the three of us.

'I think …' I started, 'I feel sort of haunted by my grandfather. It's like I can't reach him … you know those dreams where you're reaching out and the other person escapes your grasp? That's what it's like. I feel like there's a gap in my life.'

Charlotte reached across the table and put her hand on mine, looked me in the eye and gave me an almost imperceptible nod. She knew, she understood absence.

'Will you come with us … to the wood?' I asked Charlotte impulsively. It suddenly felt important to share the experience with a Belgian. Through her eyes it would be real, authentic. Dom and I had no knowledge, no understanding, of a bleak world of destruction, death, damage. We were from the raw, scratchy, somehow immature, new world; Charlotte was from the weary old, world.

'Yeah, come,' Dominic added, typically perky, friendly. 'That would be great. Plenty of room in the car.'

Charlotte hesitated a moment longer with a minimal frown, looking at the tabletop, mouth slightly open, considering; I held my breath. She glanced at me quickly, then spoke with a sigh.

'OK, I will come. I have been before. I'll show you the cemeteries, the roads that were the boundaries of the two sides. My great-grandfather, he was a soldier too, somewhere in this area. I don't know much more than that. My great-grandmother died giving birth to the child of this soldier, to my grandmother, in 1919, and then my grandmother grew up with nuns and other orphans.' Charlotte halted and looked around her, at the people milling at the bar and out into the square. 'There is not the same appetite in my family to know all the details of those who go before us. I don't even know if my great-grandfather was belgique or français, perhaps australien ... even maybe canadien. There were many soldiers stationed here in the second half of the Great War.'

'In Australia, there is a craze, a fashion, to find your family history; there's a boom in companies who'll search for things like birth, death and marriage certificates. Maybe it's a desire to work out what we're here for.' I was over-explaining, inadequately, aware that we must appear as spoilt children seeking a Disney experience of war, not sympathetic to the reality of Belgium's suffering.

'First-world, whiny problem if ever I heard one.' Dominic forced the conversation to ground abruptly. When he was out of his depth, he had a rough way of speaking and his face closed down.

'The way you speak ... it does not make sense with your trip. Why *are* you here, Dominic?' Charlotte snapped back, a little feisty. 'Why do *you* want to go where your grandfather went?'

'Well,' he said, twisting his mouth, 'I guess I just want to see it. Sort of complete the jigsaw ... and somebody had to keep Tara company.' He gave an unconvincing laugh.

'Yeah, right, Dominic. You're just as determined as I am to have some kind of revelation. You just don't know how to say so.'

'Oh, pah-leese.' Dominic concluded the serious subject matter good-naturedly. He could laugh at himself; it eased the tempo of the back and forth. 'But I am sorry if I sound like a lightweight, Charlotte. Tara's right. I'm not very good at expressing myself. I really do want to see it all; experience it, I guess.'

Quick as a flash, Dom snapped back to his crowd-pleaser persona. 'Who's for another round?'

Charlotte told me and Dominic that our grandfathers may well have drunk together in this particular bar or in one of the two adjacent establishments. All three estaminets had existed prior to the war, had been full every evening with soldiers and townspeople before their destruction, and then the bars were rebuilt, faithful to their original architecture. They catered for the latest invaders now – tourists, those seeking 'authentic experiences'. Regrettably, with a serve of self-loathing, I put us in that category.

'So really,' Dominic persuaded us with a gentle slurring, 'we are obliged to try each of these places … take in the atmosphere … sample the local produce, as it were, only of course to know our grandfathers better.' He got little resistance from me or Charlotte.

'It is pretty amazing though. I mean, Alex could've sat right here,' I said, once again overwhelmed by coincidence and echoes. '"The past and present here unite",' I declaimed.

The other two looked at me like I was a creature from another planet.

'Wha-at?' I said. 'It's Longfellow. You know, the American poet?' I sat up straight, cleared my throat and gave them my best (but slightly tipsy) rendition:

The Past and Present here unite
Beneath Time's flowing tide,
Like footprints hidden by a brook,
But seen on either side.

'Uh-huh,' was Dom's response to my literary offering.

'Very … apt … is that the word?' Charlotte was not quite so disparaging.

I didn't mind. I was wrapped up in the atmosphere, the history, the place. I wore a contented smile, leant back in my chair, half a world away from normal life.

Friends of Charlotte's drifted in and out of the bars' courtyards, and I told myself that Dominic and I were a Saturday-night novelty of the Ypres twenty- and thirty-somethings. I stayed close to Charlotte throughout; her laughter was like a warm breeze that rippled on the pond of the humans surrounding her. Dominic flirted half-heartedly with Charlotte, to which she responded with a negligible frown, a guffaw if it became too outrageous. He lapsed into long descriptions of Rachel, how much he loved her, and of course he made Charlotte smile when he told her the story of how they had met.

By one in the morning, the three of us were drunk. During the fifteen-minute teetering walk back to the hotel, we three made our way along the cobbled Veemarkt. It was as quiet as a tomb, lined with low-rise housing. Clearly, the residents were asleep.

'It is the place of the medieval cattle market,' recounted Charlotte in a whisper, which set Dominic off, loudly moo-ing, so Charlotte and I had to shush him – just as loudly.

'Hey, I've just had an idea,' I gushed with Dutch courage, a rush of enthusiasm. 'Why don't the three of us camp overnight in Ploegsteert Wood for the complete experience in "real time"? We could follow the path of the troops at the same time. They moved into the trees at nightfall; jump-off was at 3.20 a.m.; they made their way to the top of the rise to the west of the wood, and then fought the Boche, who were controlling the town of Messines.' I stepped in front of them. 'Let's make a pact.'

'Good God, Tara. You're such a Brownie, a Boy Scout, a … what is it? … A Girl Guide.'

'Come on. We'll truly follow in our grandfathers' footsteps.'

'Yes. I'll come,' said Charlotte.

'We'll go native … prehistoric … commando!' Dominic postulated.

*

We lingered at the entrance to the staff quarters where Charlotte would catch a few hours' sleep before her next shift. Dominic and I kissed Charlotte goodnight on both cheeks in what we imagined was the European way. When I reached my room, I opened the door to the balcony and stood quite still in the dark night, eyes closed, the buzz-hum of alcohol in my head – anticipating, in a gentle, abstract way.

It wasn't a complete surprise when Dom knocked on my door. It was more of a surprise to me that I opened the door.

He stepped in and without hesitation pushed the door closed with one arm and gathered me to him with the other. Smooth as silk. He kissed my neck, and whispered huskily, 'Can I … can I stay with you?'

I veered between irritation – the cheek of him – then all the way to desire for his company. I liked the idea of telling him to fuck off *and* the idea of lying in bed with him, fooling around. The two ideas of equal influence existed all at once, both at the same time.

I knew his question was not built on grand love, arguably it was about friendship, but quickly I realised he was using me, a convenient receptacle for his drunken dump of affection.

'It's not going to happen, Dominic,' I said, pushing him gently away. 'It is not right on so many levels. Off you go. Go to bed.'

He looked at me as though I had genuinely hurt his feelings, as though his feelings were indeed genuine, and I felt myself slipping into an idea of a charity fuck. I had to look away.

'Um, OK, OK, OK. You can stay.' I said it – and meant it – half-heartedly.

He smiled that ridiculous clown smile, the one I normally loved, and because of it I found the strength to see that what I had just said was appalling. I sobered up, quick smart.

'Sorry, Dom, I take that back. It is all wrong: it's a betrayal of our friendship and our work partnership, let alone our respect for Rachel, respect for ourselves.'

I imagined he might explode in anger, in rejection, as his face seemed to twitch in indecision.

'Come on, Tara. No one has to know.'

'Fuck off, Dom, I'd know. You'd know. Two of the only three people that matter would know, and the third not knowing makes it worse.'

I'd found anger, and it felt powerful. I was clearheaded. 'You're more pissed than I thought, Dom. Off you go, please.

He plonked himself down on my bed, put his hand to his forehead, and I sat down in the chair on the other side of the room, suddenly exhausted from the trip, the excitement and now this betrayal.

'Look, Tara, Rachel and I are over.' He took a deep breath, gasped and coughed, out of sorts. 'She's given me an ultimatum. I have to have given up drinking by the time I get back. You know that is impossible for me. I'll fail.' He caught my eye. 'But you, Tara, you understand me, you get it, the alcohol, my demons …'

He'd slurred a little, but I realised he wasn't as drunk as I'd thought. I stared at him a moment; I rubbed my eyes, and then my face as though I'd rub it right off. I collected myself.

'Oh, I'm really sorry, Dom. That is very hard. But, look, I can't help you, and certainly not by sleeping with you. Really, you have to go.'

There was a silence in the room, not a sound from outside nor from either of us, but there was enough light to see his tears.

'Please, Dominic, can you just go?'

CHAPTER TEN

THE WOOD

As it was summer in Europe, it was still daylight when Charlotte, Dominic and I set off from Ypres and we arrived at the wood at about 9 p.m. It was 6 June 2017, one hundred years since our grandfathers found themselves at this very same spot. We knew it would get cool in the wee hours, so we'd dressed 'sensibly' – as my mother would say – not only anticipating the weather but also in our expectation of having to walk in brush over an uneven forest floor: long-sleeved shirts and jeans, walking boots. Dominic wore a beanie with his football team emblem on the front, a white swan on a red background.

Things were strained between me and Dominic ... not in a harsh way, more a mixture of embarrassment and resignation. It crossed my mind that Dom might not even be clear on the details. He couldn't look me in the eye, and frankly, I was fine with that.

Charlotte must have noticed but chose some kind of polite discretion. She ignored the mood between us.

We walked the several hundred metres from the otherwise deserted car park to the wood. It was quiet except for the ubiquitous Belgian birds and the rustle and hustle of the millions of leaves in the tall trees. We had it all to ourselves; no other battlefield tourists were there. The next day, in Messines, memorial events would take place – brass bands, official mayoral splendour and speeches – but that was not the experience I was looking for.

Moving along the dirt track, the first hundred metres of the wood were stippled with rosy, golden light. We fell silent among towering evergreens, dark earth, shrubs and forest debris, and soon reached the first commemorative cemetery, Toronto Avenue Cemetery. Seventy-six identified and two unidentified Australian soldiers lay there, in a neat rectangle of mown grass, white blocks of regulation gravestone marking each man's allocation. The place was shaded from the last of the daylight by rows of mature trees and there was a dense, clipped hedge of rosemary around the low brick wall. This cemetery was almost on the edge of the wood, too close to the surrounding, neatly farmed fields that can be seen from the manicured plot. It was too tidy to represent the great rip in history that caused these men's deaths.

We went deeper into the trees and turned west to follow a dirt track. It was wide enough, I supposed, for the cemeteries' maintenance trucks to move along, bearing gardening tools of the twenty-first century: mowers, leaf blowers, chainsaws, noisy enough to wake the dead lying there. Six hundred metres on, the second cemetery could be seen. This was a British cemetery, and after a cursory look we left the track and waded into the long grass and fallen branches between the trees, negotiating the irregular surface of the wood's floor.

Of course, there was no knowing exactly where our antecedents had stood or settled for the night in question, but with something of a nod between us and gallant determination, we decided to work our way further and further from the track for some ten minutes. When I signalled that I thought we were in a truly remote place, we chose a cleared spot, spread the groundsheet, and positioned the basket of food and wine just so. Each of us took a corner of the groundsheet. Like a yogi, I sat cross-legged, having retrieved my Bean reference book, *Anzac to Amiens*, from my backpack. Dominic reclined on one elbow; Charlotte sat on her folded legs.

'So … here we are then.' Dominic stated the obvious, looking at the dirt, plucking at the weeds. He seemed disappointed.

'Yep,' I said. 'Now we wait. Says here that the shelling started at about 11 p.m. and then after the gas, those who were able to moved up to Anton's Farm about four hours later.'

'I wonder why the troops just sat out the shelling. Pretty stupid … unwise to say the least, to have sat here and waited for it to come over. I mean, once the Germans had found their range, the jig was up, wasn't it?' As usual, Dominic acted like a picador, looking for a rise from me. This was not new, not payback for the night before. It was a kind of semi-mocking he resorted to. Wasn't he suggesting our grandfathers were fools?

'I don't know. I guess you're right. Maybe it was more dangerous to move.' I always seemed to take the bait: I'd prevaricate, then try to turn the provocation into reasoning.

'More dangerous! What could be more dangerous than sitting and waiting for gas or any kind of shell to fall on you?' snorted Dominic.

'I reckon it's almost impossible, a hundred years on, for us to expect them to have thought like we do. I guess they thought that shelling was a normal part of war. The new warfare, drones and the like, it's now so advanced that any real contact between soldiers is unlikely, the opposite to 1917.'

'Maybe', Charlotte joined the discussion quietly, 'it was another example of the leaders paralysed by … well, men's politics and male egos.'

'Thanks, Charlotte, very helpful.' Dominic dismissed her – infuriatingly.

With a frown, Charlotte arced up. 'What? You want me to accept all this crap about "courage" and "sacrifice"? Dying for "freedom"?' She used air-quotes furiously, waving her arms in the air. 'That is the thing, that's the cliché now, eh? What the fuck is "courageous"? "Sacrifice"? Where's the "freedom" in this context? Maybe the whole thing *was … just … stupid.*'

A pause.

'Maybe.' I couldn't help it. I tried to keep the peace. 'I look at it this way: in this day and age, now, the opportunity to display courage is almost non-existent, in war or just in our normal lives; I think what we call "courage" has had to change.' I glanced at Charlotte to check she was listening and not bored of my lecturing. 'Maybe men now must live in a semi-permanent state of physical hostility just to feel alive, authentic? Or maybe, nowadays, modern men have to squash all that down.'

Charlotte seemed interested in this angle.

'And maybe women live like that too,' she answered.

'And as for sacrifice,' I was encouraged to continue, 'yep, the question is: did the men who sat here a hundred years ago *really* think what they were doing was sacrifice? I don't know: the society, the culture – completely different.' I completed my train of thought, happy with my caboose.

Charlotte responded to my attempts to soothe.

'I guess' – she nodded as she spoke – 'you're right that we are completely different as people, more educated, healthier, but their own lives, their own families, their land … in the case of your grandfathers, their land thousands of kilometres away … these things must have been just as important to each one of them as they are to us. And they gave it all up, came here and fought someone else's war.' I could see her plaintive face in the diminishing light.

'Funny, I never thought of that … the distance, the other side of the world … must have been an enormous leap of faith,' I said with an uncomfortable shrug. 'Shall we just listen for a while and try to hear what they heard here in the wood?'

'Sure, pass us a beer first.' Dominic continued to press buttons, disrupt. 'But … hate to burst your bubble … what they would have heard was the hundreds of men all around them, surely? A bit hard for us.'

'Jesus, Dominic. Can you try to enter into the spirit of the thing? Please. Don't spoil it. We've come this far.'

'*Qu'est-ce que je fais ici?*' Charlotte whispered to herself. Dominic must have seemed like an ill-mannered buffoon.

A kind of diplomatic neutrality emerged, and each of us passed the time in our own way. We had agreed at the outset not to bring phones into the wood – no social media, no music.

We worked through the picnic: baguettes and cheeses, a peach and oranges, the beers, the wine; we snoozed; chatted; stomped around the perimeter. The night progressed – twilight to darkness to a deep indigo – and enveloped us. I heard the birds call to each other as they settled in the branches around us.

At eleven o'clock, I reminded them: 'The shelling started about now.' I referred to Bean again, this time with the aid of my small torch. 'Hundreds of them were completely incapacitated by the gas shells, so much so that they had to reorganise the groups to make sure they were going to achieve their objectives,' I paraphrased.

I came to realise that Dominic was asleep; the beer and last night's booze had seen him off. Charlotte and I spoke in whispers, and we moved closer to one another for reassurance, the two of us conscious of the significance of our experience. Our self-made wormhole worked, and we considered Ypres's dreadful past. We talked about how our experience here in the forest required our own brand of twenty-first century pluck. We whispered about the ghastly, claustrophobic gas masks, the terror of an explosive landing nearby, the awareness that the experienced soldiers must have had as to the horror that was to come. So many young men, so much pain, so much loss.

Dominic snored.

At 3.10 a.m., I was dozing when Charlotte woke from a short sleep. Inexplicably, she was shaking uncontrollably. I couldn't understand why. Tears dripped and rolled down her face. She turned away from my worried, perplexed look.

'I'm so sorry. I had a bad dream. I've got another headache, it must be the alcohol … and the lack of sleep. I don't know why I'm so upset,' she wept. 'I'm really not like this.'

'It's OK, it'll be OK,' I reassured her, 'it's this whole crazy expedition. Come on.' I hugged her, feeling useless in the face of such heartfelt emotion, ineffectually patted her back. But there was something happening to Charlotte, something I couldn't take part in. 'It's time to move on now anyway.'

With a hand on his shoulder, I gently shook Dominic to wake him.

'Dom, it's time to move up to the jump-off line.' I shook him again. 'The big mine explosion happened about now. We've got to go.'

'Later … later,' Dominic mumbled and shrugged me off.

'No, we have to go now. It's the time that Alex and Edward … all the soldiers were on the move. Come on.'

'No. Fuck it. I'll go later.'

I shot a look at Charlotte and by the moonlight I saw her nod. I tried again.

'Dominic, we can't leave you here. Get up. Pack up. We've got to walk up to the line.'

'Oh, for fuck's sake,' bellowed Dominic, making Charlotte startle. He threw off his blanket and hauled himself to sitting. He tossed the picnic debris into the basket, tied his bootlaces, stood.

'Alright, Bear fucking Grylls, which direction do we go?' He was so loud in the forest's heavy atmosphere, it was an affront.

The three of us left our clearing, stumbling over fallen branches and the odd rock. It was dispiriting and cold; the wine's glow had worn off. Dominic continued with his railing.

'This was an idiotic thing to do. We're bloody lost, aren't we? Christ, I've just walked into a tree. Whose fucking stupid idea was this to come here anyway?'

We made it to the defined dirt track, and while Charlotte and I figured out where we were with a torch and one of the maps in the Bean paperback, Dominic kept up a slurred, sleepy tirade.

'I'm such a fucking idiot … to think I could … find out anything. For fuck's sake! What a fucking debacle.' His tone shifted to exasperation. 'This doesn't fucking bring him back! We'll never know them, Tara, for all your stupid dreaming. We should leave Time bloody well alone.'

He demanded the car keys.

'I'm going to sleep in the car. When you two have had enough, that's where you'll find me.' He stormed off, blanket around him, beanie awry, without waiting for a reply.

Dominic became just a chaotic torch beam heading out of the wood.

I asked, 'Do you still want to do this, Charlotte?'

'Yes,' she said with a hesitant nod. 'I think I have to. It seems … important to see it through.'

'Only if you want to …'

'I feel I … I need to.'

'Me too. OK. Let's take our time. If we go along here for a while, I think we come out north-west of the farm and we can work our way more north over the fields.'

CHAPTER ELEVEN

THE BATTLE OF MESSINES, 1917

Having watched Edward dissolve into the darkness, Alex hangs his gas mask around his neck, ready. A little awkwardly – he's a shy man – he starts to make his way among his charges, his hand on a shoulder in a gesture of support here, an adjustment of tubing or canvas there. He finds himself looking for Jim Williams – not deliberately, nor overtly – just checking the faces of each man he addresses more closely than otherwise. He is not sure what he'll say if he finds him. He is surprised at his quest, and suppresses it, immersing himself in the more pressing necessities of the moment.

For the next couple of hours, the shelling – a lottery of gassing, injury and dying – continues. Sometimes explosions occur where a man or group of men find themselves. Within this normally quiet, green wood, the blast may kill a man outright, take off a limb or eviscerate. The terror of it is intractable, but the horror of the seeping gas is worse, sapping resolution and courage. The trees and undergrowth of the wood aid the gas's purpose, trapping the vapours.

'Right,' Alex calls to the officers around him at an hour past midnight, lifting his mask. 'Let's get them going.'

The moonlight is fleeting now, sometimes obscured by clouds and smoke. With a neutral expression on his face, he accepts the setback of just how many hundreds of men have been affected by the gas. The number of able-bodied troops available is much diminished, and stretcher-bearers ply their trade constantly, to and fro, from the wood to the rear. The unlucky ones moan and grunt, swearing under their breath. There are huddles of men around medical officers and stretcher-bearers coughing, tears streaming. Alex sees that his sergeants are reorganising their groups, pushing men into unfamiliar partnerships, reallocating arms, shouting new instructions. Alex counts, delegates, reassigns in the moonlight, reallocating the attack teams into a formation that was designed before the shelling's toll. They will get to the jump-off line by hook or by crook, if the NCOs have anything to do with it. Alex's men – teens, the middle-aged, fathers, sons, fiancés, husbands, the courageous, the terrified, boasters, loners, boozers, good men and not so good – are leaving the wood in something of a line. They are spreading out as planned along the ridge below the town of Messines by the River Douve.

It is nearly 3 a.m. when Alex's section is brought together and moves forward up to the area known as Anton's Farm. On arriving, they hunker down in assembly trenches, gulping water from barrels brought up by the mules yesterday.

They are crouched forward, squatting on haunches, in a four-foot-deep trench. Waiting.

There is a flash of the mighty, fluorescent moon: its grey and yellow pockmarks are clear. The sight of the chalky, cheesy orb is hardly dulled by exploratory flares.

Trench etiquette requires the other troops to allow any man to have a moment to themselves if their head is bowed and eyes closed. Alex takes such a moment and, again, he thinks of Private Williams. The impression Williams has left is curiously deep. It feels right to Alex to think of him, to care. It is as though Private Williams has entered Alex's consciousness as Everyman, Every Soldier. Alex is more aware than ever of his responsibilities, and Private Williams has come to represent them all. Yet it is more than that. There is a fraternal quality in Alex's recognition, an almost familial frame of mind.

A bundle of khaki tumbles into the trench and lands beside Alex, disturbing his reflection – it is Edward, with a relieved smirk across his face.

'Mate, couldn't find you back in the wood. You alright? Gas didn't get you?'

Alex finds a smile, a nod and a shake in response.

'Thank God; well, just popped back to see you're OK.'

'Good to see you too. How's it going back there? Are you having tea and scones while we deal with the Boche?'

'We're hard at it,' Edward says sheepishly. 'Tell you what, this show is bloody well organised, and the Germans don't know what's coming. All hell is about to break loose.'

Alex grins through the hasty words and Edward slaps him on the back, preparing to tear off, south, along the line.

'It's starting! See you in Messines,' Edward stage-whispers.

'It's just the beginning. Careful as you go, Ed.'

*

At 3.10 a.m., the earth shudders, heaves. The trees sway abruptly to thirty degrees and back again. The sky lights up with a yellow, then a red, then a violet tint. Nineteen huge explosions rock the surrounding area. For ten minutes, every man in the wood believes this is his cataclysmic end – surely the end of the world – as all nineteen blasts burst from deep, deep tunnels along the front line. The detonations are without rhythm, without warning – enough to terrify any person near the epicentre and alarm anyone within a hundred miles. Some men scream like the Devil is on his tail; all the men crouch and are buffeted by shock waves. The massive pulsations rock every living thing and inert object in the area. It rains chunks of displaced rocks and clods of dirt. It hails with airborne pebbles, sand and vegetation.

For many months, men from both sides have worked to undermine their respective enemy's position. English, Canadian and Australian former miners have filled the buried *culs-de-sac* with explosives, waiting and wishing for the stupendous moment to deliver a dreadful reality to the enemy. It is the greatest explosion yet known to mankind. For the tunnellers who have lived and breathed the damp scent of clay and stink of mine gasses in the tiny tunnels for too many days and nights, the cataclysm is satisfying, a relief.

Alex assumes that, as the British and the Allies had hoped, the noise and vibrations stun the Germans and shatter their confidence. Surely, the explosions will wipe out any momentum German successes over the last weeks might have given them. Hun intelligence has seen the mounting preparations by the British, obvious to anyone hereabouts, as major and minor guns were moved into the area, as thousands of troops amassed, and the road traffic behind the lines tripled. The Germans knew something big was on, but the hubristic senior officers opposed the suggestion that their troops might move back to better-protected trench lines. However, as Alex knows, British and Australian Command believe the Germans have no idea that the British and Commonwealth troops have mined so extensively, so widely, so deeply, and have deposited the huge quantity of explosives beneath their feet.

At least now, after the explosions, the enemy's shelling of Ploegsteert Wood ceases briefly.

As soon as the ground has ceased its heaving and Alex is able to jump to his feet, he blows his whistle and gives a choreographed wave, as was predetermined, signalling for the groups of men to move. It is time to cross no man's land. In their minds, it is a wasteland of great distance, but it is only a mere twenty to forty yards along a three-mile snaking line. It is a dotted line on the map at divisional headquarters but for the men it is a slog over churned clay, under falling dirt, ash and rocks. The world is upside down. The respite from the shelling finishes; the enfilading machine-gun fire commences.

Alex draws his Colt service revolver. The metal is cold in his hand. The gun is clunky and longer than a big man's hand span; its size persuades the user of its authority. He is glad for it: something this heavy and awkward is bound to prevail. He moves off, into the crucible.

It is the wee hours of 7 June 1917. The Battle of Messines starts.

For several hours, it is bloody, a raucous cacophony, wet and gritty. Alex's men don't take one step back. It is progress for sure: taking one turret, one bunker, one machine-gun nest, each by laborious effort. In the field, Alex uses his whistle a couple of times to direct the play, but in the clamour, sound is snatched away from its source, hijacked, and he shoves the metal gadget back into the opening of his tunic. In any minute, each man's face slips from fear, to anguish, to exhilaration. Alex registers the state of each of his men, then moves to the next goal. Images, bits and bobs, freeze in his mind: on Alex's left, a soldier named Turner and two others are thrown back from the powerful blast of a shell, and then Turner starts to shake and jerk his arms and legs, his skull open, his brain displayed on a rock; a German turret explodes spectacularly, revealing the intricate craftmanship of the brickwork in the walls; smoke or fumes or is it a cloud of dust suddenly causes Alex's nose and lungs to lock down – must be a different kind of gas; men's bodies, like ants working, like mice scuttling, like rats, bringing harm to others.

There is no space, no time to consider bravery, courage, pride. The drills of the preceding years unfold unconsciously in him, all the practice manoeuvres, the training, the exercises. One, two, three: he is an automaton with such a state of hyperawareness as to have no sense of presence at all. Alex solves tiny problems over and over, every moment a flood of information and learning clattering through his mind. He has no time to think, plan, deliberate. The script is in place, and despite the chaotic circumstances – or perhaps because of them – the drama plays out.

The faces of the opposing force are parodies to Alex, caricatures of men. Their hob-pot helmets are now an icon of bastardy, their uniforms with their military gewgaws – no doubt meaningful to them – are loathed by Alex. Their savage eyes, grey skin, brutal weaponry – the sheer size of these giants! – revolts him. It is not courage he sources from within himself to fight these animals: he summons repugnance. Insufferable noise, horrendous sights, the uneven, lumpen floor of the rucked field, unendurable smoky mist: the ghastly environment antagonises his abhorrence – that these invaders, interlopers, have such an arrogance. He'll teach them a lesson.

He fires, runs, ducks, bobs down, cranes his neck. He waves at those behind him to come through, giving a nod of respect and regard. He charges again, up, over, down into a German trench, and this time he smashes the jaw of a Hun with his heavy pistol, experiencing the thud and cracking-crunch of living bone. Then Alex fires into the body of the man, who jolts and makes to rise. Alex fires again, eyes locked on eyes. Done. Move. He repeats the actions over and over again: fires, runs, ducks, bobs down, cranes his neck.

*

In the minutes before dawn, the metallic, murky-grey sky is just light enough to see the features of the man beside you. The battle is largely over, and Alex is on his haunches in a steep-sided crater on the north side of the River Douve with his officers, receiving a situation report.

'Has … the town … been taken?' The words are staccato because of Alex's persistent shallow breathing.

'Yes, sir – I understand … the New Zealanders.' Voices are hoarse.

'Good, good. And what of losses?' Alex tries to wet his lips, but his mouth is dry.

'Many thousands, sir, not an accurate number yet.' The not unexpected tally of terrible losses is no longer shocking to any man who has been in Europe for longer than a few months. Command predicted tens of thousands would die overnight, and many tens of thousands would be injured. Many of the injured are assumed to be as good as dead.

A pause.

'Well then, we have been effective, and the Huns are retreating or dead.'

In these first moments that allow some reflection, there is no glee; it is more like waking from a nightmare. Alex and his colleagues begin to perceive their bodily discomfort as adrenalin wears off: dirt in their boots; uniforms stinking wet with sweat and urine, theirs and those of injured and dying men; parched throats; aching muscles. The oddly rusty smell of blood and earth is irritating to breathe. The occasional snatch of pained cries drifts into their shell hole every few minutes.

As the debrief concludes and the group moves to split up, scattered rifle fire and machine-gun bursts are heard to the north-east of their position. Alex raises a finger to forestall the others. He rises cautiously to confirm the position of resistance. Just as his helmet, head and shoulders emerge above the ragged mud-lip of the crater, he is spun around one hundred and eighty degrees with a sniper's bullet to his left side and he falls back onto the wall of the crater, then slides to its base, slipping in the loose dirt, his head pointing down, his face dragging on the earth.

Disoriented, trying to unscramble the hundreds of messages coming from all over his body, cognitive alerts in his racing brain, he gasps and splutters. The mud and dirt are in his mouth, his throat and nostrils. An explosion, a shell-burst ten yards away, is a direct hit to his senior team. Bloody bits, bone fragments and chunks of the skin and hair of his fellow officers rain down around him.

Time goes by, perhaps five or ten minutes, unobserved by Alex.

Someone is standing over him, then crouching down: it is Williams, the man, the brother, the friend.

'Stretcher!' A boom, a foghorn of bass sounds above Alex. 'Stretcher, for God's sake!'

Am I safe now? I am breathing. I can feel. Alex's thoughts are loud and clumsy and form somewhere at the base of his throat. Sounds pour into his ear on hot breath; are they soothing words? Alex is unsure, but it doesn't matter. Williams speaks to Alex, or is that the rumble of artillery? Alex responds, but do the words escape their formulation? Alex reaches, but … does he touch him? He breathes out, relaxes, before the … the pain is like white light, white noise, telescoping sight, blurring vision, blaring like a klaxon through his nervous system.

'Are you there? Are you still there?' Alex cannot unravel his reality. Is someone beside him? Is it a shadow? 'My brother? Are you there? Is this a memory? Am I dreaming? Are you there?'

Alex sees stars, gags on the dirt in his mouth, is aware of wetness on his arm and chest, and can't move. Rough fingers dig the mud from throat. Gaps, a sequence of dreamy images: stretchered across a soggy quagmire of clay and topsoil; tufts of grass; branches hanging in ribbons of wood and bark; weak, golden sunshine on strangers' faces. Odd glimpses: did they give him something … morphia? Snippets, a collage of what is right in front of his eyes, but with no depth of field: the midriff of a tunic; a red face; a tooting, distorted, deep sound in muted waves; a spray of water covering him with muddy chunks and showers of earth pellets.

CHAPTER TWELVE

YPRES

Charlotte and I walked by the dwindling moonlight toward the site of so much destruction. By 5 a.m., there was enough pre-dawn light for us to get our bearings. There was a feathery, almost warm breeze, just enough to move the topmost leaves of the tall silver birch trees lining the fields adjoining the wood, and we arrived at the jump-off line, just as my grandfather had a century before.

The former jump-off line was now an anonymous stretch of dirt road, dividing a recently built farmhouse and its yards from the crops.

'There's not much to see here. I mean, remnants of the battle.'

I was disappointed. There was no watershed moment. Mostly, I just felt weary, and I saw that Charlotte was tired. She looked a little anxious and there were red shadows under her eyes, like the beginning of bruises. She was wan, none of her liveliness apparent.

Beside the road there was a memorial wooden cross, some two metres high, and on it was inscribed 'The Khaki Chums Christmas Truce'.

'This happened in quite a few places, and there are these crosses here and there,' Charlotte explained almost inaudibly. 'I don't know whether to be cynical and think that it's a myth … or maybe hundreds, perhaps thousands of soldiers *did* actually climb out of their trenches, all along the front line, on Christmas Day 1914. They made a truce, played football, and returned to their lines at nightfall.' She said this while walking up to the memorial and placing her hand on the timber cross beam, and by touching it, she seemed to craft a surreal connection with the event. 'Do you believe it?'

'I don't know. I guess I'd *like* to believe it.'

'Ha. Quite the fence-sitter, Tara,' Charlotte chuckled.

'Well, if it did happen then it didn't include Australian troops. They weren't here in 1914. And football – soccer – I am pretty sure wasn't played in Australia at that time to any real degree. I recall some historian saying that it couldn't have happened any later in the war, because in 1914 there was little animosity between the troops at ground level, and I guess there was still the sense that they were still comrades, like a class thing.'

I placed my hand on the other end of the beam, joining the mood, touching the talisman. 'Maybe they ignored the orders of their officers, who they didn't imagine to be their mates.

They just wanted to have some contact with a similar guy from a trench a hundred metres away. The loss of that kind of camaraderie between the adversaries came later, as their spirits … their humanity … was ground down. Just a theory.'

Charlotte shrugged, and said sarcastically, 'A utopian workers' dream in the midst of such violent attrition?' She appeared to me to be thinking further on it, but then surprised me.

'Hey, Tara, I am really pleased that I came here with you. This is really … valuable to me. Perhaps we Belgians want to immortalise only *our* tragedies but ignore the troubles of so many other people from all over the world. It does me good to get off my Ypres high horse … as though we were the only ones to suffer. It is good to meet you, to consider your families' involvement. I guess it makes me a better person.'

We locked eyes, smiled. 'And I'm really pleased that you came too. Thank you. You can see that Dominic is not quite the right person for this … investigation … adventure … this whatever it is we're doing here.'

'And it's good to make a new female friend too … though it's costing me a night's sleep.' Charlotte laughed, enough to put me at ease.

We moved on up the track at a slow walk. We looked for the Douve, a stream that ran west to east through this battlefield landscape. I figured we must be close; it divided Mesen – as Messines was now known – from Ploegsteert Wood. While it was essentially just a channel, it was a landmark described often in the accounts. At the War Memorial, I'd seen the artefact of a small timber footbridge that the troops used to cross it.

'I think the Douve must be this way.' I gestured.

We turned and walked north for a few minutes along a different track. We came upon a trickle, a marshy stream with a few rocks and some modern pipes.

'Hmmm, not particularly impressive,' I observed, 'and it's conclusive evidence of my ridiculous, romantic tendencies. When I was in Australia, I built up these few fields into a grand scene in my mind, the location of a grand battle. I pictured a huge plain or deep valley! Ha! This waterway is so small compared to my imagination. The Douve turns out to be a creek … and only just.'

'It's all just my home, just Belgium, to me,' said Charlotte, head to one side. 'I probably see Australia all wrong. Perhaps I see it as smaller than it is. I can't imagine the great distances I see on a map of Australia. They are simply not in my experience.'

'One day … you should come and visit us, me and my daughters,' I said enthusiastically, pleased that I'd used the plural, glad that I'd so deliberately included Charlotte and Persy in my future, something I might not have done a week ago. Perhaps I was getting better at being a mother, more complete.

'Sure.' She smiled. 'One day.'

*

At six the sun was up, and Charlotte and I found a clearing on the edge of the field, full of rustling sunflowers like a million Cyclopses: intensely yellow petals surrounding wheels with darkly black centres, observant single eyes.

She put her hand on my forearm and used it to balance, swaying a little.

'Can we sit down for a minute, Tara?' Charlotte asked, blinking rapidly. 'I'm so tired.'

We sat on the patch of dry, cut grass. To reorient us, to place us back into the hundred-year-old scene, I pulled the Bean volume from my backpack and found my place.

'Apparently, there was a counter-attack, around 7 a.m., around now.'

I read ahead silently for a moment, aware that the disassociated tone of Bean's report didn't gel with my feelings and would disrupt our experience. Bean sounded too cool, too calm. My grandfather was in danger: I felt a threat, tension in the air.

I looked up to see if Charlotte wanted me to continue with the account, and saw that she was weeping again, big tears rolling, spilling.

'So, all the while we've been walking and talking, they've been fighting?' She sounded exasperated. I was surprised by her reaction and thought it was a lament, for the past, for the dead, for the suffering.

'Yeah. I guess so. Shells, gunfire, bayonets, hand to hand: the works.' I was quiet for a moment, watching Charlotte. 'Do you want me to stop reading?'

'I don't know why I'm so affected,' Charlotte burbled, shaking her head. 'God, it's probably because of this headache I just can't seem to shake off … and we've had so little sleep.' She smiled wetly, looked up at me and saw my empathic tears. We laughed a little and I crossed the space between us to comfort Charlotte. I thought both of us were simultaneously overwhelmed by the enormity of the battle, of the consequences. The solidarity between us was intuitive. Grief was oozing from the ground under our feet and hanging in the air all around us.

Charlotte took a deep, slow breath. 'I'm OK. Let's walk a bit further; we'll get to that last ridge.' She indicated a slight rise to the north less than a kilometre away. 'That was the Black Line, yes?' It was the finishing line for the Allies that morning … and for us on our day.

I stuffed the Bean book back into the front pocket of my daypack and left it on the ground, got to my feet and turned, extending my arm. I took Charlotte's hand, helping her to stand.

'You look pale, Charlotte. Are you alright?'

Charlotte looked back at me and her eyes widened slightly. She stared for a moment too long and then did not seem to see any longer. Her legs gave way and she crumpled back to the ground like a marionette, not quite on her back, not quite on her side, her legs drawn up. Her face became grey, pink, red, then puce, while her body was quite still but for the arching of her back and her neck to an unnatural degree. She gave an almighty gasp and then a long exhalation, and then failed to breath.

'Charlotte?' I knelt beside her.

'Charlotte?' I rocked her shoulder, then sat back.

'Charlotte,' I repeated, frowning.

She was open-mouthed, her eyes partly open.

'What's wrong? What's wrong?' Too many seconds went by; I was frozen in place.

'Oh my God … God … God … what …

'Dominic!' I yelled in a panic, bewildered, desperate, knowing but not knowing that he couldn't hear me. 'Help, help, Dominic!'

I tried again; I shook Charlotte. 'Wake up, wake up. What's wrong? Please, please.'

Should I do CPR? I leant in, pushed on her shoulder to turn her. I needed her more on her back than her side. I gave a couple of half-hearted chest compressions and sat back again, defeated. *Am I harming? Healing? Hurting her? Do I do the breathing bit now?* I didn't know how to do it.

I tried to lift her upper body and her arms flopped wide; her eyes were still open. I laid her on the ground again. Her trousers were wet at the crotch. There was saliva – or was it vomit? – at the corner of her mouth. Gulping, guttural noises escaped from me – disbelief.

I doubted I could leave her: it was wrong somehow, but I had to find some help. *Where's Dominic? The car park; OK, where's the car park from here?* He could drive for an ambulance, a doctor. The best I could do was go for help, and I jumped to standing. Overwhelmed then with a need to run, I backed away from Charlotte, my eyes on hers, hoping she'd blink or move, just a little. I backed away till I reached the track and could only see her legs past the sunflowers and the high grass lining the road. Then I wrenched my body away from the scene and sprinted the kilometre to where we had left the car, heaving great breaths of air, hurting all over, light-headed.

It was an hour before an ambulance arrived with sirens sounding – that particular, peculiar European alert, which to Australian ears is curiously high-pitched, like a child's klaxon. The ambulanciers, guided by Dominic, found me back beside Charlotte's body, dazed. I could not maintain a single thread of thought. A jumble of phrases, images and sounds presented themselves and I had no inclination nor ability to sort them.

I held her hand but could not look at her. I could only look away at what I wanted to believe was Charlotte's last sight: the scattered dark clouds around us that were still touched with the pink of the rising summer sun. I wanted to think she had heard the pulse of the land, a deep drumming, the thrumming of insects, the rustle of wind – not the angry and defiling echo of this place a hundred years prior. I tried to imagine her death as a gentle process: maybe her fingers and feet came to seem a long way off, and in between, her flesh, her torso, limbs and organs lost their heaviness, became insubstantial. I hoped she'd smelled the earth, the minerals, and, at the last, felt linked to this place. I wanted her to know that she was all that had gone before and all that was to come.

CHAPTER THIRTEEN

THE CLIFFTOPS OF WIMEREUX

At a first-aid post, Alex is placed next to a groaning pile of bloodied uniform, legs missing. He turns his head, slowly, deliberately, to look at the injured man.

Not long for this world.

Alex forms the elastic and elongated words; they reverberate in his mind. The man beside him exhales a last shuddering breath.

Goodbye. Alex farewells the man, wistful. It seems a shame not to have shared a few words, to leave him quite so abruptly.

Time passes: ten minutes, ten hours? And someone in authority, some moustache and peaked cap, waves his stretcher onto a rack in a wagon drawn by a team of weary Clydesdales. As he is stretchered past the sturdy creatures Alex notes their fat necks, hogged manes, and feathered hocks caked in ruddy mud. For all their care, the stretcher-bearers can't limit the vertigo-inducing pitch of the carry, and in his dreamlike state of morphia, blood loss and pain, Alex conflates the horses' scent, the sound of their hooves pawing the ground, and the rolling and wobbling of the ride with a distracting conviction that he is astride his own horse. The happy fantasy passes in a moment. He returns to the business of agony, weak resolve, disappointment.

Lurching and lunging, sliding on the muddy roads, the wagon travels through the congested back area to a train station. More agonising time sees him lie as still as possible on the jolting, jarring train during the eighty-odd mile journey to the 2nd Australian General Hospital. It is near a town named Wimereux, close to the harbour town of Boulogne and a stone's throw from the Channel's sea cliffs. On the rare night when the wind dies down, the incoming whoosh and outgoing sigh of the swell at the base of the cliffs can be heard. The hospital is in fields formerly bordered by hawthorn hedges and dedicated to dairy cows. It is made up of mostly scruffy timber huts, plus a series of interconnected tents holding one hundred beds of medical and surgical cases. The tents are like big tops but with none of the circus folly taking place inside. When Alex arrives, he is admitted, then carried via duckboard pathways to his assigned bed in his assigned tent. He believes he can still hear the shelling, but it is only a war-time tinnitus that will stay with him for weeks, beating, chiacking, pulsing independently of any real noise. With a bolus dose of morphia, he drifts into an even more disjointed relationship with this chaotic, canvas world.

The women who cut his crusty uniform from his body, scrape the muck from his wound, then bathe his grazed skin, are past their early bloom. They are gentle, committed to care, but tetchy about being in this godforsaken place. They coo soft noises when they cause Alex pain and speak firmly when he pulls away. Their coaxing penetrates their patient's consciousness, and soothes with reassurances, with shushing and pursed lips. They hold themselves together as best they might amid this war's inhumanity in such small and significant ways.

When the nurses move to and from the wards or walk on the clifftops among the wild and windblown rosemary and gorse, the women wrap themselves in their dark-red wool capes, the colour of arterial blood. The capes hang to just below their hips. In winter's chill, they clasp them tightly to their bodies, and on warm days the capes flap about or are slung over a shoulder. The wool-weave comforts them with its weight, its origins, its hug.

*

Coming to: awareness, sight, frown, smell, sound.

Swimming into consciousness, Alex quickly recognises and records terrible pain. His left arm, shoulder, chest; broken bone, lacerations, bruising, aching, sharp, unbearable. Yet bear it he must. There is no courage that can stare down this kind of pain. Pain like this is not ignored but endured. His groans are met by a pinkness, a face coming close to his, the face of a weary, middle-aged woman, surrounded by light and clean, white air. The Australian nurse wears a Rising Sun brooch at her suprasternal notch, and when Alex catches a glimpse of the symbol, and hears a hen-like clucking, a maternal ooh and aah, he is heartened.

'You're awake! Good-o. I'm Sister Cuthbert; you can call me Edie when Matron is not around.' She takes his wrist and feels for his pulse: it's rapid, but not dangerously so. 'You're in 2AGH in Wimereux … you say it like *why my roo*, as in kangaroo.' She waits for some sign of acknowledgement. No response. 'It's Saturday and you've been unconscious for two days.'

Edie wears a much-faded, grubby, grey linen uniform. Soaked in the sweat of twelve-hour shifts day in and day out, the nurses have found their laundry can no longer be washed clean. The dresses are stained, torn, worn, and repaired again and again. They are framed by white collars and cuffs which are doubly hard to keep clean. Often, Edie works with rinsed collars and cuffs damp around her neck and forearms, with the smell of bleached material in her nostrils – at least that's preferable to the odour of the men's wounds. The women ran out of starch long ago, so the fabric of both the grey dress and now off-white collar and cuffs is limp and deformed, stretched with constant laundering.

The image, the voice, the noise of flapping tents – it's a lot to take in through an opiate fog, weariness and pain. Alex doesn't answer. His weight on a horse-hair mattress, and the tangible, harsh weave of scratchy canvas sheets on nude limbs, buttocks and back. The pillow's ticking comes into focus.

'Are you in pain, then?' Edie asks. Alex's eyebrows rise slightly. 'Righto, I'll get the morphia for you.' With a moderating pat on his right arm, the nurse's face fades from view.

It gets easier to wake. Images that could be memories return in a haphazard way. He's confounded by their sequence, their relevance, their authenticity. Certainly, there are a string of recollections from the landscape of his injury – the crater, the dirt in his mouth. There's someone beside him, and a precious pressure on and in his right hand. Someone is caring for him and it is very important. Is it life or death? Never again … or is it forever? Nothing makes sense. Alex can't see the face. Perhaps he imagined it; but no, the images continue to surge into his mind. Alex recalls the stretcher-bearer saying, 'Mate, you're gonna have to let go of his hand. We're off.'

Alex remembers more fully now: himself whimpering, 'Don't let go, please, please,' and a response from the form above him.

'It's alright, mate. It's me, Williams. I'll pop in and see you in the hospital. Just think about tomorrow, and tomorrow, and tomorrow. You'll be right. You'll see.' Their hands are pulled apart.

A young English doctor tells Alex that the gunshot wound has caused his left humerus to be fractured and ripped an open wound; the bone has pushed through the muscle and skin of his upper arm. That is the centre of the acute, blinding pain on movement and the constant ache felt viscerally, dominating Alex's every thought.

'Horrible infection is likely, old chap, and you know what that means; but we'll give you a day or two and see how you get along.'

Delivered as though a parody of an English medico, the news is barely registered by Alex, who can hardly understand the rapid delivery and oversimplification that passes for diagnosis. He supposes the doctor is talking about an amputation, but the question of exactly why, he can't say. It tires and defeats Alex; he swims upstream then down in the swollen river of morphia, dreams and hyper-reality.

'There you go, duckie. You're going to be fine,' he hears the nurses say. They do their best to keep the injury clean and dry.

'Mmmmmargh.' Alex holds his breath and clenches his teeth when they turn him in his bed before they change the sodden dressing. Before they pull off the old dressing, the nurses sluice warm saline fluid over his ripped and torn bicep to make sure that, when removed, the bandages don't tear off any new tissue. They apply a dilute iodine solution, lanolin salve to the pat-dried edges of the wound, and a thin layer of woven gauze. The arm is padded with cotton wool, and a firm bandage holds it all in place. Alex's good health does the rest, responding with a physiological default: raised temperature and blood pressure, a rapid heartbeat.

A day and two nights pass in a dream with snatches of sleep and short periods of awareness. The doctor returns to inspect the wound several times, raises his eyebrows, whispers with the nurses. On the third day, from the end of the bed, he delivers a new plan for Alex's recovery.

'All clear, so far … excellent. Looks like you'll not need an amputation, hey, what? Good news? hmm?' It's a similarly odd performance, almost as comedic as the last consultation, the doctor's version of camaraderie between an English gentleman-doctor and a wounded Australian soldier-officer. 'What you need is what we call a Thomas splint, hmmm, a Thomas splint, and you'll get that in the hospital in England. You'll be off tomorrow, 0600, with a group of other Aw-straylians. Good luck, old chap, and don't worry: we expect you will return to your regimental chums in a few months.'

A middle-aged orderly, at the foot of the bed during the exchange, witnesses Alex's wry almost-smile and raised eyebrow as the doctor moves on. They share a joke, the Londoner dragooned into his thankless wardsman role, and the Australian who shares none of the English class schism.

'He's a piece of work, eh?' the Londoner says, jerking a thumb in the doctor's direction, his nicotine-stained fingers on display.

'Oh, he's just doing his job.' Alex is not fussed by the doctor's attitude.

'Tell you something for nothing, you Australians are a treat to care for. You don't expect the world on a platter from me and me mates … like some others.' A theatrical jab of his raised thumb is aimed at the few English officers sharing the Nightingale ward with Alex and twenty other Australians.

'Glad to hear it.'

Alex grimaces as he brings himself laboriously to more of a sitting position, the clang and stab of his broken bones becoming a backdrop.

'Having said that, can I ask you to do something for me?' Alex asks. 'I don't know how to contact my friend … a fellow officer. I think he'll be in the camp down the road. The Battalion was to regroup there after the battle. How do I get a message to him? I don't know if he knows I'm in here.'

'Not a problem, squire. Give me his details and I'll get a note to him.'

The orderly finds Edward in the makeshift officers' mess that afternoon in the Division's camp of three hundred tents, not three miles away, and gives him the scrap of paper. At midnight, in the ward's low light of a couple of hurricane lamps, Alex is woken by husky whispering: it is Edward, smelling strongly of whisky, breathing in his ear.

'Wake up, shhhh, it's me.'

Waking abruptly from a morphia-induced, dream-filled deep sleep, Alex moves suddenly. The bandage tears from the unstable wound. The pain floods back through his upper arm, shoulder, neck. His face contorts with agony and turns to desperation. Alex begins in a rush through dry, cracked lips, 'Edward, Edward, you've got to help me find him …'

'Who?'

'Williams. He saved me, saved me in the dirt, held my hand. I've got to thank him, see him. That bloke, the one who spoke to us in the wood. You've got to find him. They're moving me to England tomorrow; no, it's today. Is it morning? At 0600 … they're moving me. You've got to help me, please, Edward, you can find him.'

By now, Alex's voice is loud enough to cause a stir. He's grabbed the front of Edward's jacket; he is wide-eyed, and his face is greasy with a sheen of oily sweat. The sharp *clip, clip* of a nurse's shoes comes toward them across the decking in the creaking, billowing tent. She's carrying a candle, the light swaying with her movement and the incidental breeze she causes.

'Seriously, Edward, you said you'd be quiet,' the volunteer night nurse implores, eyes darting up and down the rows of beds. 'You're waking everyone. I'll get in terrible trouble.'

Edward sneers at her. 'Alright, keep your shirt on. It's not me … it's him!' He switches abruptly to his most charming, boyish smile, a little marred, slurred with drink. 'He'll be quiet now. I'll keep him quiet now.'

Alex waits for the receding footsteps to cease and turns his head again to face Edward. In a whisper this time, 'Please, you've got to find Williams.'

'Oh, come on,' Edward says, but on seeing his friend's face, he is at a loss. He cannot fathom the hold this nobody, this Jim Williams, has on Alex. Edward resolves to kid Alex along; surely it's the pain talking, and it's late, and after all, he's injured – beside himself. Later on, Alex won't even remember that he asked for this favour. Ed draws out a notebook and pencil stub from his upper left pocket. 'What's his unit?'

'I can't remember.'

'Rank?'

'Er, I don't know.'

'How about his full name?'

'No, but you heard him say it too; can't you …'

'How am I expected to … I can't find him then.'

'Didn't he say he was from Ballarat … or was it Darwin? That'll help.'

Edward sees grief sweep over his friend's face as Alex forces his panicked eyes to close. He croaks, 'It's important. Please.'

'Yeah, alright, alright. I'll do what I can,' Edward replies without conviction, disappointed in the enthusiasm his friend shows for someone else's company, the man he so dislikes.

While he tucks the notebook away, Edward asks about Alex's injuries and is sobered by the description.

'You'll be alright though, won't you? A bit of a break across the Channel and you'll be top notch. See you back here in no time.' Ed grips and squeezes Alex's right forearm. 'Yes, yes, you'll be alright.'

The hour, the desperation, the morphia catches up with Alex and tears spread over his face. His mouth is drawn down in the tragic mask of Aeschylus.

There is no accompanying noise; it is a quiet, bereft sadness.

Not one for sad scenes, Edward takes his leave. He needs a drink.

CHAPTER FOURTEEN

YPRES

'Charlotte died from bleeding into her brain. It was an unde-tected aneurysm, deep in her head. My darling daughter … she died quickly, as fast as it is possible to die, in the blink of an eye.'

Bereft, Charlotte's mother, Ingrid, told me this, these inti-mate details, on the day she returned to Ypres with Charlotte's body after the autopsy. At Ingrid's pharmacy and home in the cobbled street lined by other flat-faced terraced shops, the funeral parlour's men lifted the coffin out of the hearse and onto a narrow trolley. They had manoeuvred it into Ingrid's small living room. It occupied much of the space.

Ingrid and I sat at her kitchen table for hours at the open French doors, with the foot of Charlotte's coffin just in sight. The sun passed left to right across the flagstones. The birds persisted, not knowing of our sadness. A lorry's reversing beeps were heard from further down the road.

'There had to be a medical examination. I travelled to Brussels in the funeral director's vehicle, with Charlotte's body. I didn't want to be far from her – even for a minute. I can't tell you the pain, the pain I am in. My heart is broken. My breasts tingle, you know? You remember from your own children? The sensation of "let down"? From so long ago, but now, again, so strong. I long for skin-to-skin contact with my baby.'

She sat, round-shouldered, her grey hair pulled back in a tight lump at the back of her head. She bounced her foot in agitation. She was the picture of agony.

'I understand the need for an autopsy; I'm a nurse after all. But more than that, I wanted all the answers. How did my Charlotte die? How did I fail to protect her?'

I let her talk. What could I have said to comfort her? I was a stranger; she knew I could not judge her. I stayed close to this grieving woman, borrowing her misery. Her grief, her tears and her trembling became mine too. Charlotte's death and Ingrid's grief led me to grieve over my own life. It gave me licence to weep for sad things: loss of innocence and friendship; my failure as a daughter, wife and mother; violence and mortality.

I couldn't sit in the hotel. I couldn't walk the streets of Ypres. I had offered to help Ingrid organise the wake, though in all honesty, I would not be of much use. We ended up drinking endless cups of coffee and too many glasses of alcohol. Someone – a neighbour, perhaps – brought us a cheese platter and the cheese cloyed in our stale mouths.

'I am nearly sixty years old, and now quite alone – not another living relative. Maybe that's why I will tell you the family history.' Ingrid was driven to tell interlocking stories – Charlotte's backstory, which was of course Ingrid's own. She had a need to account for the dissolving past, a desire for a validating witness. I leant forward, attending, watching her tired eyes and her face, elongated in misery. I squeezed her damp hand.

'I'm listening, I'm listening.' A mantra that comforted me, gave me a role to play.

'You know what that fool said, Tara?' Ingrid said with a sardonic smile and squinting eyes.

'Who? What fool?'

'The Brussels inquest official.'

'What?'

'With a pat on my back, he said, "Don't worry too much about why. These things can happen for no reason." That explanation is *not* enough. It's *unforgivable* to say such a thing!' she raged. 'There can be no such thing as *no reason* for a mother who is grieving.'

She made a dismissive sound with her tongue. 'That's why a grieving person worries, with guilt … self-recrimination. They need … something, something to explain, hang on to.'

I remembered the Ypres curse that Charlotte had referred to that night in the bar. It seemed offensive to mention it now.

'I drove back from Brussels with the funeral director; the hearse followed us, with Charlotte's coffin. The car … it smells of those cheap deodorisers.' Ingrid wrinkled her nose, then sighed. 'I was overwhelmed, done. Out of the window,' she explained to me, 'I *see* the flat countryside rolling by, but I do not *look* at it. It is peppered with awful brick-veneer villages – you know, they wanted to rebuild it all again, after the last war, so they tried to make the buildings look *traditional*. It is now, simply put, ugly. Ha! This country ... we all ... have seen so many things die ... people, animals, trees,' Ingrid continued. 'Relentless, cruel ...' Her reflections tapered off to nothing.

As Ingrid shared her pain with me, I could only nod and make those pointless listening noises. For the mother of a child who dies inexplicably, there is no comfort in the face of such a loss. I did not launch into homilies. This woman already knew death well. Even if I had the capacity, there would have been no benefit in instructing or comforting her; no platitudes would have eased her pain.

*

'Ta-rah.' Ingrid's Flemish accent made my name sound lush, European, her own version, when she telephoned me the next day. 'I'm ready. Let us have the wake now.'

Soon Dom and I, plus some thirty to forty people, were at Ingrid's home, and perched on chair arms, leaning on walls, sitting in the courtyard or on the front step – quiet, smoking, drinking wine. On the morning of the following day, Charlotte was to be buried.

Charlotte's friends were gentle people. The men wore beards, long hair in ponytails, glasses, dressed in Euro sophisticated cool – chinos and tees, leather lace-up shoes. The women were also mellow; blonde, big smiles, lean, in pastels.

We'd met some of them on our night out with Charlotte. Was it only six or was it seven days ago? Seemed, as the cliché goes, like a lifetime.

We, Dominic and I, were out of place with our inelegant Australian bodies, with my teary, bleary face and Dominic in his dirty boots, unshaven, ruddy with a hangover. We felt awkward – we *were* awkward – in this austere Belgian setting, at this difficult wake. The others spoke some English and they did their best to make conversation with us. They had known Charlotte for years; Dom and I knew her for only days.

We had stayed on in Ypres. I felt unable to leave and Dominic stuck by me – there by association. In the days following Charlotte's death, I found myself weeping almost without stopping and Dominic was at sea, not knowing what to do or say. Periodically he patted my shoulder or gave me an awkward hug, made doubly awkward as we had not yet talked in any serious way about what had happened – or not happened – between us. That being said, I didn't control my desolation just to preserve his equanimity. I didn't thank him for his efforts at kindness: I had no room for such graciousness. Mostly, Dominic just wanted to go home, to Sydney, where people didn't cry as much, nor was there tragic death in clouds of mourning hanging over every living thing and piece of the landscape.

'I just want to get this over with, have the wake, say goodbye and fly home,' he had said to Rachel with a slightly desperate tone when he rang her to explain why he was still in Belgium. We were sitting in the quiet garden of the hotel on the morning of the wake, birds chirruping in the silver birches. I heard the conversation clearly.

'I'm glad you're staying to look after Tara. I mean, she was there; it must have been really upsetting. Hey, I can hear the birds in the background. How lovely.'

Dominic shot me a look. 'Yeah, but she'll be alright, won't you, Tara?' Mock-daring me to disagree. 'But I'm over it. Getting to know Edward more thoroughly can wait; even better, I will do it via the internet. Never has Google Earth seemed a more attractive way to research the battlefields.' His irreverence could still make me smile.

At Ingrid's, there was ubiquitous cheese, wine, pâté and schnapps. We were easily persuaded to drink shots of *oude jenever* from traditional tulip glasses. At forty per cent proof, the two of us were quickly reeling. I switched to black coffee – *more* black coffee – but it was too late. My grief became maudlin. Some guests told stories about Charlotte, but they were unintelligible to us; our French hardly enabled us to order a drink in a bar let alone share the intricacies of a lost friendship.

Among us all, there was her pine coffin – plain handles, pale-yellow wood. I found myself resting my hand on the cool surface and saying, 'Goodbye, Charlotte,' in my mind, but after a second or two I said it again, this time out loud. I was aware that I should withdraw my hand. The others might have thought it odd for me to leave it there for longer than a few minutes. But my hand remained, flat against the glossy varnish, about halfway up the box. I noticed the distended veins on the back of my hand: *It must be hot*, I thought, distracted. *I must be getting old*, I thought: more trivia. Someone brought me a chair and my hand stayed there, on the coffin, while I sat down. I was very glad when Ingrid came over to sit beside me; I told her about my daughters and, with no filter, a ten-minute monologue about how lovely they were, how guilty I felt, what a lousy mother I had been so far.

'I'm not going to comfort you, Tara, and especially not today. When you go home, be a good mother. Stop losing time … no, that is not how you say it.'

'Wasting time?' I looked at her dejectedly. 'You're right.'

I'd been hoping for … what? Sympathy? Understanding?

'And be gentle,' Ingrid added. '*Doux*, you know?'

'I am gentle, *doux*,' I started, protesting my innocence at this charge.

'No, I don't think so. But this' – and she gestured around the room – 'might make you so.'

I hung my head, ashamed. She had been so generous to include me and Dom, two unsophisticated Australians, fools: Dominic in his resistance to grief, me in my indulgence in grief. Perhaps Ingrid thought – knew – we were just like children suffering inexplicable loss.

I stood, swayed a little with the effects of emotion and too much wine.

'I would like to propose a toast.'

The roomful of people raised their eyes to what must have appeared to them a dishevelled, overwrought stranger, but one by one they stood too and lifted their glasses to shoulder height, their arms outstretched.

'To dear, dear Charlotte,' I offered inadequately.

They murmured an echo of the toast, turned, carefully made eye contact and clinked glasses with the mourner beside them – with me too. They drank. We drank. A new wave of sentiment flowed through the room and the guests embraced one another. The hugs were prolonged, heartfelt and restorative.

Many of the guests stayed at the wake through the afternoon and into the soft June evening. When the golden light was slanting through the windows, Ingrid brought out a cardboard shoebox of old family photos to share; she sat near me with the box on her knees, and several people gathered around. Ingrid spoke in English after seeing the lost look on my face.

As she sifted through the photographs and memories, fragments of dried rosemary scattered in her lap. There were stalks of it at the bottom of the box and an old lavender bag embroidered with images of flowers, the purple thread almost entirely blanched with age. There was no true scent from either the rosemary or lavender, just a dusty hint of the fragrance.

'"That's rosemary … that's for remembrance",' I slurred a little. 'You know, the bit from *Hamlet* … Shakespeare, when Ophelia is … I can't remember the details. Anyway, she says "rosemary is for remembrance".'

'I don't know that reference. Belgians certainly wear sprigs of it for just that … remembrance. I suppose that's why someone put some in the box.'

Dominic pursed his lips a little and nodded in recognition. It was nice to see the notion had touched him.

He murmured, 'Yeah, rosemary,' and gave me a doleful smile.

'And this picture is my mother, Charlotte's grandmother, Charlotte Marie.' Ingrid fished out another photograph. 'She died … oh, about forty years ago. Charlotte never knew her but was named for her.' Ingrid's tears flowed again; after several days, her tears were no longer neat drops, but waves of saline on macerated cheeks.

'So, Charlotte Marie, ah, she was born … when?' I asked, making weary, sad conversation, losing track of the Charlottes.

'It was 1919, and her mother, Charlotte Eva, you remember – I told you, I think – died in childbirth. Her father, we think, was a soldier, never returned to claim the baby. It must have been a terrible time. The people of Ypres lived in ruins, as poor as church mice, for years, near starving and working only to grow food. I think I've got a picture of her. Yes, yes, here she is – another Charlotte, Charlotte Eva, *our* Charlotte's great-grandmother.'

'She is so young,' I said.

'Yes, only twenty when she dies.'

It was a thick *carte de visite*, a small photograph, heavier than it looked. The young woman in the photo looked like a painted porcelain doll, characteristic of any sepia-toned, hundred-year-old studio portrait. Her big-eyed gaze was slightly raised, seemingly to see over her right shoulder; her hair was dense and piled in layers on her head, framing her face, but allowing her improbably thin neck to emerge, slightly strained. The backdrop was a screen, typical of the time, featuring an idyll replete with a grassy landscape, acquiescent grazing sheep, Roman columns.

'We don't know anything about the father, the soldier, not if he lived or died,' Ingrid continued.

I turned the *carte* over carefully. In faded, well-formed, nineteenth-century-schooled script, there was a message:

Regards from Jim Williams, Darwin, Northern Territory, Australia. I'll be back soon. I promise. Marry me? X

*

It was in the cool of the evening when Dominic and I left the wake; we said our goodbyes to Ingrid and Charlotte's friends with kisses to both cheeks, heartfelt hugs. We promised to return and to keep in touch, though all parties knew – even with the best intentions – it was unlikely. We returned to the hotel, walking without conversation under a dark sky with few stars. In the foyer as we retrieved our room keys, I asked Dominic to come to my room.

'I've got to look through the records again. That inscription on the back of the photo that Ingrid showed us, well, I think … Charlotte's … could be …'

'Jesus, Tara, you've got to let all this go, you know, and soon.'

Dominic saw my face and understood that it was important to indulge me a bit further.

'OK, alright, let's go. But tonight, this evening, I'm going to book our flights home. I've had enough, and so have you. You need to go home. I need to go home. We're going home as fast as any bloody Qantas jet can carry us.' He looked older tonight, the shape of his face and the set of his mouth, as though the death, the wake and the shift in our simple friendship had aged him.

'Yep, I know, Dom, I know. Just come and keep me company for this search. I think Jim ...'

In my room, I opened my laptop and Dominic pulled a chair over to the blond-wood table by the open French windows. It was not long until I had reached across the world and tapped into my grandfather's digitised records on the War Memorial website. I moved through the thirty or so pages, looking for something.

'I didn't pay much attention to these pages earlier. They were unresolved and didn't seem to lead anywhere. I had no reason to, but now I think ... I think Charlotte is ...'

'Jesus wept, Tara, spit it out.' Dominic was exasperated.

'Here ... here it is. Alex wrote these two letters to the Australian War Office. Here, have a look, in his file, one written and received in 1932. See the office stamp there? And the other ... yeah, here it is, 1933. Why he wrote them then, I don't know, but look, read this.'

I spun the laptop around, and Dominic read out loud:

11 November 1932
Dear Sir
    I write to seek the details of a soldier named Williams,
J. He was known as Jim. I believe he was from Darwin. He
was at the Battle of Messines, probably in the 43rd Battalion,
a private or perhaps a sergeant. I am desirous of his current
whereabouts. It is quite important that I contact him.
    Yours sincerely
    Major Alexander Twigg-Patterson, Ret'd

'No official response to this first one is in the file, recorded.'
I moved the cursor and, with a tap, the screen displayed the
following page. 'A year later, Alex writes this one.'

11 November 1933
Dear Sir
    When I last saw the man I seek, it was in a misty dawn
light, at the tail end of the Battle of Messines.
    The years roll by, and I appreciate Jim Williams is a
'common name' as you suggest.
    In fact, the 'digger' who found me unconscious and arranged
my evacuation directly remains anything but common to me. He
saved my life perhaps in more ways than just bodily. He was a
most remarkable man. I shall continue to search.

Thanking you; regretting trouble caused by your searching for my saviour.

Yours faithfully

Major Alexander Twigg-Patterson, Ret'd

'Shit. Was he …?' Dominic broke the silence between us.

'Yeah. He was looking for Jim Williams, Charlotte's great-grandfather. I guess to thank him or … put to rights … that day when Alex was injured, just after the battle. I think Jim Williams must have saved Alex's life. But it's too much of a coincidence, isn't it? Seriously, what are the odds?'

'I don't know, Tara, but what are the odds of us meeting, our grandfathers knowing each other, us returning to a spot so important in their lives and us working out connections. Perhaps … maybe it's not so amazing. We went looking for connections; I guess we were going to find them.'

We sat in unusual peace for a while, each of us considering chance, coincidence and our own crazy search for meaningful links.

'You know, Ta, I go on a lot in a negative fashion, but in truth, I am glad we came. All this living history … and we found our little bit of it, lived it in a small way, and are now part of it.'

Northern Europe's long summer night was pink-golden through the window now. There was a water feature gurgling in the courtyard restaurant below, and we could hear the other hotel guests scraping chairs, laughing, talking, knives and forks clattering against crockery.

Dominic leant back on two of the four legs of his chair, reached into the minibar and extracted two small bottles of Duvel. He knocked the lids off the beers, placed one in front of me and drank from the other.

'OK, my friend. I'll go book the flights.'

CHAPTER FIFTEEN

THE EARLY YEARS OF JIM WILLIAMS

That his grandmother is Aboriginal is never a concern of Jim's. He loves her: the skinny old lady who lives in the shed at the end of the run of shacks in the home paddock. Her place is under the row of silk trees that seem to bloom all year long: wafty, frondy flowers that look to the boy like rosy-pink, giant spiders. She is sweet and soft, and he remembers the many times she sang her lullabies to him, when he was very small. He remembers, too, the occasional remark by a white stock-man, or the boss's youngest son, a remark meant to wound and criticise. The malice never penetrates his safe place: he is loved, he is a brave boy who can ride all day, tend a camp-fire and kill a snake. That is quite enough. The colour of his grandma's skin doesn't matter to him.

Jim's father was born to Grandma and the boss man a long time ago when the Northern Territory had fewer than a thousand white people in it. There are Chinese, Afghans and Aboriginals, but they're not counted literally or figuratively. It's a time of mavericks, and tough conditions prevail, sorting out the physically robust from those who can't take the heat, the predators, the lack of food and water, the disease, the injuries. To survive, let alone thrive, a person must be resilient, hardy. A bloke must be singularly bloody-minded to stay in this unforgiving country. Jim's father, as a boy, gets some ribbing for his colour and his bastard status. He is beaten perhaps more than his younger half-brothers and half-sister, but he manages to live in a netherworld between the big house and the workers' shacks, until it's commonly recognised that he's the boss's son, and has a job for life on the property. This boy learns two cultures, but neither thoroughly. He knows his two totems, his two languages, his two places in the world. He knows that he belongs to the land, but that his father thinks the land belongs to him. The disparity of his dual identity is only occasionally disruptive to his quiet and cheery nature: he is nourished by the red dirt, the blue-sky canopy.

Jim's father marries his mother, Eliza, in 1893. She has come from the south, from Adelaide, as a maid to assist the nanny in the nursery. There are three children to care for and Jim's mother spends most of her time washing and ironing their clothes and bed linen. She has plenty of opportunity to play with them, and there are swings in the big trees out on the only watered patch of grass: the boss's wife calls it 'the lawn'. Most late-afternoons the group of them – the three children, Nanny and Eliza – spread a canvas and then a woollen picnic blanket, and drink slightly warm lemonade, eating fruit cake.

Jim's father first sees Eliza there, and thinks she looks pretty in her violet-and-white paisley dress, and with her brown hair, in a soft French roll held by turtle-shell combs. It takes a year of sitting beside each other in long silences, chaperoned by Nanny, until Jim's father proposes on bended knee on 'the lawn'. Eliza's parents are long deceased, so Jim's father asks his own father, Eliza's employer, for permission to marry her – a curious hierarchy of authority and patronage in this turn of events, but not unhappily so. Indeed, the boss's young wife, never comfortable with Jim's father's existence, welcomes the idea that he might marry, leave the station, strike out by himself and, frankly, take his coloured mother with him.

It doesn't turn out as she'd hoped.

In a flurry of pain and blood, the boss's wife dies in childbirth shortly after Jim's parents marry. The newlyweds are obliged to stay – to help with the remaining children and with the running of the station – and are happy to do so. They want to make a go of living there with the boss as more of a father, father-in-law and grandfather than an employer. Jim is born a couple of months later and grows up in an atmosphere of a more unified family, where the boss and his son build on their difficult start until there is no remnant of the ill-will from the boss's late wife. By the time he is five, Jim is invited to call the boss 'Grandfather'. He has learnt humility and gratitude – not as a sop to his indigenous background, but as a humanist. He has learnt to be gracious.

Jim is a fine boy: he is strong, hardy, endures and enjoys all the physical challenges an outback life throws at him. In spirit, he is generous and respectful with a flexible intellect, curious about the natural world. He's a scallywag: his laughing smile wins any disagreement, and when he successfully catches the eye of any person, he grins like he's conquered Goliath. But staring at the *Encyclopaedia Britannica*'s pages, interpreting complex diagrams, mouthing the hard words, is his favourite pastime. He's mostly a quiet boy and in time becomes a contemplative man, and when he senses that his listener is truly interested, he visibly brightens and is a fount of facts, trivia, enthusiasm and metaphor. He becomes a great reader, consuming any and all of the books that his grandfather sends for through the post.

Like his father, he learns the land in two ways: in its physical, all-encompassing form and by abstract, horizontal paper mapping. His Indigenous kin show and tell him the land's secrets, its history, its ups and downs, its ins and outs. His white family and fellow jackeroos teach him how to exploit it, its value, its assets. He can quickly weave the concepts: the two notions slip-slide together in an agile mind. Every annual round-up and cattle drive, Jim rides confidently across the land, along the creek beds, through pandanus, with the cacophony of the herd echoing off the sheer red-rock faces. He admires and acknowledges the noble jabiru and feisty cockatoos, the supreme crocs and robust rock wallabies. He feels the land's power when the thunderclaps near-deafen him, and he is repeatedly renewed by the torrid sheets of rain.

When the newspapers – three weeks' old by the time they arrive at the property – tell of the conflict, the Empire's fight, Jim discusses his duty with those around him. Is his duty to king and country? Or his parents and grandparents?

Looking at the dirt, arms crossed, his father asks him not to join up. 'It's not our fight, son.'

His mother pleads with him not to leave, with tears and wringing her hands. 'It's dangerous!'

His grandfather orders him not to set foot off the property. 'No, young man. Your responsibility is to me, to your family. You'll stay here, you hear me. There's work to be done.'

But his grandmother, she grins when asked and, with a twinkle in her eye, says, 'Go find out for yourself, Jimmy.'

And he does. When he joins up at the post office in Darwin, it is the first time he has experienced a town. In this small place and in any of the cities he visits subsequently, he is not fazed by the chaos nor seduced by the humbuggery. He is not at the mercy of his naivete, rather released by it to watch and listen, all eyes and ears, no history, no rules, no borders. He continues to take life as it comes, at face value, and each day he fair bristles at the opportunity.

The long journey to Europe is an eye-opener. He chuckles out loud when he first sees the sea, filled with the glory and the mischief – the sheer inventiveness – of Nature. He had thought the landscape of his homeland was expansive, grand, but the oceans are magnificent: their surge, their grey-green tones with ever-moving white peaks. But then there are trains, deserts, forests, lorries, weapons, manners, food, men of all shapes and sizes – all quite different to his experience, exhilarating in their variety.

Jim arrives at Salisbury Plain and is allocated to the 11th Machine Gun Company. He is twenty-three years old, lean and strong; all six foot of him, muscle and sinew. He lives with thousands and thousands of men on a windswept expanse of cold, flat earth, in rows of tents, tidy and regular, just as the army likes it. At night, his canvas stretcher is uncomfortable, perhaps precarious; giving his weight to it is an act of faith. His shared tarpaulin home becomes stuffy with too many bodies inside it, and Jim draws unwanted attention to himself – and a negative response – by asking if he might be allowed to sleep out under the stars.

A machine gun is a revelation. What an instrument! What engineering! Jim has never imagined the like. He takes to it as he does to most mechanical things: deliberately, focussed, thoroughly.

He digs trenches, learning how to plank the walls and where and how to place a machine gun upon them. He labours with his shirt off, causing a ruckus among the British officers walking about, supervising.

'See here, put it back on, there's a good chap.' The bristling moustache wriggles; then, *sotto*, 'Bloody Australians.'

Though they are not Jim's specific responsibility, he spends a lot of time with the Company's horses and mules. Whether through a sleek or a rough coat, their warm skin is a joy to feel, and he scratches them behind the ears, pats their rump, finds the velvety patch between their nostrils, and he talks to them in low, affectionate tones.

'Nice creatures, you are. There's a bit of a scratch, my fine laddie. Look at us, eh? England no less. Whaddya reckon, eh?'

Jim is standing to attention in the Company's very back row when the king trots by inspecting the troops, and along with his teammates he doesn't understand the fuss. Instead, they admire the king's mount, a fine specimen of horse flesh. The king? He's just a man: just like any of them.

At last – and it feels like they've been stuck there a bloody lifetime – Jim and the Company are ordered to prepare. They're off to France. Though it's cold and the Channel is rough, he's glad to be on the move. It's cowardly to sit on Salisbury Plain while others are fighting without him.

Jim and his mates tramp from the Calais dock to the train station, to the forward area, a town called Bailleul in northern France. There is a boyish, adventurous atmosphere among the lads, but Jim doesn't participate in the joshing and mock-boxing. He doesn't need to express the trepidation, the tension, the nerves. Now they can hear the guns – irregular, muffled booms of varied tones. Now they hear the stories from soldiers returning from the front – fragmentary, differing impressions. Injured or not, those returning are all tired. They are dirty with grease and the human detritus of the trenches. Jim listens, nodding or offering a reassuring word.

Jim quickly becomes known in his unit as a good bloke. It's praise indeed, from these laconic men, who have been raised to conserve one's admiration, just in case you need to tear down the tall poppy at a later date. But Jim can be relied upon for a kind word, a shared brew-up, a generous pat on the back when the chips are down. 'Big-hearted' is the word the Australian officers use for Jim when reviewing their men's potential.

The Company moves into a camp near Armentières. They've had to walk through the outskirts of the town, past the medieval terraces on cobbled streets. Much of the rest of the town is levelled with curiously jagged corners and half-walls dotted along interrupted streets, pitted with the holes of artillery fire. Jim stares at the old buildings, agog with the history, the foreign architecture – foreign in time and by virtue of their design. Tall and thin and curving slightly, these buildings line the street with a lean. The remaining dwellings are mostly boarded up.

One or two old folk stand in their doorways, watching the troops tramp, tramp, tramp by.

'G'day,' Jim tries with a nod and small smile to the few townspeople, but he receives no response.

Soon, he is at the front. He steps down and descends into a maze, marked with street signs of sorts, chalk boards indicating the compass points and giving directions to send the various groups to their designated location. Down more steps, along a rabbit run, past shallow, broad, man-sized holes in the walls roughly scrabbled out of the clay. There are clacking, clanking, mechanical sounds, and booms and crashes with no synchronicity or rhythm. The air is foetid and clear by turn: smells of stale urine and iron or cool countryside breezes. Underfoot, there are duckboards made slippery by the wet debris of hundreds of live bodies and rain. Jim's uniform is already wet through, clinging to his knees and thighs, clammy over his chilled shoulders and back.

'Stand aside, stand aside, ya bastards. Injured man coming through,' someone shouts, and the jostling stretcher-bearers jog by. They have the body of a man under a muddy, dark brown blanket. Only his pale face is showing, contorted in pain. Jim frowns, whispers, 'Poor lad,' then pushes on, the picture of the injured man-child directed to the back of his mind. He has witnessed the anguish and torture of the first man of his Company to be wounded. It is New Year's Eve, 1917.

But the first death of the Company is Tommy Quigley, a comrade of Jim's. They were assigned to the same mess group of eight men, to share a brew-up billycan and a tin of tea leaves. After a week, Jim finds himself on the other side of a dugout when Tommy is brought in mortally wounded. Jim stays in the space, allowing the doctor and his assistant to do their work, calling out, 'You'll be right, Tommy. It's all goin' to turn out right, mate,' craning his neck to see.

But Tommy dies quietly: the arteries, veins, bones and muscles of the left side – pelvis, abdomen, ribcage, head – have been smashed and ground to an unviable pulp.

'He's dead,' says the stretcher-bearer, turning his head to Jim. 'Give us a hand to move him back, will ya? I have to haul him to Armentières.'

'Yeah, righto.' Jim could choose to sleep or merely rest, but to help with Tommy's body is the right thing to do.

It is a gruelling trudge back to Armentières, and after, Jim slumps, exhausted with it all. It's been some two miles with the stretcher of Tommy's heavy corpse between them. He sits on a rock in some rubble and accepts a shot of burning liqueur – perhaps it is Cognac – that heats his mouth and throat in an invigorating way. It is served to him in a mess cup, by a barman in a stained apron. The man is standing in an area defined by two half-walls, open to the street, with just a wooden crate of unlabelled bottles, half a dozen mess cups.

Hearing a thrumming far away in the sky, Jim looks up and sees a biplane, a fantastic mechanical bird, and he wonders at the beauty of the invention, the millennia of thought and creativity it has taken to get to this point. He rises, stretches, thinking of how a plane could be used in the outback.

'I'm off,' he says to the stretcher-bearer and barman, dusting off his trousers, buttoning his tunic. 'See you again soon.'

Over the next five weeks, four more men from his Company die. It is disconcerting to have the men – friends, comrades – disappear from their intense shared lives. The tempo of their days is such that the bonds are deep, formed in extreme conditions by ferocious challenges. A sudden absence is disorientating. Other things flare at the edge of his mind: the distance between him and his family, the fragility of mortality, the joy that will be experienced on his return.

The winter is very cold, and Jim finds his clothes becoming looser. Food is scant, but Jim's resolute. He's here because he's here. He learns the art of surviving while giving the enemy merry hell. He's good at catching snatches of sleep; good at taking off his boots and drying his feet almost daily; good at keeping his kit clean and dry – well, when possible.

By the start of March 1917, the cold of the terrible winter is abating, and with it, the number and size of the skirmishes increase. Jim and his mates have been sent on mission after mission, day after day for weeks on end. They get a few days' respite every few weeks, and Jim sleeps for the first twenty-four hours of his break, then emerges from under his blanket to eat as much as he can forage, and walks around the village he finds himself in. He looks at all the damaged places with a neutrality that could be construed as uncaring, but Jim's equanimity is acceptance. He sees this war as inevitable, an entropy of sorts, a prelude to renewal, what mankind does to itself periodically and has done through history.

It is April when, behind the lines, life is reasserting itself in a glorious spring of wildflowers and an array of greens in leaves and grasses. But at the front, Jim is gassed for the first time. He uses his mask and avoids the worst of it, but it's impossible to function under that weight and confinement of the heavy canvas and tubing. He just has to take the damn thing off. He breathes the poison, knowing full well that every breath is injuring him. To Jim, gassing – by either side – seems like evil, wickedness. It is the ultimate, ghastly undermining of all the good things that humans could do for each other, one of the worst barbarous acts among numerous barbarous acts. But while the incident increases Jim's dissonance, he returns to his duty – killing, destroying, damaging – with a diligence and expertise that makes him a valued soldier.

The Company's actions allow Jim a good deal of travel up and down the lines, for which he's grateful – far better to be on the move. It would be too much to bear to sit in a trench or a dugout and wait for trouble. His ability to move competently – safely – between the various countries' forces around the area means that he is assigned as a messenger or as a way-finder for teams that need to move through doubtful territory. He can move between the dreadfulness of the front to the beauty of the still-preserved villages and towns: he stays sound, lucid, collected.

He gets to know the area around the Division: Armentières, Ypres, Erquinghem, Messines, all so utterly different to his homeland. How could two corners of the earth be so opposite? Europe's seasons seem like a fairytale and are just as unreal. And the water! Everywhere and all the time as opposed to rare and rarely. The colours of France and Belgium are soothing – subtle and appealing; but the deep reds of northern Australia's gorges and plains and the lapis lazuli of the sky-dome have been sustenance for Jim to date. It's a challenge to reconcile. His mind, his senses, explode with the variety.

His awe and admiration for all these new places makes him stand up straight, tilt his head back to see the sunlight on a terracotta-tiled roof or the rain coating the slate of a steeple. He especially loves the city of Ypres.

May sees Jim and much of the Division move by stages all the way back to the coast near the intact and busy city of Calais, which is overrun with military forces, and the locals are consigned to servicing the troops. Here, the 11th Machine Gun Company, along with the rest of the Battalion, are gathering resources, rehearsing clashes, receiving further instruction – building their capabilities. Something is different; something is afoot. It could make a man jittery. Soon they're on the move again, en masse, holus-bolus back to the Ypres area.

This time – *snap*! The sight of the destruction of Ypres takes Jim by dreadful surprise. It is during *this* visit that he is deeply affected by *these* wretched ruins, *this* tragic waste, the scandalous profligacy. The loss of *this* city – its architecture, its citizens, its culture – breaks his heart more than any other terrible sight. It is an affront. Perhaps by a cumulative grief, all that he's witnessed up until this point in time has made him more vulnerable and sensitive. He senses he is breaking. He mourns the late beauty of this ancient city – a first for Jim, who till now could take all the misery that the War's futility and malevolence had shown him.

Yet in this sad place, he has met a woman – got to know her, learnt to love her – Charlotte Eva. She displays dignity in the face of the destruction of her home, city, family and livelihood.

She confirms his faith in kind people and reminds him that for every terrible person or incident, there are a hundred marvellous people and a thousand good deeds. While he doesn't understand the depth of his response to her, he knows he loves her for all time. For him, that is an easy deduction. He wishes to care for her and, as though *she* is Ypres, rebuild her, restore her. And when one sunny afternoon, with her permission, he can kiss her, he can scarcely contain the flood of elation he feels because of this pearl of a woman, who says she will be his. Each time he is required at the front and must leave her, he gathers all the strength of character he's amassed over his twenty-three years and resolves anew to make sure he comes back to her. He's now seen how easily a life is extinguished; he must not let it happen to him. He must not.

Charlotte Eva gives him a studio portrait of herself, a big gesture of commitment on her part. Though he longs to keep it on his person, he begs her to hold the keepsake safe for him, and he writes a message for her on its back, which he asks her to read often.

Regards from Jim Williams, Darwin, Northern Territory, Australia. I'll be back soon. I promise. Marry me? X

One evening they make love in the gloaming, under one of the few remaining apple trees, near the farmhouse where she and her family have taken temporary refuge. Jim and Charlotte Eva lie in long grass and it is sweet, innocent; their embrace is gentle and genuine. A new life is created amid so much heartache and yearning.

*

At the base of the muddy crater, Jim Williams gathers his rifle, his limbs, his courage, and his gaze follows the direction the stretcher-bearers took moments ago.

The early daylight is enough to see where to place his feet in the churned soil – he doesn't want to stand on the remnants of his fallen comrades. It looks to him like a huddle of officers, perhaps four or five, caught a mortar directly.

The captain must have moved away just in time.

Wisps of fog-like smoke reduce visibility a little and add an eeriness to the scene. He is quite alone; no other surviving soldier is in sight.

It was quite a fight, quite a battle that Jim Williams has just survived, and he considers his luck as he walks up the crater's wall, slightly bent over for just a little bit of extra safety. He is aware that he brought more savagery to this battle than at any other time; he didn't know he had it in him. This time, this battle, he didn't want any of the enemy to escape retribution. He wanted vengeance and it scares him.

'Am I hardening? Am I deserving?' he says out loud. Charlotte Eva's reserved profile comes to mind.

Almost at the edge of the crater, he catches a glimpse of the trees of Ploegsteert Wood. Its deep green, its fullness, its natural power, brings a quick smile to his mouth.

What a grand thing Nature is.

As he emerges at the crater's lip, satisfied that it's safe to do so, the sniper's bullet catches Jim Williams in the neck on his left side, ripping open his carotid artery and travelling upward through the centre of his brain, its trajectory halted when it meets his skull. He is quite dead in less than two minutes. One hundred and twenty rapid heartbeats and most of his ten pints of blood are all over his woollen tunic, his trousers, and soaking into the Flanders earth on this miserable day.

There is no witness to Jim's death. A shell bursts close to him, and his body is torn apart, beyond recognition.

CHAPTER SIXTEEN

EDWARD'S EUROPE

'It's the pain, sir. I can't move when it comes on. I need some pills to take the pain away. Then … then I can get back to it.'

'Can you tell me a little more about the pain, Lieutenant Fitzgerald?'

The same flat monotone in Edward's voice has been heard many times now by the army doctor, from many mouths. Around the clock, the clinic in Bailleul has queues of distressed men presenting with symptoms that are not technically signs of disease or physical injury.

'A terrible headache, pounding. I'm blinded by the lights in my eyes. I throw up. Pain … everywhere.'

Since the Battle of Messines, Edward has lost his centre of gravity. As though in an echo chamber, Europe's white noise of destruction resounds in his mind. He can't recollect his core memories, or the basis for living on. He is unable to recall the comfort of his mother's physical presence, the tone of her calm voice: she is too far away and has been for too long. His surviving brothers are scattered across Europe and there's one dead on the Somme. To some, Edward appears as well adjusted as ever, but those who know him observe that his eyes are just a little too wide, his responses just a little delayed: his smile, his handshake, his nod.

'Are you drinking too much?' The doctor knows the answer already. On Edward's breath, above the aroma of mint sweets, there is the whiff of whisky. He is found every evening in his tent or dugout, drinking alone, no longer the amusing clown, but with a guilty look, his big brown eyes moving in his gaunt face. He drinks too much for days on end, dodging any decisions and judgemental colleagues – he hides from his own ignominy.

'Well, I … I … I don't know …'

At the centre of it all, Edward is shaken by his friend's distress in the hospital tent at Wimereux, but he just can't face him, let alone look for Williams. He turns away from the doctor, blinks back acid tears and clasps his shaking hands in his lap. He is rent with shame – he has failed Alex. 'I d-d-deserted my friend,' he blurts, as though this might explain, heart turning in his chest, sweating.

There is no time for the doctor to deal with this man's problem: there is simply too much heartache and grief among these men.

'Look here, Fitzgerald, I'll not be giving you any kind of sleeping draught. What you need is a few days' leave in England, a bit of normal, eh? Get some sleep, get something decent to eat, eh?' He tries to smile at Edward, to reassure.

It falls flat; Edward's face is a picture of pathos. 'You sort your-self out and come back here and do your duty. Savvy?'

He's just a boy. The tired officer justifies his dismissal of Edward to himself, running his hand through his salt-and-pepper hair as he signs the forms. *It's remorseless, too much for him … for all of them … for all of us.*

*

London is the same as when Edward and Alex visited a year before. It is Edward that is different, and he sees the city in a different light. To him it's a miserable place of complaints and dichotomy. He is lonely but chooses to drink alone. He is hungry but chooses to eat sparingly. He is tired beyond somnolence but cannot sleep.

On a night of cold drizzle, Edward walks the streets searching for the house where he and Alex met Robert and his family. What a night that had been: the sweet wife, the dear children, the golden candlelight. It had been full of barely disguised hints as to what lay in store for the both of them. Edward had not listened, had not heard the warnings. When he finds the right door, he knocks, but no one is there. Edward slumps, with the damp and the cold and his singular desolation. He walks on aimlessly. He slips into the Cadogan Arms on the King's Road. At the bar, from a rickety stool, he watches a team of young British pilots celebrate some mile-stone in their training. These young wingmen are noisy and joyous. At first, Edward is angered by their impudence, their nonchalance, their hubris.

Why, those lazy cowards don't even have to fight. Flying around, dodging the hard life, the trenches, the … the …

As he stares at the bar top's sticky surface, and skols the several whiskies placed progressively in front of him, the anger turns to envy, then realisation. He could be a pilot – he'll fly over the battles and never have to face man-to-man combat again. He'll never have to witness another man die in agony from his hand.

I'll be as far away as is possible from the noise, chaos, smell, wet and cold like these stuck-up bastards.

In the following days, Edward pulls every string he has, pushes for a transfer to the nascent Australian Flying Corps, and is taken on immediately: not many other serving men are rushing to increase their odds of almost certain death in the flying machines. Edward masters the art and the skills of flying and survives the most dangerous of training days – that is, the early ones, when others, those younger than he and almost as able, die at a high rate, crashing to earth because of just one small mistake. Edward resolves to be the best pilot there is. His stomach lurches at the thought of telling his mother, to be able to say he'd achieved something great. He'll be a hero.

To this end, he reluctantly gives up the drink; and soon he is scheduled to fly back to France with one other fellow in a Sopwith Triplane. This plane is used for training, an unusual two-seater, but the pair will use it in developing combat methods; they are charged with further testing the battle capabilities of this model. He and his partner will be stationed in a little airfield in France, near Cambrai, and they will fly reconnaissance and drop grenades on the enemy lines. A couple of years younger, his partner is a decent chap but no help to Edward. The boy has not yet seen war, let alone been troubled by it. Edward is plagued by what he's witnessed already: all the seven veils of decent, humane society have been torn away.

Each day Edward rises early, checks his take-off schedule, determines his specific task, washes, shaves, brushes his clothing, shines his boots. Ignoring every screaming physical reminder of anticipation, he tries to eat some breakfast. He can tolerate the soft part of the crusty loaves if he is able to chew very slowly and carefully. Some days when he's eating, his body makes too much watery spit and he panics: will he drown in it? Other days, his mouth is so dry he must slurp his cooling tea to swallow the crumbly bread. If a comrade sits beside him at breakfast on the upturned barrels outside the airfield's camp-kitchen, Edward must put down the bread and try to smile at the appropriate time in the conversation, laugh at the right moment. The smile is sometimes a grimace, the laugh sometimes mistimed, but this is Edward's holding pattern. He is functional; to his superiors, he is a useful soldier again – useful enough, sent to attack, again and again.

*

At take-off, they view a carpet of green fields in northern France or just into Belgium, neat farmland and petite villages; then, on they fly to muddy desolation where the trench lines stretch, zigzag, out of sight. And when the biplane must dive so that the two in it can almost see the eyes of the enemy, and one of them must pull the pin and throw a hand grenade, Edward sees stars and his legs tingle. In his mind, the bullets are already ramming into his lower body through the canvas structure. It is unadulterated fear – but not unreasonable – too deep and too wide to fathom or curtail.

Through the latter part of 1917 and into 1918, Edward need never get closer to the mayhem of trench warfare than the thirty yards aloft, the optimal distance required to drop a grenade into the enemy trench. He never witnesses the damage done. He can't hear the noise of men with shrapnel in their abdomen, can't smell the blood, doesn't stand in the stinking mud. He can pretend that the harm he creates happens far away and is therefore not relevant. He need feel no responsibility; the dogs of war are not barking in his face.

Edward considers Alex abstractly. The image of Alex's face against the sweat-stained hospital pillow flares – but is banished just as quickly as it appears. He is unable to find relief from his sadness regarding his friend, and so it is assigned to the edge of his mind, corralled there. He does not try to find Alex, choosing to assume Alex is safe, recuperating, recovering, perhaps even rejoining the men of the Third Division. He decides to feel satisfied with his fantasy: he cannot dwell on any responsibility for his friend's well-being; his own is almost too much to preserve.

Aloft, Edward witnesses the big push from the Boche – Operation Michael – climaxing for the Australians in the battle for Villers-Bretonneux. From the cockpit, the battles of April and May of 1918 look violent and brutal as the destructive waves swerve back and forth, east and west. The bombardment from both sides is continuous and overwhelming: arrhythmic booms and blasts, day and night with no respite. Recognising the battle's horror but not participating in it at ground level has a peculiar effect on Edward. It is dreamlike; his mood blank, his heart numb. He plods through each day of the battle with little enthusiasm, but no rancour, nor cynicism. His voice and facial expressions strike his companions as strangely inanimate.

Adding to the desert of his ubiquitous guilt – his wearying self-recrimination – Edward survives, truly against all odds.

CHAPTER SEVENTEEN

ALEX'S EUROPE

Through the summer then autumn of 1917, Alex spends nearly four months at a Red Cross auxiliary hospital, in the grand, eighteenth-century Harewood House, near the city of Leeds. On his arrival, he relishes such beauty: its architecture, the gardens, the surrounding rolling fields. By Australian standards, the building is a palace, but Alex is not overwhelmed by the size, wealth or importance of the place; he scarcely notices those aspects. But the green of the parkland with its island-stands of dark evergreen trees, the seemingly confused groups of black-faced sheep and the constant melodies from the thousands of pretty birds make for a human place, a human space where he can find some peace.

The acute pain of Alex's wound site, plus the constant ache in his elbow, the bones of his upper arm and his shoulder, disallow much contemplation. Any momentary reflection of the Battle of Messines and its successive days brings him to stinging, pricking tears, and then, like the turning on and off of a tap, self-preservation forces him to cease to recall, and he stops his near-crying just as immediately. During all those months of recovery, he does not progress beyond this: a shocking recollection, momentary anguish and then a subconscious, self-imposed neutrality. Any thoughts of his friend's whereabouts are vague: Edward is simply somewhere and must be safe because Alex can't – won't – entertain the idea that he might be hurt.

The idea of Jim Williams remains elusive, ghostly, tenuous, just out of sight.

*

'It's not too bad,' Alex reports, when it's time to be judged as ready or not to return to the fray.

The concept of physiotherapy is not yet well developed but the throwing and catching of calisthenic pins and many long walks through the forested areas has worked well enough as a recovery regimen for Alex.

'Ah, that's the spirit, Captain. Not too bad.' The doctor gives Alex the all-clear, though he knows full well Alex's elbow will never be the same and his arm is far from restored. 'You're to report to your headquarters in London. I understand you'll again lead the 11th Machine Gun Company. A big push is on.'

In truth, the big push has been on for some months, but Alex is in time to catch up with his troops as they enter the battlefield for the October assaults at Passchendaele. The generals, buoyed by the success of the Battle of Messines – albeit temporary – continue to make for the Channel's coast, like overconfident moths to a disastrous flame.

Alex is somewhat numb – not catatonic, merely functional without warm engagement. He speaks rarely, listens mostly; his men wonder if he's become just one more strange bastard, an officer out of his depth. He sleeps, he eats, he cleans his firearm. But when the time comes to lead his Company, Captain Twigg-Patterson does so without drama, though the Battle of Passchendaele takes more than four hundred thousand lives. Among the horrors of cold and wet and mud and shelling, Alex's men drown while their friends can only watch; some blow their brains out in plain sight of their comrades; four of his draughthorses – magnificent equine behemoths – squeal and thrash for sixteen long hours before succumbing to their deep trap in the clay mud. The men cannot leave their shelter to put the creatures out of their misery and they listen to the horses' last laboured breath. Most of the Company's guns and light cannons are rendered useless by the water falling as rain or rising in shell pockmarks. Mud falls from the sky on Alex and his men as each shell plummets to earth and explodes in the muck.

'Gas.' Alex recognises the cloying scent, among the mouldy smell of mud and clean aroma of rain. 'Again.' He fits his gas mask, and the noisy, monotonic world shrinks to the size and shape of a canvas balaclava; it's a curious respite.

If I don't fight the claustrophobia, I'm pretty alright, he observes, removed from the scene, distant even from himself.

Beyond his headwear, the battle proceeds in slow motion.

On the fourth day, Alex receives permission to recede from their original jump-off point and withdraw five hundred yards. Here, they are to hold. This is a nonsense, an order that is impossible to achieve. There is nothing – no *place* – to hold on to. For acres and acres, there is only clay and mud, stones, charred timber, splintered tree trunks, and corpses – animal and human.

He must report this to a senior officer – the last one alive in the present arena, assuming command in lieu of any other directive. To reach him, Alex must dodge shells, machine-gun fire and snipers, wade through ice-cold, hip-high pools of murky water, balance across teetering duckboards and stand to attention.

'Of the Company, sir, sixteen are dead, fifteen are wounded, twelve are incapacitated by gas. We lost the horses and nine mules. Most of our arms are somewhere out there.' Alex waves a dismissive arm toward the area where the town of Passchendaele used to be some thousand yards away, now only recognisable by the single-skinned brick wall of the former bakery.

'Of a single Company? What's that? Forty-one? Forty-two? Dear God. You left here with a strength of a hundred and forty-four; it says so in your original orders.'

'It's forty-three. I lost forty-three men, sir, in four days, sir.'

'What a total, bloody shambles.'

'Yes, sir, a total, bloody shambles.'

There are another four days of shelling, mostly gas. Alex and his countrymen, strung out along a twelve-mile front, have no means of attack and no real protection. They sleep in shifts in mud caves scraped out of the trenches. The trench walls ooze and collapse regularly. Gravity seems determined to bury them. The Canadian troops relieve them, and the survivors of Alex's Company move – laboriously – to the rear.

Jim Williams's form has re-entered Alex's mind. He searches for Williams's silhouette with every glance and recce, especially at night when the shadows distort reality. Alex longs to see it. If he can, then perhaps, by some strange natural algorithm, all will be right with the world.

Jim, what do you think? Are we alright? Alex wordlessly speaks to Jim in his dreams. *Shall we simply pack up and go home? What do you say?* Alex never gets a reply.

*

Through November and December 1917 there is a lull, dictated to the warring sides by the weather. It is a bitterly cold winter: to a man, they are thin, they have chilblains, cracked lips. They eat every skerrick they can find, picking at anything on offer with bony fingers in cut-off gloves. Some wear sheepskin vests, which are the most valued bit of kit among the men. They drill rather despondently; they meet in a barn for a short

lecture – short because their attention span is much diminished. The men kick a footy around in a small field of soggy
turf, which brings a brief liveliness, but there's no interest in
tackling or competing for possession of the ball. For the occasional, awkward mark, the men summon a lukewarm cheer.

Alex is promoted to major and placed as second in
command of the 43rd Battalion, some thousand-plus men, and
he takes charge for a month while the usual head of the Battalion has leave. It is a time for all the components of the 43rd,
every sad and ruined Company – all those who have made
it this far – to meet the replacements, be they their equals or
superiors, and figure out how to get along with them. The
replacements are green to army customs, war conduct, foreign
ways and great hardship. Alex needs to bring them up to
speed as fast as the generals need them. It strikes him with a
cold dread that he is truly leading lambs to the slaughter.

*

Alex's dreams are not only of Jim. When awake and still seeking sleep, he sees Lottie in the dawn shadows of Brisbane's
morning nearly two years before, a foggy picture of a small
face with big eyes, and the mounds of her body are gentle
hillocks against the slivers of light from around the partially
drawn curtains. The actual dreams remain fleshy but blood-
streaked. She still smiles as sweetly, though it is difficult to
make out the curve of her mouth through the fuddle of deep
sleep. The dreams are short-lived, and Alex wakes himself

abruptly to save himself a heart-thumping adrenalin surge. The dream's narrative can escalate to a nightmare. He forces himself to open his eyes when Lottie's plump tissue merges with his, and, shapeshifting, he becomes Lottie – a version of Lottie, dead and dripping.

He decides to write to her: surely the dreams are not a coincidence. A message? A spiritual connection? Why after these many months would he be seeking her in his unconscious?

Dear Lottie, I am unsure how to begin. We've had a rough time and I think of you as a dear person in a lovely part of the world – golden and warm. I hope you are well. Please write to me if you get a moment. Sincere regards, Major Alex Twigg-Patterson.

He seals the unsophisticated letter immediately, and his hurried, wobbly script from a shaky hand makes the address nearly illegible. When the private assigned to the task of collecting the outgoing mail comes by, Alex is slow to extend the hand holding the envelope most delicately between thumb and forefinger, as though the letter is dangerous.

This uncharacteristic act is one more thing to become and remain unresolved. He never receives a reply.

*

'Sir, whaddya reckon?'

On 12 December 1917, the Australian troops must vote on conscription, the second attempt by the Australian government to pass it into law. The men discuss it in the days prior and ask Alex for his point of view.

'You want to know what *I* think?'

They sit in a burst of weak but pretty sunshine, on logs and rocks a couple of feet from the field kitchen. It is midday, still cold enough to have them exhaling foggy clouds of breath. They have had a bowl of broth and it has brought about a mellow attitude, discursive.

'Yes, sir. We're interested in your thoughts on the subject. Are you going to vote yes or no?'

Alex looks off into the distance; he no longer likes to meet the eyes of the men. He coughs a little, not so much clearing his throat; rather, after the last gas attack he has an annoying tickle at the back of his throat almost all the while. His damaged left arm aches and, while formulating a response, he indulges in the habit he has developed, that of massaging over the site of the break with the ridge of the palm of his right hand.

'Erm. I think that those who have been lucky enough … or crafty enough … to stay out of this shouldn't be made to suffer it. No one should.'

A couple of them take a drag on their cigarettes, exchanging looks. He's thought to have been 'a bit off' since he came back after his injury, but not 'gone' in a dangerous way. The men trust Alex to get it right, and they know he's not a toff like the rest of them.

'Yeah, that's what I reckon,' the most outspoken of the men states.

'And me.'

'Me too.'

'Alright then, sir. We'll be heading out.'

They cast their butts into the mud, slosh the leaves from their tin mugs, gather belongings, rise and walk off to their posts.

And Alex is left wondering if he has said what he as an officer should have said.

The vote fails, and the issue of conscription is finally put to bed.

As soon as it is in better shape, working parties and reconnaissance groups head off to prepare the way – the Battalion has been ordered to the front line. After Christmas Day 1917, Alex's troops enter the trenches just south of Armentières, patrolling both day and night. Alex joins them sometimes to keep in touch with the goings-on, and sometimes he joins them simply to keep moving: stasis is worse. The men wade through heavy snow on their way to and from the front line. Every day, day after day, is a day to be withstood. Every night, night after night, is a night to be endured. Eighty days and nights, Alex sleepwalks, never truly asleep, never truly awake.

*

'An urgent request for you, Major.'

· A rider from divisional headquarters appears in front of Alex's tent.

'The entire Battalion is to move south. The Germans commenced a huge bombardment three days ago in the Somme Valley. The losses have been … appalling. Here are your orders. You – the Battalion – are to be encamped in Villers-Bretonneux by the twenty-eighth … the twenty-eighth of March that is …'

With a raised eyebrow, Alex calmly takes in the news. He skim-reads the orders. He clears his throat.

'Logistical support?'

'Er, none that I know of, sir. But, er, I believe the Americans are arriving any day.'

'Arriving? Arriving where?'

'Er, the Somme, I imagine.' The junior officer's face lights up. 'With tanks!'

'So,' Alex's response is delivered in a monotone, 'the thousand men of this Battalion, approximately half of whom are still on the line, with no immediate relief force in sight, are to walk eighty-odd miles, bearing their supplies, gear and moving the bigger guns, in six days?' His cynicism gets the better of him. 'Then they are to be ready to immediately engage the enemy in battle conditions rather than trench warfare, in which it would be ambitious to presume perhaps a quarter of them have had any training or experience? Mmmmh?'

'Yes, sounds about right, Major.' Hesitating. 'Er, sir, where's the best place for my horse?'

Alex seconds lorries, buses, wagons, horse and mule teams. He is sworn at, cursed and praised for his unorthodox methods of moving his men. He is unshakeable, not raising his voice, threatening, cajoling or ridiculing them, like some other officers around him who have felt the pressure. Alex is not conscious of his behaviour; indeed, he'd be surprised if you suggested it is anything out of the ordinary. Polite, firm, without passion, without despair, he goes about his business, carrying out his orders, fulfilling his obligations, in the only way he can, the only way he is capable of. At dawn on 28 March, his mind in a fog, Alex shepherds the remaining stragglers of the 43rd Battalion to their destination.

Alex and his men are at a part of the front line they've not experienced before, a little north of Villers-Bretonneux. Exhaustion means he is less than conscious of his immediate surroundings; he cannot easily answer when addressed, cannot clearly make out why one or another man wants his attention, advice, authorisation. He lives only in the present with tunnel vision. On comprehending a request or question, he responds quietly, quickly, without eye contact. He forgets his discomfort: the tickle of lice, the mud and metal taste of his food and tea, the chronic sting of conjunctivitis and the tinnitus from the waves of disrupted air that have constantly swept over him for nearly two years now. Through it all, he is aware of the increased number of the flimsy aircraft overhead – theirs, ours, both just as curious. Alex can't help but recall Edward's delight in the 'planes, and he thinks kindly of his friend, hopes he is somewhere safe.

*

'Where am I? … Who are you? … is, is somebody there?'

Alex wakes but cannot open his eyes; rather, he is not certain if his eyes are open or unseeing, or is it that what he sees is not real? He cannot remember where he is, or what his duties are; who is that staring at him and speaking very loudly, incomprehensibly?

'Now see here.' He tries to sit, then stand: his legs act as though they belong to someone else – and he collapses back onto his stretcher. His head pounds, all peripheral vision is gone, he is hot, hot, hot.

It is four days since the Battalion arrived, and though this is an unprecedented period of overwhelming warfare, suddenly Alex cannot be with his men.

'I think I need … the Casualty Station,' he hears himself say to the form beside him, and is half dragged, half carried through several hundred yards of trenches, across sniper spots, past the sleeping, the dead, the alert; he reaches a fast-filling cleared area – muddy, but with a packed-earth base – that is the closest medical care. The orderly takes a quick look at Alex.

'It's another trench fever. Stick him over there, would you?' the orderly says to Alex's second, and he waves at a corner of the open-ended tent where there are any number of canvas stretchers with clean palliasses of ticking stuffed with straw, supporting four or five prone, still bodies. 'We'll move him back to Wimereux later today. Write his name and rank in the book over there, will you, on your way out?'

Aspirin brings down his fever, but Alex is still delirious as he is transported first to Wimereux for twelve hours, and then back across the Channel. As the grey waves buffet the ferry, he is certain his protector, his deliverer, Jim Williams, holds his hand – like the last time in the crater at Messines – and the solace is absolute.

'You're safe! Thank God,' Alex says to Williams, who is hovering in the air to Alex's left. He stretches his arm to touch Williams, his bony hand shaking.

'I was just going to say the same thing,' the spirit of Williams replies, and makes Alex smile.

One of the doctors nudges the other. 'Off with the birds, I'd say,' he says, twirling a finger at his temple. Alex catches sight of the gesture and Williams disappears. A sinking, heavy weight of lonely sadness settles throughout his body.

He is given a place on the ferry's deck because of his rank. The spring sunshine ought to be a comfort, and while it warms his bones after a month of mud and drizzle, his head starts its pounding again, as the sunlight hurts his eyes. He covers his eyes with his forearm. The other stretcher cases around him are in no fit state to chat, which suits Alex. The rough sea enables fractured, superficial sleep. In his disjointed dreams, there is his acolyte, his companion, Edward, muddied, bleeding; Alex hasn't the energy to feel hurt when his friend turns his back on him.

The English army hospital is in an old country house; it's not the same one he stayed in while recovering from the injury to his arm. That was nearly ten months ago; it seems like years. The ground floor of this building is essentially a rehabilitation dormitory for officers recovering from disease rather than trauma. It has a barracks feel, and the only medical person that visits is a busy nurse who calls a roll.

'Does anyone need to see the doctor today?' she shouts to the thirty men. 'No? Good. Anyone with a fever? Feeling unwell? Terrific. Alright, I'm off then; see you tomorrow,' and she dashes off to the more fraught wards, for dressing duty, where the work is concerned with healing stump wounds, and those holes that just won't mend in abdomens, chests and heads.

This illness exhausts the last morsel of reserves Alex has been calling on. Now his physical exhaustion is complete and coupled with a psychological destitution. He is a shell of his real self, his pre-war self. Though the English summer is emerging, there is none of the former joy that Alex might have found in the prettiness of the leaves, the liveliness of the birds and insects, the gentle airiness. Passchendaele and Villers-Bretonneux have done their worst. Most days, the men of Alex's ward find a spot in the sun and read, stare off into the distance or sleep. It is very quiet, no jollity or high-spirited antics. Most of the officers are British, some Scots, a Canadian and three or four Australians. They don't make friends, don't chat, don't discuss their experiences to date; the only time they make eye contact with each other is at the communal dining table with a request to pass the milk jug or the salt. This suits Alex's frame of mind: he's searching for his 'middle C', as he likes to think of it, and his need to return to it is a conscious activity. He seeks socially acceptable neutrality, even ambivalence, and he's good at it. His recent experiences are pushed down, not allowed to surface.

Occasionally one or another of the patients announces they are returning to the front.

'I'm off tomorrow, Patterson, back to the 41st.'

'Oh, righto then. Off early?'

'Trucks'll be here at 0700, I believe.'

'The 41st still at Amiens?'

'Yes. Yes.'

'Well … well, best of luck then. Won't be long before I'm off too, I suppose.'

But it takes all of May and June, even into July, before Alex's fevers cease to trouble him. Every night for eight weeks, he wakes in the early pre-dawn with his long, woollen underwear wet through with sweat. He lies still for a while, listening to the birds stirring with their exploratory tweets, a sound no longer heard in so much of northern France and Belgium. He recalls with sorrow that there are no trees left for the birds.

He is interviewed in mid-July by a superior officer and at its conclusion Alex has no idea if it went well. He is not sent back to the front and Alex is mildly troubled by it: did he give away his rocky mental state? He doesn't want to be known as a shirker or a failure. Instead, his orders are to return to Salisbury Plain. He is to complete a training course for those officers who will work with tanks and the Americans: both are present and essential to the Western Front battle arenas. The monstrous machines are awe-inspiring, and to Alex they are unnerving representations of the state of the world: huge, loud, cold, hard, unforgiving, unbeatable. The chunky, gurgling sound of them, the heavy smoke-fumes, the bone-rattling vibrations felt through the ground he stands on; it puts his teeth on edge. In the fields of southern England, charming outcrops of late-summer's wildflowers are churned over as the tanks are put through their paces for the Allied officers to see.

*

As they rush across the Hindenburg Line in October, Alex rejoins his men. They tell him what he missed, the colossal battle that took place at Villers-Bretonneux. The Australian troops – and his men – did well, and he congratulates them fulsomely, but quietly. He still can't look them in the eye.

'Bit of hush there, thank you. I have an announcement. Men of the Battalion, fellow soldiers, at 1100 tomorrow, the War is over.'

Subdued, Alex announces the end. The hundreds of men in his control stand in front of him on the sports oval of a village in central France. The village is intact – the buildings whole, civilians going about their daily life, cats and dogs, green grass and shrubs – making it all the more surreal for those whose usual sights are of desolation. It is overcast, there is a cold breeze; the men are dishevelled, unshaven, unkempt, relaxing off-duty. They stand in groups of three and four, arms crossed, slouching, disinterested. A lukewarm cheer is given.

'Right, then, a bit of housekeeping.' Alex explains the logistics of the next few weeks as he understands them. It takes a mere five minutes.

One soldier – he looks a little like Edward – crosses himself and the action catches Alex's eye. For a moment Alex is distracted, mid-announcement. He wonders how any man could still include God in his life after these torrid years. He cannot understand a faith that could withstand this war.

'Three cheers for our commander!' Alex's second in command proposes, and after the last hurrah, the troops move off.

At his conclusion, a few of the junior officers reservedly shake his hand and mouth expected responses – 'Well done, sir,' 'Good news, eh, sir?' – but he can tell they don't mean it and like him these men know the barbarity of mankind is eternal and omnipresent. The milk is spilt. The horse has bolted. Pandora's box is well and truly open.

There is no celebration, gloating, emotional outpouring: 11 November 1918, the day of the Armistice, is a fizzer.

After the Armistice, it is premature to go home, that dreamlike place, somewhere far away. Alex considers no other alternative except to work on, now with the 5th – and final –

Australian Division. Until mid-1919, he is in General Monash's inner circle, taking him to France and London. All around think him a diligent young man. They hope he will stay on in a permanent capacity in the Australian Army: but every night, the damage to his psyche emerges. His ritual goes like this: before he sleeps for his regular five hours, he curls up in a ball, trying to take up the smallest space possible. He closes his eyes as tight as he can and clamps his teeth together until his jaw hurts. He sees stars and his ears are so hot, they hurt. For half an hour, he is still, rigid. He taps his right thigh with his right index finger, metronomically, ten times, pause; ten times, pause. The pain in his joints takes over, forcing him free of his recent memories. He performs the self-imposed exorcism each night, and sometimes when it gets bad, twice a night. His ability to block emotion is finely honed.

CHAPTER EIGHTEEN

EDWARD'S RETURN

In early 1919, Edward is met on his return from Europe at the Sydney wharf by a family group so numerous it requires three wagons to transport them all. There is laughter and happy tears until Edward begins to shake and his gaunt face becomes fixed in a pained rictus.

'Mummy,' whispers the twenty-three-year-old returned soldier as he is shepherded from the wharf by his mother, like a small child unfit to care for himself. 'I tried. Really, I tried.'

'Tried? Tried to what, darling?' His mother is taken aback but recovers to soothe him. 'Whatever's the matter …? Everything is alright now … there, there, dear, shhhhh.' Her taffeta outfit rustles and creaks, her enormous feathered hat rocks as she comforts her overwhelmed boy, her defeated child.

During the first months of his recovery, Edward's mother never instructs him. She never insists that he come downstairs and join the family for dinner. She never asks him to get out of bed, dress and have tea with her. Each morning at nine, she knocks on his bedroom door, waits for his permission to enter, sits on the side of his bed and addresses the lump under the sheets and blankets and eiderdown. She describes the rainy weather, the four puppies just born to the family's new beagle, and she recounts the latest community mishap, such as the ferry's unfortunate argument with the quay, causing all kinds of havoc to the Manly day-trippers. Edward's foetal position unfurls, and he replies briefly in not much more than monosyllables. One day he reaches for her hand and holds it loosely for the balance of his mother's visit. She saves her tears for when she can close the door of her sitting room, and then she weeps for all her sons, their losses: family, friends, health, happiness. There is a lot to grieve.

Then, while soft autumn lingers, Edward chooses to spend several hours each day in the eyrie, a small space at the top of the 'tower', an overly grand name for the little room at the apex of the house. There he opens the shutters and sits in the window space, catches the warmth of the sunshine on the mostly fine days, or watches as storms roll in from the Pacific Ocean. He hears the squalls' gusts and the correspondingly larger waves crash onto the nearby beach. He takes a book to the tower but scarcely opens it, and a scrap of cake or bread and jam, with a ubiquitous cup of tea. At mealtimes, rain or shine, though the family is around the dining table, he still prefers to sit outside, on the edge of the back veranda, and he drinks his strong, dark-brown tea in a rose-painted teacup, with the head of a soft-furred dog in his cupped palm.

During a mild winter, Edward ventures out to take the air along the Corso. He recovers sufficiently to take himself out each day, all day. His mother does not ask where he goes.

'You could find yourself a delicious lunch somewhere nice.'

Ed takes the money she offers and he can produce a tentative smile of thanks in response.

He walks and walks, on the beaches, the headland, the bushland, his head full of inanities. He is entertained by a kind of intellectual pursuit: he tramps all day till his feet are sore as he muses on the equity of heroism. Every poem and story written about the terrible ordeal of the War seems to him to be concerned with 'heroes' and 'heroism'. Edward has difficulty reconciling what is said with his experience.

'Am I a hero too?' he poses, but it fills him with disgust. 'Poppycock.'

But every speech made, every painting executed, every monument dedication appears to be narrowly focussing on the 'sacrifice' and 'bravery' of the 'valiant' dead.

Was I not just as gallant? Can gallantry be quantified, identified, as though it can be bottled, preserved? What is courage anyway? He suspects that the glamorising of soldiery is done by those who did not take part. He is troubled by the falsity, the nonsense that is emerging as truth.

We all just did what we had to.

Edward reads in the newspaper that one place in Australia produced more Victoria Cross Medal recipients than any other: the Strathbogie valley in Victoria. It is suggested that this place fosters bravery to an inordinate level: 'the very air is superior by all accounts'. In spring, Ed reaches a plan. He will travel to the valley, only a couple of hours from Melbourne, and see for himself what it is that made these men 'great'.

Greater than myself?

He stews on the dilemma without rancour or envy, but he is troubled that he is not one of them, one of the VC recipients, but perhaps, he reasons, that's alright. He's starting to believe he is, and will be, alright. As his limbs feel looser and his stride extends, life – living – is beginning to seem imaginable, easier. His lungs fill and empty fully and his sighs are less frequent; instead of fraught, they are a release. He is alive; others are not. This fills him with neither joy nor despair.

Now his ribs stretch gratifyingly from his sternum as he unfolds at dawn from a less troubled night's sleep – his nightmares are keeping to a minimum. The silhouette of Jim Williams in Ploegsteert Wood continues to hover. In one dream, Williams reminds him of all that he has not achieved, will not ever achieve. The reminder is not malicious, but fills Edward with regret, not only for his failures, but because in his dreams he never seems to get where he's going, finish what he's doing, complete all he has to say. Jim Williams judges him in sorrow.

Edward's surviving three brothers are all now returned and in varying states of disability. Two were wounded: Jeremy lost a leg at the knee, and Nick walks bent forward. The flesh covering Nick's abdomen healed too tight, and the white bands of scar tissue disallow free movement. When he can stand it, the doctors will release the strictures and adhesions. The one brother who returned without overt injury, John, is arguably the most damaged, and he stays in his room day and night, silent and uncommunicative. His mind is paralysed. When pushed by the family doctor, this former golden child weeps and sobs, immune to his mother's physical comfort and his childhood home's shelter.

Edward and his brothers move around each other with care; they never discuss their individual experiences, never share a battalion tale, never swap war stories. They never mention the dead brother, Andrew. This silence is permanent. Each of them knows too much about the others' state of mind.

In the spirit of adventure, Jeremy elects to travel with Edward to the Strathbogie valley. The two brothers are close – in age, appearance, and when they were boys, especially as friends. They will find the families of the VC recipients: Leslie Maygar, Fred Tubb and Alex Burton. They will view the countryside that nurtured these bravest of men. They set out on a glorious day: bright-white cumulonimbus clouds explode in the sky over the harbour as the Manly ferry takes them to the centre of Sydney. It's an omnibus to the Central Station and they settle on a train heading south for Melbourne. They alight in Euroa, a lively, small town, sited around the pretty waterway of Seven Creeks, an eventual tributary of the sizeable Goulburn River. Surrounded by perfect green-grassy land, raising fat sheep for their world-class wool, the community is well-off compared to many other Australian towns in 1919. Food and water in abundance, commerce is thriving as this major railway stop is an important moment in travel and distribution between Melbourne and New South Wales.

One of the schoolteachers in Euroa is Michael Kelly, a distant cousin of Edward and Jeremy's. As the train slows into the station, they are on the look-out for a one-armed fellow, with burn scars on his face: there is Michael, on the dusty, tamped-earth platform – diminutive, in an oversized black suit jacket, the left sleeve pinned but still flapping about. They greet their relative with polite conventionality, but by sunset, as they sit on the veranda of Michael's neat, one-roomed work-er's cottage, and with a few bottles of dark, local beer between them, a familial ease develops.

'I lost my arm on the Somme in July '16. My sleeve caught fire at Fromelles. I was home by Christmas.' Michael begins delicately; his is a quiet voice, unwavering, able to convey his steadfastness.

There are a few moments of uncomfortable silence.

Edward clears his throat, then matches Michael's conver-sational gambit.

'I didn't arrive in France until late 1916. I flew a 'plane for the last months, a biplane. Quite an experience.'

Jeremy feels he must contribute to be polite, sociable.

'I scrubbed out during the Passchendaele push. You know, the end of 1917. The crutches … I can't roam about as I'd like.'

An awkward silence between them is broken by Michael. 'Well, I'll put on our supper then. Mutton chops and peas do you?'

They sleep well, the brothers on the cottage floor. Jeremy uses Michael's swag and Edward makes do with several blankets beneath and on top of him. Breakfast is strong black tea, plus fresh brown bread from the bakery, not four doors away, topped with local golden butter and aromatic honey. That afternoon the Euroa versus Nagambie football game is a mock-ferocious riot of young and old bodies. Those aged in-between are absent, mostly dead, their bodies in the dirt of Europe, Turkey or northern Africa; or they're incapacitated, with their damaged bodies on the sidelines with crutches, jerry-built wheelchairs or empty sleeves. Euroa wins by a goal and a behind, and by 5 p.m., the three men and much of Euroa's male population pass under the florid sprays of cast-iron lace surrounding the street-level veranda and upper balcony of the Seven Creeks Hotel. When they reach the bar, Michael and Edward place one foot each on the steel footrest and lean on the bar's chrome piping; Jeremy finds a home on a barstool. Edward and Jeremy are more at ease than for several years, and as the crowd swells, diminishes, swells and diminishes through the late afternoon and evening, they seek from the locals the background stories of the three VC recipients of whom Euroa is so very proud.

Leslie Maygar's portrait is on the bar wall, a hand-tinted photo. He is sporting a flamboyant moustache.

'Yes, that's him, God rest his soul.' The publican warms to his role as storyteller. 'He won his VC in the Boer War, but then served at Gallipoli and in Egypt. He died there; it was in the Battle of Beersheba, in 1917. He was an officer in the army, but a farmer before he left Euroa. He owned land with his father and brothers not thirty miles from here. Aw, jeez, he was a mountain of a man.'

'And Fred Tubb or Alex Burton, do you know those fellows?' Edward enquires.

'Ah, Fred.' The publican finds it more difficult to speak of him. 'He was a cousin of mine, another farmer – his land's just out of town – and an officer.' There is a bit of hush around the small group; one of the other barmen has limped up to put a hand on the publican's shoulder. 'He got his VC for his action at Gallipoli. He died at Passchendaele.'

That seems to be the limit of the publican's ability to hold his tears back; it is all that can be said of Fred Tubb just at that moment. Edward and Michael glance at Jeremy, who replies with a quick shake of the head. No, there is no way Jeremy is going to pipe up, 'I was at Passchendaele too.' There are things you just don't offer up at certain moments, when someone reveals they lost a friend or relative, and you didn't die with them.

The second barman volunteers to tell the out-of-towners about Alex Burton.

'Al was a great bloke, an ironmonger, up the road in Miller's outfit. Not an officer, mind you, but you'd trust him with your life, you would. He died at Lone Pine. They took the

Turks on, flat out, and won for a while.' All eyes downcast, a momentary lament. Then back to the business at hand.

'So, ah, refill, fellas?'

*

The next day is a Sunday and Michael borrows a buggy pulled by a small bay pony who lifts her tidy hooves with enthusiasm, and the three men share it. There *is* something about this place, an allusive energy, an invisible flow of goodwill. They roam between Avenel and Nagambie, and finally find themselves brewing billy tea on a low ridge of the Strathbogie Ranges, looking back toward the township of Euroa. They are seated on granite rocks that protrude from the hillside as though determined to assert their stony authority. There's a light breeze and a pinking sky.

'I've been thinking about the Victoria Cross fellas: two out of three of them were farmers, and the third one grew up on a farm but was living in town when he joined up. It strikes me that farming is the magic ingredient. It seems to me that the atmosphere of the land gave Maygar, Tubb and Burton the ability to be VC heroes. And I reckon we three, we should give farming a go, here in this beautiful valley.'

Jeremy and Michael both turn to stare at Edward; startled, but for slightly different reasons.

Jeremy's face twists. 'Give a man a chance, Edward. How the hell could I join in? I've only got one bloody leg.'

'You'd be a great help, Jeremy. I know you'd do your share, somehow, anyhow.'

'And me, Edward? I have nothing, no money, no bloody arm.'

Edward barks a seldom-heard laugh, and with a surge of bitterness, says, 'You're like a couple of old bloody chooks! We'll be able … we'll work together. You'll see. We can do something … make something … prove … well, together. We've got to try.'

They return to the township by the light of what seems to be a particularly bright half-moon. The infectious but fragile nervous energy that comes from Edward's idea inspires the others not just to consider the notion, but to have the three of them make plans for the rest of the night and through the following day.

*

To all intents and purposes, Edward is a recovered man. He builds a good life, productive and stable, in the green valley of the Goulburn River – but he never forgives himself. His is a self-imposed culpability: he did not seek and did not find Alex's saviour or stay in touch with Alex. Over the years, by guilt's stealth, he arrives at the delusion that he is somehow negligent of his responsibility for both Alex's welfare and Jim Williams's fate. In the quiet night, when there is no sound from the omnipresent birds or from the sheep and horses in the home paddock, he experiences a sinking feeling in his gut, reminding him of his failures. He sees again Alex's greasy, sweaty face against the dirty calico sheets of the hospital in Wimereux; he smells again the hospital's metallic wet odour of blood, the back-lane stink of urine and infection. He hears again the soft groans and muffled sleeping and stirring noises of the crowded tent ward. He feels small and useless and must get out of his farmhouse bed, pull on his boots and walk around in the dawn light until his heart stops beating so. He knows these are stupid pictures to hang on to: how was he to prevent Alex being injured? There were lots of injured soldiers. Alex was just one more, wasn't he? And surely, he couldn't have found Williams even if he'd tried?

In the day's bright sunlight, when the past's haunting images have dissolved, Edward, Jeremy and Michael work hard and run sheep competently at their property for several years. But Michael dies suddenly from pneumonia. The doctor says the gas of the War contributed to his condition. Jeremy and Edward mourn intensely, but silently, privately. It's yet another death, and grief is cumulative. Edward's night-wandering is as bad as ever.

Jeremy marries a local lass; it's not much of a coincidence that she's a sister to one of the VC recipients that brought Jeremy and Edward to the town in the first place. It is a good match. With his stump constantly aching and his good leg overworked on the farm, Jeremy is persuaded to take up a role in the township, that of assistant manager of the local branch of the State Savings Bank of Victoria. He dons a tweed suit and a starched collar, and leaves Edward to run the property alone.

Edward marries at thirty in 1927. The bride, Edith, is in modish white satin with a train. The wedding day photographs show Edward's hair thinning a little and that he has retained the moustache he first grew in Flanders. He seems a little wooden in the poses contrived by the photographer. Some of the male members of the wedding party flinch when the camera's flash bursts noisily with a crump like the sound of a shell landing at a distance.

Their first child arrives in 1930, a boy followed by two girls, four years apart. The lengthy gaps between the children reflect Edward's conflict – he keeps his desire in check. By doing so he can contain his sense of unravelling, of his life draining from him. If he can dampen any affectionate outbursts, he will preserve his hard-won life energy. Control is the key; with control he keeps his memories at bay – the smell of warm blood, the screams of the injured, the nausea of air pockets.

*

'Don't you love me?' Edith asks as they lie under the satin eiderdown, not touching, staring at the ceiling. The full moon's white light streams through the window. She is confused: has she done something wrong? She'd tried to move in the right way, say loving things; she had even followed her mother's advice about perfume, undergarments and hairstyles.

A petulant, defensive tone creeps into her plaintive query. 'Am I not good enough?'

She holds her breath, but breaks and has to beg.

'Please, Eddie, answer me.'

He remains quite still, glowering. He feels angry to be put on the spot. He's unable to answer this impossible question; all seems so hopeless. Even in the daylight, when the world ought to make sense, let alone when the wind is up and he can hear the windmill in the home paddock churning at high speed like the whirring of flying shrapnel, he still has no explanation, no excuse, no way to make things right.

'Ed, your silence is … well, it's just cruel.' She turns to face away from him.

She must accept his will.

*

At the outbreak of the Second World War, Edward is reed thin, drinking excessively, and isolates himself from his family more and more. He is short-tempered and barks orders to stock-men and farmhands. His fears are resurgent. His marriage of twelve years and the chaos of three children is confining, confounding. His night-waking is on the increase again. He jolts to upright with the sound of his own groaning; the bed is sodden with the sweat of his nightmares. In 1941, at forty-four, he feels compelled to join up again, to rectify his mistakes. He is ashamed to know that he is seeking his second chance at heroism – but he does not share that sentiment with anyone, hardly faces it himself. He is fit enough; the farming life has enabled him to stay strong.

Edward's leadership position in the 2nd AIF takes him to Singapore, then to a prisoner-of-war camp at Changi jail, and ultimately to the Burma railway, where the burden of respon-sibility for a battalion of young men plagues him for three long and grinding years of imprisonment marked by fear, scarcity and dispossession. Where the jungle flows into the river, on a flat rectangle of compacted clay, a little over a thousand men – Major Edward Fitzgerald's men – endure each long day and each long night of sad deprivation.

Among these men, on this unholy stage, Edward is tested again. Day after day he turns over and over in his mind his obsession: how to bring order to chaos in a place bereft of definition. There are no borders to the camp, no limits to the spread of bodies, no walls to speak of, no personal mitigation besides impossible individual force and unobtainable self-possession. Nothing shifts the thoughts of this terrible place, these tortured men, from his mind. There is no space – even if there was an inclination – for Edward to hope. And he is angry. He is offended by the careless brutality of his captors. If he could have, he would have sobbed like a child.

Edward is aware of his runaway dread and that he is unable to control it. His men see this in his irritability, his shallow breathing, his sudden shouts, his red-faced fury when dealing with some infraction. When officiating at the many burials, the gravediggers hear his voice, harsh with constraint; see his face stiffly held in what he hopes passes for composure. Every time – and there are many occasions – Edward thinks of his first funeral service, that of Thomas Joseph Quigley. Now, in the jungles of Thailand, half a world away and half a lifetime later, how is this any different – the waste, the profligacy of the soldiers' deaths? He departs speedily from the grave sites, head down, tripping over protruding roots, in his laceless, worn boots.

Once – and only once – does he voice his illogical anger, in a moonlit exchange on the banks of the Kwai, some distance from the others. The major he addresses is a person of equal rank, a respected leader of another large prisoner group. As the big man is silhouetted and sitting stooped on a log in the half-light, Edward sees a shape, the spectre of a man resembling Jim Williams in a startling return to that night in the wood almost thirty years before. By that illusory shadow, he sees a chance to be comforted, protected, made whole. Could this man do for him what Williams did for Alex? Give him hope? Succour?

'Now, then, Ed, you don't seem well. Tell me, what's troubling you?' The question is posed in a general way, the other officer – a compassionate man – fishing for a way to help Edward. He's noticed, as have the men, that Major Edward Fitzgerald is struggling. 'I know the obvious' – he smiles a little – 'but you ... er ... is there something specific I can help with.'

Edward drops his guard, the caution of twenty-five years.

'This war ... is not ... gentlemanly.' Edward's voice trembles and breaks. His violent antipathy escapes him. 'The Nips, they're animals, all grunts and ... hands like paws ...' – he kneads the swollen joints of his hands – '... putrid, their foul mouths and mucus ... I'm frightened, frightened.'

His face contorts in a grimace, white foam at the corners of his mouth. The other man listens, his face fixed, head lowered and to one side; he allows Edward to let off some steam.

'Every death, every bashing, every injury, wound or lost limb … it is my fault; this appalling disaster is my fault. I only ever wanted to be a good officer, a strong man …'

Pushing through a tight, constricted throat, Edward enunciates each syllable with a laboured precision: he will not miss an anguished detail of his confession.

'… honourable, brave, a leader of men … a bloody hero.'

All those years protecting, damming, curating his fear, his terror, his grief, his sadness, account for nothing and his agony pours forth.

'They … the bastards … spit great gobs of phlegm … disgusting. The sweat on their hides stink … It's not right, not right, I tell you. I'm … I'm scared.' His voice has risen to a querulous, hysterical high pitch. His wide eyes stare at the embers of the small fire in front of them.

This is out of hand by any measure; the big man cuts him off with a gruff almost-order.

'Be careful, Fitzgerald. You're giving in to their … their way: you're giving up. We are civilised, we are dignified. You can't speak like that, Ed, you can't think like that. You just can't.' He puts his big hand on Edward's shoulder and grasps it tight. 'We'll get through this, Ed.'

'Perhaps that's what gives me the greatest fear,' Edward hisses in a whisper. 'What will we be if we survive? If we have to fight like … like animals? What will we become? Like them?'

'Get some sleep, Ed. Go on, get some rest.'

Edward is still, quiet, then quite suddenly he breathes in, gasps, open-mouthed. He gets to his feet. With a guilty expression, he looks at his confessor; now he is awkward, aware, and mortified to have revealed his underbelly. He turns and staggers away.

*

When the ghastly Pacific War is over and the camps are liberated, Edward's freedom, his return to Australia, completes his suffering: he is guilty of the worst misdemeanour – surviving. The last child of Edward and Edith Fitzgerald is born in 1946; this is Eric, Dominic's father, the result of the last act of intimacy that Edward can muster. He is impotent for the rest of his life.

'I am not brave. I saved no one. I am truly a failure.' He mutters this or a version of it annually, each Anzac Day, deep in his cups. No one hears this, or anything like it, until one day he drops his guard and starts to tell his grandson. When he sees young Dominic's confused face fall, he stops just in time: he doesn't make a fool of himself again.

CHAPTER NINETEEN

ALEX AT HOME

'Eila, dear, Mother's gone. I'll have Raoul run for Dr Miller. There, there, dear, she is at peace.' Alex holds the sobbing Eila and they both stare at their mother's slumped, plump body in her worn-velvet armchair in the bay window of the 'front room'.

'She always said the dropsy would take her in the end. Oooooh, what will become of me? What will we do?'

'How about you make us all a cup of tea then, eh?' Leslie, a kind brother, knows the remedy for Eila's theatrics – keep her busy. 'Come on then, I'll help.'

It's a cold winter's evening and Alex has only been back in Melbourne a short time. His homecoming was subdued. Those who never left the country during the War feel they have completed the welcome home to the returning soldiers that is decently required of them, and now, well, that's enough. Of course, Alex's siblings are overjoyed at his arrival; they've not seen nor hardly heard from him for more than four years. Still, Alex concludes that even they have moved on from the War and its meaning. For his part, Melbourne is overwhelmingly stolid:

the unharmed buildings, the long rows of green, green trees, the orderly gardens, the intact infrastructure, and scarcely, to his eye, an amputee or uniform to be seen. He somewhat reluctantly sheds his own khaki, made uncomfortable by what it reminds others of. Yet civilian clothes are uncomfortable too for reasons he does not understand. He doesn't know who he is and what he is supposed to be doing at any moment of the day. His conflicts, his emotions, lie like eels in a pond, camouflaged, mostly still, ugly.

His mother takes with her to her grave any regard she had for her eldest son. She had almost entirely ignored him on his return. Alex assumed that for her to admit her weaknesses – that she had missed him, worried about him – was a bridge too far. Perhaps in a state of relief, on his safe return, Alex's mother gave up her fight to stay alive, if only to spite her children.

Unusual for a wife at this time, Jean leaves a will and Alex is the executor. The local solicitor advises Alex that Jean has left Alexander Senior everything, which only amounts to her paltry personal possessions. More importantly to Jean, in making this legal, formal, humiliating document when death has ultimately parted them, she has left her husband a reminder that at least one of them had done their marital duty.

Alex's father must be found and notified. Alex hires a private detective and writes to his father in late December 1919. Some months later a letter addressed to 'A. Patterson, Poste Restante Cairns, Queensland' reaches the sought-after man:

Dear Father

I write to inform you of Mother's passing in September of this year. You are nominated as the beneficiary of her will. Are you able to attend the offices of Mr. J. Phillips, of Phillips, Phillips and Greene, 231 Ferrie Road, Hawthorn, for the purposes of completion in this matter?

Mother is buried at the Kew Cemetery.

Yours sincerely

Alexander Twigg-Patterson

After more than a decade of troubled times and with so much dark and dirty water under the world's bridge – Alex is required to make an adult son's peace with this man. His unconscious wish never again to have to deal with his father, this stranger, tests his resilience, his capacity for tolerating weakness in others. He doesn't particularly like this trait. Sometimes he wishes he could feel anger, act on it, punish idlers, bullies and the self-indulgent. Perhaps his tendency to please, forgive, accept was honed when dealing with his mother's narcissism. As a child he'd thoroughly absorbed the Victorian maxim:

Life is mostly froth and bubble;
Two things stand like stone:
Kindness in another's trouble,
Courage in your own.

Alexander Senior arrives in Melbourne six weeks later. He is thin; his worn clothing hangs from bony shoulders. His grey skin is greasy, perhaps because of some unidentified, low-grade illness or a lack of thorough washing. He smells a little: a liverish odour. His children have difficulty looking him in the eye, and he is pitiable, humble and quiet as he takes his place as a grieving widower, sleeping in the marital bed again – in Jean's bed – in the room that has not been touched, let alone occupied, since her death.

Eila sleeps in the only other bedroom, while the three brothers share the sleepout, an enclosed veranda at the side of the timber house. None of them has chosen a spouse, and Eila lost her only marriage prospect in the Battle of the Somme.

Mr Phillips, the solicitor, is decorous as he describes the legacy to Alexander Senior in Alex's presence.

'Mr Patterson, as the marriage was never concluded, by divorce or annulment, nor by any other avenue, Mrs Twigg-Patterson did not *own* anything in her own right, except her personal possessions, her jewellery, her clothing. Indeed, Mr Patterson, you own the residence, the family home, at 1 Millicent Street, Kew, its furniture and chattels.'

The solicitor falls silent briefly, allowing the information to be absorbed while the grandfather clock in the corner of the office audibly tick-tocks some sixty times. He isn't quite sure that Mr Patterson is the same man who disappeared all those years ago – not literally, it is just that Mr Patterson doesn't seem to hear or understand what is being said. It is as though the man is a little simple.

'Have you any questions then, sir?' Phillips uses a slightly raised voice. Perhaps Patterson has become a little hard of hearing. Tick-tock. Tick-tock.

'Ah, no. Ah … no,' Mr Patterson says, clearing his throat with an empty sniff.

'Well then, we can conclude. I assure you the major asset never left your possession and is in your exclusive control.'

*

Alex finds he's unsettled. Is it the awkwardness of his father's presence? It is a new phenomenon and not well understood. His thoughts move on to Lottie, a distraction, perhaps: but he said that he'd see her after the war; he ought to keep his word. He chooses to ignore her lack of reply to his letter of late 1917 and imagines she'll be pleased to meet him again, as a friend or as a … what? A chum, perhaps.

Alex writes to the Reverend Brown.

Dear Sir

I recall with much fondness the kindness and hospitality your family showed me in 1916.

I am travelling to Brisbane on family business in early May and ask that I might visit your home again.

I look forward to your response.

Alex is not bold enough to ask after Lottie, but the letter contains a lie: he has no family business in Brisbane.

The reply does not confirm Lottie's presence – nor absence, it must be said – there at the rectory. In a flare of optimism, Alex assumes the best and sets off on the long, arduous, three-night train journey from Melbourne to Brisbane.

Four full years since he was last there, Alex knocks on the front door of the manse of the Kenmore Presbyterian Church. Its chintz-covered sofas in the front room can be seen through the window from the street, just as they were in 1916. The manse maid shows Alex into this room, bobs a curtsy, and shortly after, the Reverend Brown joins him, all wringing hands and dripping red nose. Inevitably, the clichés begin, those that serve as polite conversation concerning the War.

'We prayed for your safekeeping against the terrible Hun. And we prayed for all the gallant young men who sacrificed their lives for our delivery from the Germanic monsters.' The mucus drip wobbles. 'And I have thanked our gracious God for your return.'

Alex's thoughts fly through his mind and skitter across his face. *How does he manage to make it sound like I should still be there, six bloody feet under? As though* God *allowed my return, such an obliging, polite deity.*

Alex is not particularly good at this contemporary dance between returned soldiers and civilians. Good manners require him to maintain a slightly forlorn poker face. He is supposed to feel and display reasonable, but not excessive, grief for the sixty thousand fellow Australians who died. Little do odious gentlemen such as the Reverend Brown know that

the abiding grief is so immense that the socially appropriate
face is a parody of the true discoloration of Alex's character.

'Ah, yes ... well, thank you for your prayers.' Alex blushes
with the effort of civility.

But for the maid and the large tortoiseshell Persian cat
purring from its throne on the reverend's knees, it seems they
are alone in the house, and Alex must engage in polite subter-
fuge to gauge Lottie's whereabouts. He begins by asking after
Mrs Brown.

'Oh dear, oh dear, God rest her soul. Mrs Brown
succumbed to pneumonia in the winter of 1917. It was 7 June
that God required her company. And do you recall my poor
orphaned ward, Lottie? You'll not have heard of Lottie's
untimely demise. How could you have? A dog bite led to a
ghastly infection. Horrible, horrible. She lingered for eight
days: fevers, grinding her teeth.' The reverend shakes himself
theatrically, but the drip on the end of his nose remains.
'She's buried next to my wife in the cemetery.' He indi-
cates beyond the small window of the front room and Alex
recalls the higgledy-piggledy gravestones of the town's burial
ground, naked without the ubiquitous tropical undergrowth
of Queensland or any of the big native trees: the Moreton Bay
figs, eucalypts and wattles.

Alex's fortitude melts, his face collapses, beyond his
control. The sides of his mouth turn down, his eyebrows rise
and eyes widen. The random sorrow of it, Lottie's suffering –
so alive in his memory, a life force. He has been relying on his

meeting her again more than he thought. Had he hoped she'd restore his equilibrium? Love him through his troubles? Save him from despair by her lust and vigour? Had he seen her as the midwife to his rebirth – someone to make him cry, make him breathe, make him live again?

'My dear man, are you alright there?'

Alex composes his features and spends an agonising twenty-four hours in the Reverend Brown's company pretending. He travels three more nights on his train journey home, a solitary man. Quite out of the blue, he thinks of Edward; he discovers he would quite like to have shared his pain with him. The realisation makes him laugh out loud in the rocking carriage, so accidental is the rather poignant memory of his friend, his companion – when it is so very important to have one.

*

Over the next couple of years, the male children leave the reoccupied family home: Raoul to marry a nice lass, Leslie to become a missionary in Fiji, and Alex to farm. Eila remains a financial captive of her father for the rest of his life: a companion, a nurse, the maid, a slave.

The soldier-settlement schemes are in full swing and Alex formally requests acreage near the tiny town of Mortlake, Victoria. Mortlake, in the Western District, has a wild and often stormy coastline, with swells rolling in from the squalls and gusts of the Roaring Forties, and where, Alex imagines, the wind will blow away his 'cobwebs'. The area is famous for its supply of bluestone, on display in the old buildings already there in the tiny township of Mortlake when Alex arrives in the early 1920s. He is thirty-three years old. In keeping with his age, weariness and breathing difficulties, he slowly builds a one-room, bluestone dwelling on his land, plants a hedge of rosemary around its perimeter, and stocks the few acres with dairy cows. They seem sufficiently placid to him, manageable: he knows so little about farming that he believes that gentle animals would be best for his abilities and enterprise.

During this long and lonely period, two dates emerge as triggers to haunting war recollections: 7 June and 11 November. In June, when the icy wind of the Great Australian Bight roars past his shack, he thinks of Edward, his happy face and infectious laugh. Alex wonders where he ended up, if he's well, if he made it through. In tandem, he hears the battlefields, his arm aches with hindsight, and he feels nervous, unmanly, childish, reduced by this reaction. But in November, when the other ex-soldiers of the area ask him to come to the hotel to spend the day drinking and recollecting, Alex learns that he must stay close to home. On this day, his thoughts of Jim Williams spear his gut – irrational, silly, uncontrollable. Alex wants to weep, leaning his head against his milkers in the morning and night sessions, for the misery of his loss, for the joy he might have uncovered if he could have known the man. The memory of Jim Williams is now an ideal; he represents noble men, leaders, mates, unattainable qualities for the imperfect, and Alex feels their absence in his life.

He meets a young local woman at a Christian Friendship meeting. Her name is Cressida, and he finds that he likes her enormously – her physical solidness, her quiet assuredness. It's enough for this day and age to inspire a proposal of marriage. They marry in 1935 when Alex is forty-four years old. His son James is born in 1937 and the child is always known for his 'chesty' condition. They are alike, but the son fusses and whines, though he hasn't earned the right, whereas Alex wears his troubles gently.

Alex's daughter is born in 1938 and is the apple of his eye. He doubts life has ever been more wonderfully manifest, and he tells her so every day. He desperately wants to give her a French name but ultimately the christening proceeds, under Cressida's instruction, with the local reverend pronouncing her name as Mary Eliza Twigg-Patterson. Alex always calls her Marie in benign defiance.

*

One day, Mary, as a nine-year-old, is neglectful of her chores: she was to have let the cows through the gate from the home paddock to the milking yards and commence the milking. It is a job Alex would normally do, but he has had to go to town. Several hours later, Alex returns home and can hear the cows' distressed mooing, trumpeting their disquiet as he turns the van's engine off. Mary hears the van and remembers her undone chore: now she is sure she'll cop it, get a hiding with the leather strap – her mother keeps the two children on the straight and narrow with a belting when she feels they need it. Alex takes Mary aside.

'Darling, the cows are very unhappy.' He takes her hand. 'Why didn't you look after them?'

'I just forgot, Dad, I just forgot.' Her pixie face crumples.

'Poor, dear cows. Let's go and comfort them?' He places his free hand on her soft, bronze child-hair, a blessing, a forgiving.

As he moves off toward the cows, Mary bursts into tears.

'Why are you so nice to me, Daddy? I made the cows sad.' She wails in shame.

'Well, darling, it's not for me to chastise you; you'll be miserable enough about the cows without me adding to it. I don't think you'll ever forget them again, will you? Come here, love, and give me a hug. We'll make it up to these dear creatures.'

More than gracious, more than forgiving, almost subservient, for the rest of his life Alex is not riled, nor driven, nor angry. But he's not a saint, and Alex cannot help but occasionally compare Cressida and Lottie. Lottie is, after all, the only other woman with whom he shared that most intimate of moments – of congress, of skin, of vulnerability. Even he knows the comparison is not real; idealised-Lottie has become a bonnie, kind-hearted young woman who adores him. He catches a glimpse in his mind's eye of her inner thigh and feels a little troubled at this lust, shocking to his own sense of self. Over the years, he has eradicated the remnants of humiliation, the sense of rejection. He never thinks of her as loose, nor immoral for giving herself to him so generously. He can't imagine licentiousness in someone who showed him love and loving.

Cressida, of course, suffers from familiarity in the comparison, especially as the years go by. Child-bearing, old age, poverty and working as a dairyman's wife leads to incontinence, bleeding, sagging dry skin all over, rotten teeth. After a few minutes of self-assessment, it is hard for Cressida to see just what is left of the strong young woman who followed Alex to the windswept, rain-drenched, isolated farm. Sometimes she sheds a tear or two for what she might have achieved. It is just as much of a delusion as Alex's dreaming: better left alone. She senses his occasional wave of disappointment that laps at the shore of their marriage, but it is rare enough. She knows Alex well; she understands his need to reconcile what *is* with what *might* have been.

'We all do it sometimes,' she justifies, while leaning over the steaming copper, scrubbing and pummelling the weekly wash. 'And anyway, he's a dear old thing.'

*

When it comes around, Alex is too old to serve in the Second World War. He doesn't consider it for a moment; indeed, he rather ignores the War's news. And he is unwell: his lungs give him merry hell and the local doctor says they'll never improve. As for his left arm, it aches on good days, and with activity there is a grinding sensation under the skin as though bone rubs on bone. For a few days of each month, he grimaces with the shooting nerve pain. He rubs his upper left arm with his right hand, and sometimes he resorts to aspirin. Alex hides his pain and the arm's imperfections from Cressida, Mary and James.

The farm fails. Alex is not unhappy; there are many other returned soldiers around him in the district who are also struggling, each with his own problems. Sometimes, a farm's failure is just a sad fizzle of incompetence or drunkenness or suicide. The Twigg-Patterson family abandons the farm and moves to Manly in the 1950s, where it's a comfort to Cressida to be near her sister. And though he is too old and frail to be lumping the heavy machines from door to door, Alex turns his hand to selling vacuum cleaners. It is not a success. He has no care or ability to close a sale and spends much of his day drinking tea with the lady of the house, bringing comfort by listening to her observations and worries. He remains mum about his war experiences, and anyway, people have stopped asking him about it; anyone under thirty years of age has, of course, no memory of those times and certainly no interest. That's fine with Alex. He doesn't dwell on it either, except perhaps when his breathing is very bad, or his cough exhausts him. It is then that tears of grief and loss make his eyes swim. The small voice in his head declares, 'It is all too bloody sad, such a bloody waste.'

When she has lived long enough to see her first grandchild born, in 1960, Cressida dies. She was asleep beside Alex when she took her last breath. He is not distraught, knowing it was a gentle death for her, and he's been grieving since 1917. It has become a permanent, gentle state, that of letting others go, letting everyone go. He's been practising this state twice a year, every year, when he says an introspective hello and goodbye to Edward Fitzgerald and to Jim Williams with memories of Ploegsteert Wood, and then again with the public outpourings of Anzac Day. He is not irredeemably attached, connected, to anyone. He knows cognitively that death comes to all – but he can *feel* it, just beyond his tacit reality.

Cressida's death heralds his permanent withdrawal; he only sees his immediate family now. He lives with his daughter, son-in-law and grandchildren, spending all day, every day, pottering in the shed and in the backyard tending the vegetable patch. It means a lot to him to plant seeds, nurture seedlings, replant, protect and finally reap a crop. The family is well supplied in all the basics: potatoes, pumpkins, beans, peas, and in summer there are stone fruits, which Mary bottles. His speciality is sweet, luscious strawberries – the trick is to keep them well watered – and the grandchildren love him for it. He sees his son when he visits – it's not often – but it's good to know James is doing satisfactorily in real estate, though James's asthma troubles him.

Alex wants to die at home but his daughter panics when he stops breathing at the kitchen table. It is 5 p.m. on a Sydney-grey winter's day. Alex's cold has lingered as a cough for weeks. He is acutely aware of being a burden to his family, so much so that he wishes for his own death weeks before it comes about. Again, he does not grieve prospectively for his own life in those final weeks; that grieving took place after the Battle of Messines. His familiarity with near-death and death – his own, his friends', his Cressida's, his colleagues', his troops' –

enables a resolved view of the end of life. At this late stage, he regrets not trying to find Edward, during all those long, intervening years. He hopes it wasn't pride, a petulance, that without knowing it, he had been waiting for Edward to find him. He doesn't know why and doesn't search for an answer.

Mary calls an ambulance; and at the hospital, Alex manages to squeeze her hand in thanks and farewell. His final coherent thought is not particularly grand; it takes him back to June 1917.

These sheets are cold, scratchy, like the ones in Wimereux.

CODA

We met at lunchtime in a hotel in Pyrmont, an old-fashioned pub, which was still wearing its 1950s colours: faun walls and pale-green tiles. It was near Dominic's office, on an asphalt island, landlocked by freeways and busy streets, heaving with fast-moving traffic. The carpets squelched and the place smelled of stale beer.

Dominic had not spoken to me since our return, even after weeks back in Sydney. I thought perhaps he felt too awkward to reach out to see me, in light of the drunken episode in Ypres, a barrier for him to any conversation, casual or significant. I assumed Dominic just didn't know what to say to me, but I needed to talk to him, to sort it out, and – a difficult admission for me – I missed him.

'And what brings us to this charming dive, Tara? The decor? Their refusal to serve any boutique beer?' He had launched the sarcasm defence, even before I'd challenged him. He looked very chic in a Sydney ad agency way in what was surely a designer linen suit, and he had had a very short haircut. He had ordered a tomato juice and a packet of peanuts … which had given me pause for thought.

'Can we cut the bonhomie, Dominic? We need to talk it out. First, I want to thank you – thank you properly – for getting me home: booking the flights, driving to the airport, shepherding me onto the plane. I was really struggling.'

Dominic shrugged off my niceties with a smile and a big gesture of out-stretched arms. 'Aw, come on. No need for thanks.'

'Seriously, Dominic, just for once can you be gracious and accept my feelings of gratitude?' I insisted, though I was aware that I sounded like some pompous relative. I tried to soften my Hallmark sentiments. 'You did me a good turn. I was really at the end of my tether. I guess I was really shocked, stunned, by finally understanding that experiencing loss is the only way to appreciate what you have.'

'OK, OK. Graciousness is not really my strong point, Tara. Hadn't you noticed?' He took a slurp of his juice. 'And if we're going to be all lovey-dovey about it, I guess I have to thank you for taking me to Europe at all. I could have just continued to hide under my rock here in Sydney, having a perfectly good time. In the end, I have to acknowledge that it was … therapeutic.'

'How so?'

'Fuck, I don't know. Haven't got that far yet,' he said with a hoot and a theatrical shrug of his shoulders.

'Well, Dominic, one thing I've decided because of it is that, in the interests of being a better person, I'm going to be a better mother, and friend, and daughter, and ex-wife' – I drew a big breath – … and I'm not going back to work.' I found I was nervous to say it out loud. I was certainly humourless in the face of his jollity, made tense by anticipated criticism.

'What … taking the afternoon off?'

'No. I mean I'm quitting …'

'Quitting?' He was genuinely taken aback, the levity gone. 'Why?'

'… and I wanted to tell you first because I owe you, because … because of the BEER! account.'

Playing for time and composure, I moved my glass of spritz and took to shifting my drink coaster around, a few centimetres here, a few centimetres there. I spun the coaster on its corner, flicking it with my middle finger.

'I can't go back, Dom, and anyway, I wouldn't be any use to you, because, well, I don't want to be there. That's over for me.'

'But … er, is it because of … you know, what we did in Ypres? It's not a "me too" thing? I'd be mortified if you thought that.'

'No, no, nothing like that. But let's talk about it. Don't ever do that again, OK? It really hurt my feelings. I felt you were just going to use me and you didn't care. It was a shitty thing to do.'

Dom hung his head for what felt like minutes. 'I literally don't know what to say. I feel so ashamed … and that doesn't sit well. "Sorry" sounds stupid and trivial.'

'Yeah, I guess so.'

We both took a slurp of our drinks, both looking out at the traffic roaring by on the roadway beyond the big open doors.

'So, we OK then?' Dom sounded like a small boy, humble, chastised. I smiled and we turned back to face each other.

'Sure. I think so.'

'And you've really quit JJMcK?' One of Dominic's eyebrows popped up, an ironic look, smirking, pseudo-chiding. 'The agency will be seriously pissed off.'

'Yep. I'm expecting that. I've moved back to my mother's – Persy and Charlotte just love it there – and let my flat for some income. I mean to write up Alex's life, the War, and our experience. Like a novel but based in fact.'

Dominic smiled even more widely. 'That'll be great.'

My latent self-doubt was activated. Like so many times before, I was helpless in the face of my own tendency to believe that criticism was the world's natural response to the things I care about: my passions, my disappointments.

'OK, now I know you're just being a bastard, Dominic.'

'No, you big boofhead, I'm serious,' he said, and he gently play-slapped me up the side of my head. 'I'm in the same boat. I no longer give a flying fuck about BEER!, if indeed I ever did. I don't know what I'm going to do next. I've got to work that out.'

'So, you're OK with it then? You seem …'

'… very relaxed, Tara. You think you were the only one changed by our experience? I assure you, that's not true.'

'You're changed?'

'I don't really know how, but I'll work it out. I will,' he said. 'You won't believe it, but I've not had a drop of alcohol since we returned. I've not given up' – he raised both hands in protest – 'just taking a very long, long break. I've discovered it's easier to think about if I say that.'

Dominic told me that since he had returned to Australia, he had been uneasy – unusual for him. Sleep was elusive and he was plagued by images of Charlotte's dead body; he'd never seen one before. For him, there was a new, low-level, niggling anxiety.

'I find I *need* Rachel. She's noticed and is a bit weirded out, as they say. I hope she'll stick it out.' His voice had dropped to a whisper. 'And work is not fun. For the first time in a long while, I see the pathetic affairs of my colleagues as just plain tedious. In days of old, I thought my life was filled with marvellously distracting stuff and *I* was absolutely *relevant*. At this point …'

'But what about the fact that I'm going to want to write about Edward, your grandfather? I want to do a warts-and-all kind of thing. I'm going to swipe Alex's and Ed's past, and I'll have to fabricate the bits I don't know about and then I'll probably have to make assumptions about them. I hope *they'll* both forgive me. But, you, Dom, are *you* OK with that?'

'Sure.' He was looking at the floor, making me worried.

'It's a liberty, I know, on my part, but this book just won't work otherwise.'

'Yeah, no, really, it will be great.' His eyes met mine and I could see they were full of tears.

'Well, thanks for your support.' I took his hand, and couldn't help but think that Dominic represented Edward in giving me permission. 'You know, it will probably just end up on the remainder table in every Australian bookshop.' I winced at my own truthfulness.

'Ha! Let's have lunch … your shout.'

*

The next day, I was seated on the swings in the Kirribilli toddlers' playground. The mayhem and cacophony of fifteen or so under-fives was remarkably soothing to me. There was so much life in the chaos: dirt and tears, wails and laughing. Pudgy limbs and staggering gaits propelled little bodies up ladders, down slides, across dusty tanbark. Charles, 'The Ex', as handsome – and cold – as ever, sat on the next swing. He too had had a short, very modern haircut – unlike him, but very cool. I remained immune to his charms. He was quiet, perhaps not yet believing that all the time I was spending with the girls and my newly found cordial attitude were something he could rely on. Little Charlotte and Persy were springing up and squatting down, collecting scattered sticks, happy as gambolling lambs, piling the twigs in neat mounds, some few metres away from us. I had just finished explaining that I had left the ad agency to write.

'I know this book is just a small-scale tale – minute, even! Everybody's grandfather did something at least remotely interesting to someone else. But my determination to share this story is important to me. God, I don't seem to be selling this idea very well. Can you … can you bear with me?'

It meant financial hardship for us all. Charles remained silent, processing the implications, not impressed.

'Thanks for letting me come with you today.' I tried to de-escalate the tension. 'We've got a lovely sunny afternoon for it. They really love this playground, and so do I.' I gestured toward the little girls in their winter-weight jersey dresses and matching beanies. 'I've got a new favourite word: cherish. I cherish my time with them.'

Reflexively, Charles answered by raising both eyebrows.

'Look, more broadly, Charles, I'm sorry.' I felt a rush of accountability: not just to own it, but to declare it. 'I really am. I feel largely responsible for allowing us to fall into this … this mess.'

He kept his eyes looking in front of him. This was a first. Normally, he interrupted, lectured me, always had the last word. Between us it was quiet. I hoped it indicated some kind of amnesty.

'I didn't call it when I knew that we shouldn't go forward with it – the marriage, the house, the kids. I was a coward.' I plunged on. 'Look, that is clumsily put … God, I sound like Yoda: you know, from *Star Wars*?' I said with a laugh. It was my turn to focus only in front of me, watching the busy girls for a full minute. But, no, that would not do. I meant to say it. I ought to say it. I would say it. I turned to Charles and caught his eye, saw his hesitant look, grabbed his hand. 'I just want to say: I. Am. Sorry.'

'OK, OK.' He shrugged, took his hand back but not in a dismissive way. 'It'll be alright. We're alright. Really.'

A sudden squeal of delight from the swings was mixed with a cry of pain and anguish from the slides; the two of us looked up immediately, sought the outline of our girls among the tangle and bedlam of little bodies; there they were, OK, absorbed in their stick forest in the mounds of dirty sand that surrounded the playground. We were both instantly relieved: it was some other child who'd cried out.

'Have you ever experienced an intense sensory change?' I tried again.

'A what?'

'I don't know how else to put it, but in the past few weeks I have become aware of seeing things in brighter colours. Reds are redder; blues are bluer. My peripheral vision is wider. I … absorb … what I see.'

'Uh-huh.' Charles looked up at me, perplexed.

'No, really. I've probably got a brain tumour,' I said, deadpan.

'What?' Truly alarmed, Charles reached for my arm.

'Hey, I was just being hilariously funny.'

'You've never been hilariously funny.'

'Hence, the evidence that I'm a new woman.'

Charles tipped his head back a little; a small, gentle smirk gave it away. Maybe he comprehended that he didn't have to defend himself from my pessimism anymore. Since I'd returned from Ypres, I'd been saying to Charles over and over again that I wanted to truly know the girls and I wanted them to truly know me. He understood we'd never get back together and had no regrets nor anger; we both appreciated that we could forge a happy detente. I was hoping that he was thinking that I would start giving to – rather than taking from – him, my mother, my friends. I was hoping that he was thinking, *Maybe she really is whole.*

'So, are we going to eat the cheese sandwiches I brought, or what? Shall I call the girls over?' Without waiting for an answer, I hollered, 'Girls! Time for our picnic!' and I picked up the rug Charles had placed beside us, shook it open to cover a grassy patch, and very soon made the girls roll around with giggling as I began to sing from *The Sound of Music.*

Fräulein Maria always made them laugh.

*

Days later, Dominic and I entered the monumental War Memorial at Canberra. Dominic started to amble past the lions from the Menin Gate, but I couldn't let him pass them without him knowing their story. I got him to sit on the same seat as I did months earlier and I told him the tale. He touched the lion's paw too and looked at them with a look of … what? Affection, recognition, acknowledgement?

We made our way to the archives room. Dom took the folder of notes from the archivist with resolution. I let him take the lead – this trip was more his than mine. *He* was going to search the records and Edward's handwritten memoirs for mentions of Alex or Jim Williams, and I was going to help him.

Dominic took his time. While I flicked through Charles Bean's volumes, he enjoyed his grandfather's presence

314 · DIANA O'NEIL

contained so thoroughly in the memoir and the papers: the soldier's turn of phrase, the speech patterns of Edward's generation, florid yet earthy, straightforward. Dom pointed out a meaty sentence or two to me and we had a mute laugh in the silence of the archive room, as quiet as any library. He lingered over Edward's pen sketches: one of the camp in England, one of men asleep in a dugout, one of a landscape of churned earth and a single tree. There was something intimate about the inky script and Dominic felt close to the man, dead now for many years.

After some hours, Dominic turned the last page and spied just the corner of an envelope, caught under the cardboard fold of the archive's pannier. He drew my attention to it, looked at me, mouthed: 'What's this?'

I shrugged and mouthed back, 'I don't know.' The envelope was open, and Dom read the document that was tucked inside first. It was a single sheet of paper and looked like a handwritten letter, but I couldn't see what it was all about.

In the hush of the archives room, the staff and other visitors heard Dominic's rapid, inward breath and the slower expulsion of all that air when he finished the letter.

'What the hell …?' I asked in a whisper.

'It's a letter from Alex to Edward, from 1967. Hang on a tick. You should read it … in a minute. We'll read it together when we get out of here.'

It was nearly five o'clock, closing time at the Memorial. After making a copy of the letter, returning the boxes, folders and stacks to the librarian, with thanks and promises of seeing them the next day, Dominic and I found the exit.

Outside, Australia's inland winter warmth was lovely even for those not used to it. The busloads of Chinese tourists exiting the Memorial and clambering into their huge vehicles at the bottom of the steps looked surprised by the blue and gold glory of the light and the gumtree- and wattle-scented breeze. But Dominic, in his baggy shorts, soft leather boat shoes, ubiquitous windcheater, seemed mercifully restored by the sun on his cooled skin: we'd moved from dry and warm air-conditioning to chilly, delightful daylight, full of sunbeams preparing for sunset. He raised his face to the sunshine, and closed his eyes briefly, took a deep breath.

'Just wait, can you just wait a minute?' Dom said to my request to see the letter as we stood on the step of the main entrance. 'I have to call Rachel before you read it. I've got to do something.'

'What? Dom, what's going on? Are you alright?'

'Sorry to be so weird, Tara. I seem to have been granted that sense of completion I was looking for,' he added, his familiar smirk returning.

He pulled the phone from his right pocket, stabbed in the code and the number, and then jangled the car keys in his left pocket while it rang. He looked down the vast avenue of giant eucalypts that stretched for a couple of kilometres. His eyes reached for the mid-distance, then all the way across the lake, past Old Parliament House and on to the new Parliament House. The warm air rose off the Memorial's entrance-way steps after another day in the sun. The wispy cirrus clouds flickered white against the famous blue dome, Canberra's sky. We came to sit side by side on the top step.

'Let's get married, Rachel,' he said as soon as she answered. 'Really, I mean it. I can't think of any reason we shouldn't, only reasons why we should.'

I couldn't have been more surprised, but Rachel didn't miss a beat. It was almost as though she'd been expecting something to shift in him.

'Wow. What's brought this on? Are you alright, Dom?' I could hear her reply in a calm voice, with just an edge of anxiety for him, which I shared.

'There's something about what I've been through with Tara in Belgium and these papers today. It's made me think. I'm absolutely sure about this, and you, and us. Forever. We have to close off the doubts. And I do really love you,' he said, his voice cracking. 'And you *really* love me.' He smiled his big, winning, toothy smile and he made her laugh. 'So, let's do it. What do you reckon?'

Dominic and I could both hear the smile in her voice when she said, 'OK.'

He nudged me in the ribs with a smile to match hers and I was chuffed – touched – to be part of this. He finished his call with a flourish of 'Love you, love you, yes, yes …' and we returned to the business at hand.

'OK. Here it is, a letter from Alex to Edward, from mid-July 1967. I think this is it: the closer. This is where we find out that they – Edward and Alex – were firm friends, that they …' Dominic stumbled a bit. 'Look, you just read it, read it out loud.' And I took up his offer.

Dear Edward

After all these years, it is marvellous to receive your letter.

Yes, I'm still alive! Only just, the doc tells me. The gas from 1917 has caught up with me, and I live with an oxygen bottle as my best friend. I hope you fared better.

You tracked me down here in Sydney! I never thought of you living here too. I should have. I recall now that you came from Manly way? Shall we catch up? In person?

I live with my daughter, Mary, and grandchildren now in Fairlight. I work in my vegetable garden and help around the house where I can. I have a son as well, James. My wife, Cressida, recently passed away.

I want to respond to your apology. There is no need at all to feel distressed about not finding Jim Williams all those years ago. When I asked you to find him, I was half out of my mind with pain and fatigue. I'm sure I sounded desperate and probably crazed! I tried to track him down many years later, sometime in the 30s, I think. Armistice Day has always brought out tough memories for me, and once or twice I thought I should seek him out. The Army administration was not very helpful, though it was always a long shot.

I suppose he's gone. So many were killed in that terrible time. I just wanted to thank him. He really did save my life, and I wanted to acknowledge his kindness.

I want to sincerely thank you for your friendship during that period. It was tough for us both and you helped me in so many ways. I could count on you to cheer me up, not in a superficial way, but with your caring and support. And we had some fun, didn't we? Oh dear! This old man's getting sentimental. Forgive me.

I do hope you can come for a cup of tea to my home. Next Sunday? 21st July?

Regards, old friend,

Alex Twigg-Patterson.

'And look,' Dom pointed, 'there's a note in the bottom left-hand corner of the page. That's Edward's handwriting. See? "Deceased 19th July 1967". That's today's date. Today's! Yeah, another one of your beautiful connections. You couldn't make this stuff up.'

Sitting on the steps of the cold monolith of the War Memorial, both Dominic and I were choked up for all that was between us, for all that was between our grandfathers, for loss, for friendship, for fine feelings and tragic deaths, and a couple of moments of stillness between us were broken only by one or other of us sniffling a little.

*

That evening, I picked up the Canberra hotel's complimentary pen, opened the complimentary notepad and started my book – this book – in which I tried my hardest to explain to the world why it's so important to know, understand and treasure the past. The damp, mouldy past is all about the present –

and the future. The interconnectedness is messy, ragged and fraying with every day that goes by. It's all around us, above and below us, through us, beside us. I saw it in Dominic and Rachel, my mother, my daughters and even Aunty Mary. I experienced it with Charlotte, Ingrid – everyone I spoke to in Belgium. With an open mind and heart, I just had to look to find it – an important bond, something to hold on to and to pass on.

Evidently, Rachel, too, had been changed by our trip and discoveries. When summer arrived, she insisted we come for brunch one Sunday and while we sat on the plump couch in the open-plan kitchen, coffee in hand, she told me she was pregnant.

'Three months!' she said, as though no one had ever reached that milestone before. Her eyes were shining and she grasped my hand.

Perhaps she saw my hesitation – I'd remembered that Rachel had previously decided not to have children and perhaps the look on my face showed confusion. Regardless of whether she registered my faltering, she felt the need to explain to me.

'Look, it began to feel like a denial for me to withhold, to be selfish and refuse to take part in what is so terribly important to Dominic.' She let go of my hand, turning away. 'I think kids are the distillation of longstanding love. Now it seems like a natural progression – love, dedication, continuation.' She hesitated, looked down and plucked at a stray thread. 'After your trip to Belgium, probably because of it, for the first time in our lives, Dom and I have spent the past few months thinking hard about mortality ... other people's mortality ... its finality. It makes you consider your own. What do you leave behind if not something of you, really of you ... hopefully, a good part of you, something good you created and shaped well.'

I nodded as she spoke. My two girls were playing with an assembly of teddies and other soft toys in front of us – shiny, healthy little cherubs, pink-cheeked in sunshine. I could hear their chirrups and cooing as I looked at Rachel's face, and it was utterly clear to me that it was the right thing for Dominic and Rachel to do.

'Fantastic, fantastic, fantastic,' was my inept but heartfelt version of congratulations, and I hugged her with a proper embrace – not the social kind, but a thoughtful one, arms right around, slow and deliberate – mindful of how much I loved my friends.

*

Dom and Rachel's baby girl was eight weeks old when they held a naming-day party. They managed to keep her name secret from everyone right up until the speeches of the day, when the baby, slumbering peacefully in her mother's arms, was surrounded by a roomful of admiring adults and numerous children of friends and relatives.

Dominic's speech was all that it should have been – blustering, romantic, witty – and then, when he was sure every glass was suitably charged, he announced:

'Our darling daughter will be named … Rosemary Charlotte Fitzgerald …'

'Rosemary!' I called out involuntarily, surprised, elated.

'"… that's for remembrance!"' Dominic concluded, and the crowd erupted with clapping and hooting, enough to wake the sleeping baby.

*

This book is the story of when I went looking for my grandfather. He died twenty years before I was born, but I wanted to *know* him: about his physical self, his mind, his particular friends, his mentors, his acolytes, his sweethearts, his sense of achievment, his sense of failure. I discovered a great deal about him, plus some universal truths, and I learnt about some dreadful tragedies.

It is not humility that makes me emphasise that this story is a tiny moment in the timescale of humankind. It is in no way important; its telling will not change anything. It's personal, so why tell it at all?

I wrestled with the why *and* the who: who owns the knowledge? Who has the right to tell this story? Who can speak to us from the past and has earned the right to be heard? Whose is that voice that I hear and I want you to hear? Why am I driven to tell you? Why might you be driven to listen?

I've got the story down now – a higgledy-piggledy record – and the guts of it make a certain looping sense to me now: unfolding, hiccoughing, hither and thither, joyous, grim, exhilarating. You can decide; judge it as a story with a point of view, or just a tale of small consequence. The facts of it meant something to someone, somewhere, sometime.

ACKNOWLEDGEMENTS

I am very grateful to Robert Sessions, who held my hand and endured my whining while I agonised over this book: his kind support was all important. My love and thanks go to Adam Oakes, for being an excellent friend. Thanks to author Tony Park for mentoring me via the Australian Society of Authors. Thanks to my sister, Helen, and brother-in-law, Stephen, who said very little about an early draft, which, of course, said a great deal. Thanks too to my cousins who generously let me use their surname with blind trust. Many and sincere thanks to everyone at Whitefox for their supreme professionalism.

ABOUT THE AUTHOR

Diana's experience spans across various fields – from book and magazine publishing to TV and nursing, with an interesting stint in the armed forces. Splitting her time between Italy and Australia, she finds solace in swimming in the sea, eating tomatoes and olives, and indulging in a glass of wine. When not engaged in a game of Scrabble, she loves to read. *Sorrows Yield* marks her debut book.

Printed in Great Britain
by Amazon

47328906R00192